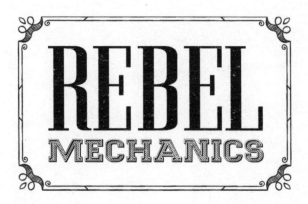

REBEL
MECHANICS

REBEL
MECHANICS
ALL IS FAIR IN LOVE AND REVOLUTION

SHANNA SWENDSON

MARGARET FERGUSON BOOKS
Farrar Straus Giroux • New York

Farrar Straus Giroux Books for Young Readers
175 Fifth Avenue, New York 10010

Copyright © 2015 by Shanna Swendson
All rights reserved
Printed in the United States of America
Designed by Andrew Arnold
First edition, 2015
1 3 5 7 9 10 8 6 4 2

macteenbooks.com

Library of Congress Cataloging-in-Publication Data

Swendson, Shanna.
    Rebel mechanics / Shanna Swendson. — First edition.
        pages cm
    Summary: In 1888 New York City, sixteen-year-old governess
Verity Newton agrees to become a spy, whatever the risk, after learning
that the man for whom she has feelings sympathizes with rebels developing
non-magical sources of power, via steam engines, in hopes of gaining
freedom from British rule.
    ISBN 978-0-374-30009-8 (hardback)
    ISBN 978-0-374-30017-3 (e-book)
    [1. Governesses—Fiction.   2. Spies—Fiction.   3. Magic—Fiction.
4. Insurgency—Fiction.   5. New York (N.Y.)—History—1865–1898—Fiction.
6. Science fiction.]   I. Title.

PZ7.1.S94Reb 2015
[Fic]—dc23
                                                                        2014041381

Farrar Straus Giroux Books for Young Readers may be purchased for business or
promotional use. For information on bulk purchases please contact Macmillan
Corporate and Premium Sales Department at (800) 221-7945 x5442 or by email at
specialmarkets@macmillan.com.

For all the people who were instrumental
in the very long journey from idea to publication:

Michael *and* **Angela**
for brainstorming and antique show browsing

Mom, Debbie, *and* **Jenny**
for the reading and helpful feedback

My agent, **Kristin Nelson,**
for never giving up (and not having to eat her hat)

And my editor, **Margaret Ferguson,**
for forcing me (sometimes kicking, screaming, and pouting all the
way) to make the book the best it could be

CONTENTS

AUTHOR'S NOTE

This novel is a work of alternate history that explores what might have happened if something in our country's history had been different. What if the colonies had never gained their independence and the British continued to rule? What if that ruling class had magical powers?

That would have changed a lot of things, including technology, industry, and the social order. And many other things might have been different. For instance, Great Britain abolished slavery in 1833, and if the American colonies had still been part of the empire, there might never have been the need for the Civil War. The pattern of westward expansion might have changed as well, altering relationships with the native peoples.

With magic in the mix, some technologies might have come later or never been developed at all, while others might have been ahead of their time. If magic provided the power for all industry and technology, common people would be dependent on the magical classes for their livelihood and survival.

But there are other forms of power, like steam and electricity, and if people could learn about and make use of this power, they might have a way to fight against the magical classes and gain their freedom from the British.

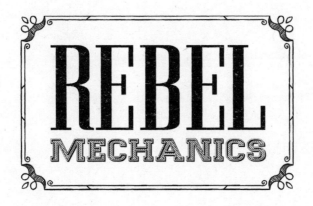

New York City
1888

IN WHICH
I FACE BANDITS
AND BUTLERS

If I'd let myself think about what might lie ahead for me, I'd have been terrified. So, instead of thinking, I lost myself in the book I'd bought at the train station newsstand—the kind of pulp novel I'd have had to hide behind a copy of *The Odyssey* if I'd still been at home in New Haven. Now, though, I could read what I wanted without my father having any say in the matter. My life had improved in that way, at least.

Although the motion of the train made it difficult to keep the paperback book steady, I defiantly held it with the lurid cover clearly visible as I read about a daring gang of bandits terrorizing stagecoaches. I was so engrossed in the story that when I heard a sharp noise and raised voices, I initially mistook it for my imagination bringing the story to life. Then I looked up to see a group of masked, gun-wielding men rushing through the connecting doorway at the front of the car. A thrill shot through me. I had told myself my life would be more exciting beginning today, but I hadn't really believed it. I picked up my bag and dropped the book into it so I wouldn't miss a thing.

"Seal the door!" the tallest bandit ordered, and one of the masked men turned to throw the latch. He held his hands over it, and I thought for a moment that I saw a shimmer beneath them. A shiver went down my spine, making me gasp. Could that have been magic? No, I decided, only the magister class could use magic, and that class held most of the property in the British Empire and controlled the magical power that ran all industry, even here in the American colonies. Magisters shouldn't need to rob trains. When I looked again, the shimmer was gone. I must have imagined it.

While the man who'd sealed the door stood lookout, the tall bandit who'd shouted the order strode up the aisle, heading toward the rear of the car where I sat. Abruptly, he stopped and raised his pistol at a man sitting three rows ahead of me. "I'll take that," he said in a soft but firm voice as he grabbed a slim black leather case the man held in his lap. The man clung to his case, and it looked for a moment as though he might put up a fight, but the bandit cocked his pistol with his thumb and held it closer to the man's face. The man released his hold on the bag. The bandit gave him a disconcertingly polite nod as he lowered the gun and took the case. He then continued up the aisle, seemingly unaffected by the swaying motion of the train as it slowed to round a bend.

He stopped directly in front of my seat, and I gripped the handles of my bag as my heart beat wildly. The bandit stood so close to me I could see his eyes through the slits in his mask. They were an icy, pale blue, hard and cold, with little flecks of gray around the pupil and a band of darker blue around the outer edge of the iris. I had never met a killer, but based on every novel I'd read, that was how I imagined a killer's eyes would look.

When the bandit stepped toward me, I reacted instinctively. I rose to my feet, swung my bag at him, and then felt the shock go up to my elbows when I connected with his head. He staggered backward, and I felt light-headed as my breath came in shallow gasps. I shrank away, fearing retribution.

Instead of being angered by my assault, he smiled wryly and holstered his gun. The smile made his eyes look much less icy and hard. With a slight bow, he said, "My apologies, miss. I did not intend to alarm you."

"They're coming!" the lookout called from the front of the car. "Hurry!"

My bandit glanced over his shoulder to see the railroad guards attempting to open the locked door, then returned his attention to me. "And now, if you will excuse me, I need to make use of your seat to reach that hatch." I followed his eyes upward to see a hatch in the car's ceiling, directly above me. The bandit put the case he'd taken on the seat near me, stepped onto the seat, placed his hands against the hatch, paused for a moment, and pushed. The hatch flew open, sending a gust of wind rushing into the car and jolting me back against the window. I worried my hat would fly off, but I was too afraid of letting go of my bag to secure my hatpin. "It's open, come on!" the bandit shouted to the others as he climbed down.

The rest of the gang ran toward us, and I clutched my bag against my chest as, one by one, they jumped onto the seat and hoisted themselves through the hatch onto the roof of the car. A couple passed heavy-looking sacks up to other gang members before climbing after them. When the others had all gone, the bandit I'd hit reached for my gloved hand and brushed my knuckles with his lips, whispering, "I hope the rest of your journey goes smoothly, miss," before he climbed onto the seat, passed the stolen case up to a colleague, then pulled himself through. The hatch closed behind him with a clang and the car instantly grew quieter.

Breathless and quivering, I sank slowly onto my seat, resting my bag on my knees. I absently rubbed my left thumb across the knuckles of my right hand, where the bandit had kissed me. It was the first truly romantic thing I'd ever experienced.

The guards finally made it through the door, and they ran down the aisle. The man whose bag had been taken leaped out of his seat to accost them. "I am a courier on official business for the Crown, and those bandits took my case of priority dispatches!" he shouted, his mustache bristling in fury. "I expect better protection than this when I travel!" The other passengers joined in, adding their complaints at high volume.

The guards did their best to calm everyone. They interviewed the courier and several of the other passengers. One of the guards climbed onto the seat beside mine—without so much as a word to me—and attempted unsuccessfully to open the hatch. All the while, I kept glancing out the window, wondering where the bandits had gone. The train hadn't slowed down enough for them to jump, and I'd seen no one running away from the tracks.

The connecting door at the rear of the car opened and a well-dressed young man carrying a large brown leather valise entered. He pulled up short and gaped at the commotion. "I say, what's all this?" he asked.

"Nothing for you to worry about, sir," a guard said brusquely. "Please have a seat."

The newcomer glanced around for a seat and took one across the aisle from me. With a sheepish grin, he told me, "There was a baby crying in the other car. I didn't think I could bear it any longer. This looks a lot more interesting." He watched the guards conducting their investigation with great fascination, as though this was the best entertainment he'd seen in a long time. I thought he seemed a little too interested in the proceedings, and his color was heightened, as though he was either excited about something or had just done a great deal of physical activity. Surely one wouldn't get that red-faced merely while making his way through the train in search of a seat. Then I dismissed my suspicions as a flight of fancy. The bandits couldn't possibly have come down off the top of the train, removed their masks and adjusted their appearance in the lavatories, and then dispersed throughout the train as ordinary travelers.

Or could they? This man's height, build, and voice were all

wrong for the lead bandit, and I'd paid too little notice to the rest of the gang to tell if this man could have been part of the group. I decided to leave the investigation to the guards. If there was something worth looking into, they'd question him.

The remainder of the journey passed without incident. When the train pulled into Grand Central Depot in New York City, I noticed upon disembarking that the third-class passengers were being searched, so apparently the first and second classes were above suspicion. I was fortunate that my father's last gesture of goodwill to me had been a second-class ticket.

In the depot, I was immediately swallowed by the sea of porters, newsboys, and passengers. After several vain attempts to get a porter's attention, I was finally able to arrange for my trunk to be held. Then I followed the flow of humanity onto the concourse toward the exit, where I paused on the threshold. Seven potential employers had requested interviews based on my letters of application, so I had high hopes of obtaining a position and a place to stay by this evening. Beyond those doors lay my future, and I was ready for it to begin.

I was entirely unprepared for the assault on my senses as I stepped out of the depot onto Forty-Second Street. Horse-drawn carriages and omnibuses and magical horseless carriages clattered up and down the street, their drivers ringing bells, sounding horns, and shouting. Smaller magical roadsters zipped in and out of the traffic, startling the horses. That many horses on the street left a pungent odor that competed with the smell of cooking from nearby restaurants and street stalls and a pall of smoke from coal fires that hung over the city. There were people packed shoulder to shoulder on the sidewalk, all in a great hurry. Scattered through the crowds were the bright scarlet coats of British soldiers.

In spite of my grand ambitions, I now worried whether I was up to the challenge. The city was even bigger, more crowded, and noisier than I'd imagined, and I was so very much alone in those crowds. "I fought off a bandit," I reminded myself as I consulted my map. When I spotted a lull in the traffic I darted across the street in the direction of my first interview.

A few streets away from the depot the traffic and noise were lighter, and once I entered an enclave of fine homes, the stench from horses was gone. Perhaps the city wasn't so intimidating after all, I thought. This wasn't too different from the neighborhood where I'd grown up. It was merely grander.

I soon found the first home on my list, the household that most closely met my criteria. According to my research, they were of the magical class but not titled nobility—probably descended from a younger son many generations back. I hoped that meant this family wasn't so high that they would never consider a relatively inexperienced professor's daughter as a governess. The house wasn't all that imposing, a modest brownstone. *I could be at home here*, I thought.

Feeling confident about my prospects, I boldly climbed the front steps and rang the bell. A moment later, a butler opened the door, and the way he scowled at me sapped my strength. "I'm Miss Verity Newton, here to see Mrs. Upton. We have an appointment. She's expecting me," I blurted, all in one breath.

He said, "I'm sorry, but Mrs. Upton instructed me to tell you that the position has been filled," then closed the door before I could protest.

"But she never even interviewed me," I whispered plaintively to the closed door. To hide my disappointment, I marched down the steps, my head held high, then strode down the sidewalk with a sense of purpose. This was only the first interview. I still had six more, and none of them could go as badly as this one.

At the next interview, I made it into the house before I was informed that I was far too young to be suitable for the position. That was a slight improvement. The next interview went even better, as I wasn't rejected outright but rather told that I would be considered. It was only after I left that I realized they would have no way to contact me if they decided to hire me. They had only my New Haven address from my initial letter of application, and no one there would know how to reach me.

I kept ringing bells and smiling my way through interviews until there was just one name left on the list, a Mrs. Talbot who was housekeeper for Lord Henry Lyndon. Although I had never imagined I might be employed in the home of a titled gentleman, Mrs. Talbot's response to my inquiry had been encouraging. The address was much farther uptown, on Fifth Avenue at Seventy-Seventh Street. I headed toward Fifth Avenue, leaving behind the clean, quiet neighborhood and reentering the clamor of the city.

When I reached the avenue and got my bearings, I realized that my destination was nearly forty blocks away. My feet cried out for mercy at the thought of that long a walk. I saw a horse-drawn omnibus approaching and decided I could spare a few pennies to avoid walking that far.

The bus stopped and I stepped forward and asked the conductor, "Excuse me, but do you go up to Seventy-Seventh Street?"

"Sorry, miss, but horses aren't allowed above Fifty-Ninth on Fifth Avenue. The magisters don't like the mess in their neighborhoods." One of his team proceeded to demonstrate exactly what mess he meant, and I averted my eyes. The prohibition on horses in magister neighborhoods explained the clean streets where I'd just been. "Though, if you ask me," he added more softly, "it's their way of keepin' the likes of us out of their part of town." Back in a louder voice, he said, "There's an uptown bus on Third Avenue that'll go to Seventy-Seventh."

I frowned, puzzled. "But if that bus goes to Seventy-Seventh, why not this one?"

"Only magisters live around the park up there. Farther east, it's just regular people—that is, until more magisters move uptown and shove them out. You can take a cab." He gestured as a magically powered carriage passed, looking rather naked without any horses pulling it. I knew my budget wouldn't extend that far. As the bus rattled away, I allowed myself a weary sigh before gathering my strength to walk to Third Avenue to catch the bus there.

"Hey, miss!" a voice behind me said, and I turned cautiously. A newsboy stood nearby, a stack of papers at his feet and several held so he could display the headlines to passersby. The banner at the top declared it to be the *World*, a newspaper with which

I was unfamiliar. He wore a flat cap pulled low over his forehead. Dark hair straggled past his collar in the back, and his thin face was smeared with ink and dirt.

He gave me a cheeky wink as he raised the papers he held and shouted to a passing man, "Parliament renews the colonial tax act! Straight off the ether from London! How will it really affect us? You won't read the truth anywhere else!" The man tossed him a coin, which he deftly caught while handing over a copy of the paper. The customer folded the paper and tucked it inside the breast of his coat as he walked away. When the customer was gone, the boy said, "You're tryin' to get up to magpie land by the park?"

I assumed that "magpie" was his slang term for the magisters. "Yes, I am."

"What would you wanna do that for?"

"I have an interview for a position as governess."

He raised a skeptical eyebrow. "You want to work for the magpies?"

"I want to work for someone who will hire me." I couldn't help but allow my discouragement to creep into my voice. "Now I suppose I had better start walking or I'll be late for my interview."

"Don't go just yet." He glanced around, then gestured for me to come closer. "You can get a ride from here if you wait. Some friends of mine'll be along any minute now." He flicked a small gear wheel with a red ribbon tied through it that was pinned to his oversize coat and waggled his eyebrows like he was conveying some hidden meaning. I wasn't sure what the significance of the gear was, but I nodded as though I understood. "Ah, I had you figured for one of us," he said with a grin. He stuck out a hand blackened with newspaper ink. "The name's Nat."

I shook his hand, grateful that I'd worn black gloves instead of white. "And I'm Verity."

A shrill whistle rent the air, and Nat gave a satisfied nod. "Here they come, right on time. Wait'll you see this, Verity."

With a screech and a shudder, an enormous metal contraption lumbered to a stop beside us. A horizontal cylinder on huge spoked wheels belched smoke from a chimney on top, and steam billowed from vents on the sides. Two men rode on the machine, one steering while the other monitored a series of gauges. An omnibus like the horse-drawn one was hitched to this monstrosity.

Nat rushed forward and called out to the man studying the gauges. "Hey, Alec! I've got a friend here who needs a lift to magpie land. You can take her, can't you? You're goin' that way anyhow."

I couldn't see Alec's reaction because a large pair of brass goggles obscured most of his face and his attention was focused on his device. "We might not be stopping when we're there," he said as he worked.

A head in a bowler hat emerged from the doorway of the bus. "Did you say this charming young lady needs a ride?" The speaker swept the hat off his head, revealing a shock of bright red hair and a young face spattered with freckles.

"I need to get to Seventy-Seventh Street," I said shakily, wondering if perhaps I'd fallen asleep on the train and had dreamed everything from the robbery until now. This was all so very strange.

Nat added, "Verity's tryin' to be a governess, and she's gonna be late for her interview."

The red-haired young man gave me a look of theatrically exaggerated pity and held his hat against his heart. "Oh, you poor dear. You're too pretty to be a governess. Ah, but I suppose you're the independent type and won't settle for letting a man take care of you."

I couldn't help but smile, and I felt my cheeks warm in a furious blush. I'd never in my life been called pretty. I was admired for my cleverness rather than my appearance. I suspected he was what romantic novels called a flirt, but I didn't think he meant any harm, even if he didn't mean what he said. "You flatter me," I said. "I have no choice but to make my own way in the world."

With a saucy wink he replied, "Well, if you change your mind about finding a man to take care of you, let me know, and I'll submit my application. The name's Colin Flynn, and if ever you want me just ask around, and I'll be there."

While we were talking, a few people who had been milling around on the sidewalk approached the bus. Colin replaced his hat on his head and stepped down. "One at a time, people!" he called out, his tone switching from flirt to officious conductor. "All aboard for a voyage into the future."

As the people stepped up to Colin, they each flicked something on their lapels. A closer study revealed that they were gears on red ribbons, like the one Nat wore. Colin also wore one on the breast of his frayed morning coat, but his gear was much larger and his ribbon much wider. When all the passengers had boarded, Colin turned to address the man tinkering with the gauges. "Have you got Bessie all stoked up, Alec?"

"One minute more, Colin. Look out for some competition."

Colin returned his attention to me. "And now, if you will step aboard my humble conveyance, we will take you on a journey you won't soon forget."

"How much is the fare?" I asked.

"Today we're offering a complimentary demonstration run. It's an experimental project. We're engineering students at the university."

I hesitated. I needed reliable transportation, not an experiment. "That's very kind of you—" I began, but Nat grabbed my arm.

"Go on, Verity. Trust me. Bessie'll get you there."

"I assure you, it's quite safe," Colin added. "All the explosions happened in the lab. We've had no trouble with the full-size model."

The idea of explosions wasn't very reassuring, but I didn't know how else I would make it to my interview on time, and I *had* to get this job. "Very well, then," I said as firmly as I could manage, in spite of my misgivings. "I accept your kind offer of transportation."

He grinned, sweeping his hat off his head and giving me a gallant bow. "Welcome aboard, Verity. And be prepared to make history."

IN WHICH
I LAND AMONGST
MECHANICS

Colin seated me at the front of the bus, next to a girl about my age. "This is Verity," he said to her. "Look after her." To me, he added, "This is my sister, Lizzie. Pinch her if she gives you any trouble."

"Ignore him, I always do," she said with an air of much-tested patience. She shared her brother's bright hair, freckles, and lanky build. A notebook rested on her knee, and she held a pencil. Another pencil was stuck behind her ear.

Most of the other passengers on the crowded bus were young men, and the few women were not at all what my mother would have considered proper ladies. They wore the wildest clothing, a mix of pieces that seemed as though they'd dug them from a rag pile with their eyes closed and then dressed in the dark. The men mixed formal wear with working attire, and some of the women wore their elaborately decorated corsets *outside* their blouses. A few of them wore skirts that fell well above their ankles. There was one woman near the back of the bus who looked out of place in the dull black of a widow in deepest mourning, with a black veil obscuring her face.

The engine made louder sounds, and more steam and smoke billowed from it—so much that I feared it would explode. Alec patted the man at the controls on the shoulder, then tapped on the front window to signal Colin. Colin acknowledged him with a nod, secured his hat on his head, and pulled a pair of goggles from his hat brim down over his eyes. He shut the door, then turned to face his passengers. "Ladies and gentlemen—and the rest of you lot," he shouted above the rumble of the engine. "We are about to embark on a great venture, one that will prove us to be the equal of any thieving magpie. What they do with magic, we have built with our own ingenuity. They think to shut us out of their districts with their laws, but this bus violates no law—yet. I'm sure they'll think of something after today." The passengers chuckled, and one or two shouted obscenities coarse enough to make me gasp.

"If there was any doubt as to why we do this, look to our guest." He pointed at me, and my skin prickled as I sensed every eye on the bus focusing on me. "This young lady here is the perfect example of our cause. She seeks honest employment at a home in magpie land, but how is she to get there for the interview? The cabs that can go there are too expensive for common folk, and the buses that do convey the common folk aren't allowed to violate their precious streets because they're drawn by horses. This is why we've devoted our knowledge and skills toward this momentous day, creating an engine powerful enough to pull a bus without being powered by magic. Now, hang on to your seats, because here we go!"

The engine grew even louder, making *chug-chug* sounds. After a long, piercing blast of the whistle, the engine strained forward, dragging the bus with it. At first it crept, as though moving was a struggle, but then it built momentum. The bus drew up alongside a magical carriage that had the coat of arms of a noble house painted on its door and a driver in livery seated in front. It looked like the passenger compartment was empty. Colin leaned out the bus window and called, "Nice toy you have there. Do you know what it can do?"

The driver turned to look at the engine and the bus, and his eyes grew wide. "What the blazes is that?" he shouted back at Colin.

Colin cued Alec, who pulled a cord, making the whistle sound a shrill blast. The engine moved a little faster, pulling ahead of the carriage. "This is the machine that'll leave your magical toy in the dust," Colin shouted with a laugh. The other young men on the bus joined in with raucous catcalls at the carriage. The driver glared at them, then furrowed his brow and moved a lever, and the carriage increased its speed. The engine soon responded, going ever faster. Colin leaned out the window, thumbed his nose at the driver, and said, "What's the matter, think your master'll turn you into a frog if you actually drive that thing? Or were you a frog to begin with, and he turned you into his driver?" I saw a flash of fury on the driver's face, and the race was on.

The noise was deafening. The engine chugged and puffed and made a great rumbling roar. The bus moaned and creaked alarmingly. I suspected it had not been designed for such speed. Every so often, it bounced when the wheels hit an obstacle, and there was a constant vibration from the paving bricks. Next to me, Lizzie wrote in her notebook, and I wondered how she could manage while being jostled so badly.

As we rattled our way up Fifth Avenue, crowds gathered on the sidewalks. Most merely gazed in curiosity, but there were also cheers as we passed. I was both terrified and exhilarated. Carriages on the cross streets barely stopped in time when the bus plowed through intersections. The bus swayed side to side as it wove its way around slower vehicles. The magical carriage kept up, with the bus occasionally pulling ahead before the carriage caught up again. In the brief moments when we were neck and neck, I saw that the carriage driver was focused intently, a look of sheer determination on his face. Alec and the other man on the engine made frantic adjustments, pulling levers and shoveling coal into what looked like a furnace.

Colin stood at the front of the bus, surprisingly steady on his feet. He sang at the top of his lungs in a strong Irish tenor, "'Yankee Doodle went to town, riding a steam pony. Led the magpies on a chase and made them look like phonies.'"

The rest of the passengers joined in the chorus, singing, "'Yankee Doodle keep it up, Yankee Doodle dandy. Fight the magic and the Brits, and with machines be handy.'"

My blood ran cold as the meaning of their song struck me and I realized amongst whom I'd fallen. These were the infamous Rebel Mechanics, the underground group that wanted to use machines to overthrow the magical ruling class and break the American colonies away from Great Britain. Just being with them would be considered treason.

My heart racing with the awareness of where I was, I turned to Lizzie and shouted over the noise of the engine and the bus wheels clattering on the pavement, "You're *rebels*?"

She gave me a reassuring smile. "There is nothing treasonous about what we're doing here. Do you think this is wrong?"

I honestly didn't know what to think. I'd heard rumors about this group in New Haven, where some university students had supported the cause, but my father hadn't taken the rebels seriously. He'd said it was merely young men being foolish. I didn't think it wise to say this while I was at their mercy. "We are perhaps going a trifle fast for safety," I suggested, holding my bag with one hand while I gripped the edge of my seat with the other.

She laughed. "Yes, I suppose we are, but we're merely proving that this machine is as good as any magical engine. Usually we'd travel at a more reasonable speed."

There was a shout from the back of the bus, and I looked over my shoulder to see a man positioned at the rear window waving frantically. Colin noticed the gesture, stopped singing, and nodded. Then he leaned out the front window and signaled Alec, who frowned and adjusted a lever. The bus picked up speed, making even more alarming noises. I was afraid it would fall apart around us. "What's happening?" I asked Lizzie.

"The police are giving chase. You were right about us going too fast."

"The police?" I squeaked in horror. With a criminal record, I could never find a position in a good home. I wondered if the authorities would believe this band of dangerous rebels had kidnapped me.

I glanced anxiously over my shoulder again and saw the rear lookouts grinning broadly. "They've given up!" one shouted. Colin raised his arms over his head in triumph.

His sister shook her head. "They'll signal ahead and cut us off!" she warned. "We should stop now!"

"The race is still on!" he cried out. "We don't stop until we've won!"

The magical carriage kept pace with us. The driver must have been a real gamesman, for the police pursuit hadn't deterred him. We'd reached the lower boundary of Central Park, which meant we were within twenty blocks of my destination. "Come on," I pleaded under my breath, unsure whether I was egging on the engine or urging our competitor to give up so the race would end. The park passed by in a green blur as we rattled furiously up the avenue. I couldn't even tell how many blocks we'd traveled, as each cross street went by in a flash.

Our opponent gradually fell behind until his carriage disappeared from sight. "Those engines don't have the capacity for long runs at high speeds, not without a constant input of magic, so it was hardly a fair contest," Lizzie said. "But I do think we've made our point that there are other viable sources of power." Around us, the bus full of Mechanics cheered and launched once more into their raucous Yankee Doodle song. I merely sighed in relief.

The bus slowed, and Colin came over to me. "We're near your destination, and the police will head us off at any moment, so this is where you get off." He bade me brace myself in the doorway, then jumped down to run alongside the bus. Holding his arms up to me, he shouted, "Jump, Verity! I'll catch you!"

The bus still seemed to be moving terribly fast, but I heard a police bell approaching and realized that if I didn't jump, I might never make it to my interview. I took as deep a breath as my stays allowed and flung myself out the doorway. Colin caught me easily, ran a couple of steps more, then set me on my feet and kept his arms around me until I was steady. "Now, hurry into the park and disappear until the police pass," he instructed before catching up with the bus. He leaped aboard and waved his hat to me through the doorway. "Best of luck to you, Verity!"

I waved back at him and made haste to the nearest park entrance. I jogged down a pathway until I could run no more, then slowed to a walk. The sound of clanging police bells on the street grew louder and turned my legs to jelly from fright. I collapsed onto the nearest bench and took my book out of my bag to try to appear as though I'd been sitting there all along, minding my own business.

I took no notice of the words on the page as I considered what I'd just experienced. History had shown rebel movements to be futile. The American colonists had attempted to rebel more than a hundred years earlier, but had stood no chance against the magical might of the British Empire. If there were other sources of power that didn't require magic, that would change things entirely. I'd just seen a steam-powered engine outrace a magical one. Did this mean that another revolution was imminent? That would mean violence, death, and an interruption of daily life even for those who didn't support the cause. Life for the nonmagical hadn't seemed that difficult to me because my life had been reasonably comfortable, but in my first day in the city, I could already see that there was much I didn't know about the world outside the sheltered academic enclave I'd previously inhabited.

When no police officer appeared after several minutes, I considered myself safe. I checked the watch pinned to my bodice. It was half past three, and Mrs. Talbot had instructed me to arrive before four. I returned my book to my bag, straightened my hat and resecured it with my hatpin, then rose and made my way to the nearby park exit.

The homes I faced were far grander than the ones I'd visited earlier and seemed much newer. Some were still under construction. The rebels had let me off a couple of blocks beyond my destination, which meant that my mad dash through the park had brought me almost exactly to the address I sought. When I saw the house, I double-checked the address with Mrs. Talbot's letter because it was no mere house. It was a palace.

It was larger than the others on the block, built of white marble, and it looked like an Italian Renaissance villa. I imagined
an army of servants, including wigged and liveried footmen. I
did not imagine myself in such a setting. I wasn't at all worldly.
I hadn't taken a Grand Tour of Europe. I'd barely seen the sights
of New Haven. How could I possibly hope to teach children who
were likely far more polished than I was?

But, I reminded myself, Mrs. Talbot would have known that
from my letter of application. I had been entirely honest about
my experience and qualifications, if not about my age, and she
had still requested an interview. If I didn't get this job, I'd have
to find a rooming house and start all over again answering ad-
vertisements. That thought motivated me to cross the street,
scale the majestic front steps, and reach for the bellpull.

Before my fingers closed around the cord, the door opened.
"You must be Miss Newton," a tall, broad-shouldered butler said
in a deep, rumbling voice. "Mrs. Talbot is expecting you. Please
come in." The home might have been imposing, but this was the
most welcoming greeting I'd had all day, aside from the band of
rebels.

The entry hall took my breath away. The ceiling soared far
above me, with windows of stained glass that cast multicolored
light onto the black-and-white chessboard marble floor. A sweeping staircase led to the upper floors, and statuary in niches lined
the entry hall. This foyer alone was nearly as large as my old
home, a fairly large one by New Haven standards. I couldn't
hold back a small sigh of longing. How wonderful to live in such

a place. Even as a governess, I'd feel like a princess whenever I came down that staircase.

I reined in my flight of fancy when the most intimidating woman I'd ever seen entered the foyer. She was very tall, and she had a strong, square, somewhat masculine jaw, with an equally strong, square brow. She didn't look like a woman who would tolerate nonsense or inefficiency of any sort. Her severe black dress and tight knot of hair added to the impression. She was more forbidding than my father. I hadn't believed that to be possible.

But her smile was friendly. In fact, there was a hint of sympathy to it, as though she was thinking "Oh, you poor dear." I stiffened my spine, prepared to be told that the position had already been filled. Instead, she reached to shake my hand. I hoped Nat hadn't left my glove dirty enough to smear ink on her bare hand. "Thank you, Mr. Chastain," she said to the butler. To me she said, "Miss Newton, I am Mrs. Talbot. Please come with me. We can talk in the morning room." Without waiting for my response, she turned and headed up the staircase. I had to run a few steps to catch up with her.

We passed a white-aproned maid on the landing, and Mrs. Talbot paused to say, "Please serve tea for two in the morning room, right away." She led me to a very feminine sitting room filled with dainty furniture so fragile-looking that I feared it wouldn't support a woman as sturdy as Mrs. Talbot, who looked even larger and more imposing in this setting. I felt ungainly there despite my own average size.

"Have a seat, Miss Newton," Mrs. Talbot said, gesturing toward a small sofa. She took the chair across from it. "Lord Henry was supposed to be here for this interview, but he has not returned yet. We may as well begin in his absence." She gave me another sympathetic smile. "I must say, you are not what I expected. Based on your letter, I assumed that you were a spinster, but you are very young."

"I am almost eighteen," I said, trying to sit even straighter and give the impression of age and maturity. It was less than half a year until my eighteenth birthday, so I felt I was stretching the truth only slightly.

She raised an eyebrow but made no comment. "Your letter says you have tutored young ladies and young gentlemen. You are comfortable with both?"

"Yes," I said with a nod. "And a variety of ages, as well."

"Yet you have not attended a university yourself? Nor school of any kind?"

"My father is a professor at Yale. He believed he could teach me more effectively than any school. I had received the equivalent of a university education by the time I was sixteen, and I had begun tutoring younger children long before that."

For a moment, her face softened. "You must not have had much of a childhood." That had never occurred to me because I liked books and learning, but the note of pity in her voice made me realize the loss. She quickly stiffened back into her imposing form. "Lord Henry was impressed with that portion of your letter." Although that should have been a positive sign, I got the strangest impression that she didn't want her employer to be in favor of me.

The maid entered with a tea tray, and the interview paused while Mrs. Talbot poured and the maid served sandwiches. When the maid left, Mrs. Talbot continued, "The reason I am concerned about your age, in spite of your impressive academic achievements, is that the position is not purely that of governess. You would serve as chaperone for the older children, and that requires a certain degree of maturity." She tilted her head and studied me for a moment. "You do not appear to be the flighty type, but I worry that you would not have the necessary air of authority with the children."

"I am capable of being quite stern," I assured her. "The children are not particularly wild, are they?"

A flicker of a smile crossed her lips. "No, not wild. But they may be challenging. Lady Olive is six and requires a full range of instruction. She is the one who needs a governess. Lady Flora, the eldest, is sixteen and in need of a good example, according to Lord Henry. Lord Roland is thirteen and attends school, but Lord Henry believes his education needs supplementation." Lord Henry sounded a lot like my father. "Both of the elder children must be chaperoned at any social events."

My heart sank. I knew I could teach Latin, Greek, French, literature, grammar, science, and mathematics, and I could even get by with music and drawing, although children of this class would have specialized drawing masters and music teachers. But the sort of social events that the aristocracy attended were well outside my experience. I wouldn't know how I should act, let alone what would be proper for my charges. I could learn, I told myself. I needed a job to have a roof over my head, and this would be a very comfortable roof.

"I believe I would be an excellent chaperone," I said, willing it to be true.

She raised her eyebrow again, but she didn't challenge my assertion. Instead, she asked, "Do you have any questions about the children or the position?"

In novels, applicants never seemed to inquire what had become of their predecessors, and I'd always sworn I wouldn't make the same mistake. I doubted that the last governess had been killed or driven mad by a specter, but one never knew, and there had to be a reason a family this noble would consider someone as inexperienced as I was, so I squared my shoulders and asked, "If you don't mind telling me, why is the position now vacant?" I thought that sounded properly professional.

She gave another one of those little secret smiles. "There have been four governesses in the past year," she admitted.

"What became of them?"

"Two of them were dismissed and two left of their own accord."

"Do you know why?"

She glanced around, then leaned forward and whispered, "Lord Henry fancies himself a scientist. He has *Ideas*." I could hear the capital letter in her voice, and I could tell from the way she wrinkled her nose that she didn't approve of said *Ideas*. I thought that might explain why she didn't consider the fact that Lord Henry approved of my application a mark in my favor.

"Ideas?" I asked nervously.

"About education and what is valuable for a young lady or gentleman to know. Two of the governesses proved not to live up to his standards."

"And the others?"

"He's quite the amateur naturalist, with his primary interest in insects. And Lord Rollo is a boy." She watched my face carefully as she said this, as though she wanted to see my reaction. Was she trying to scare me into rejecting the position?

"So the governesses found bugs in their bed and fled," I concluded, making sure I didn't sound at all alarmed by this prospect. "I assure you, I shall do no such thing." My suspicion that Mrs. Talbot was trying to dissuade me grew stronger when her lips puckered in distaste at my response.

A young man then entered the room. He didn't seem nearly old enough to be the master of this house—I didn't think he could be too far beyond his teens. He wore tweed sporting attire, carried a butterfly net under one arm, held a sketchbook in his hand, and had a pair of binoculars slung around his neck. His sandy brown hair was wavy and unruly, falling across his forehead, and his small, wire-framed spectacles gave him a scholarly appearance. There was a distracted manner about him, as though he'd been lost in thought and wandered in off the street without realizing he was in the wrong house.

He must have been in the proper home, though, because

Mrs. Talbot sprang to her feet at his entrance, wincing as he tripped over the edge of the carpet and then barely steadied himself. "Mrs. Talbot!" he said, pushing his eyeglasses back up his nose. "I just found a particularly rare species of lacewing in the park. I wasn't able to catch it, but I believe I made a creditable likeness." He opened his sketchbook to show her, dropping his butterfly net as he did so. When he bent to retrieve the net, he dropped the sketchbook, and it would have landed square in the middle of the tea tray if Mrs. Talbot hadn't rescued it. "Good catch, Mrs. Talbot," he said with a laugh as he took it back from her. "I nearly spoiled your tea." He then noticed me. "And you have company. Please forgive my intrusion."

He started to leave, but Mrs. Talbot said firmly, "Lord Henry, this is one of the governess candidates, Miss Newton, the one from New Haven. She had an appointment this afternoon."

"Oh dear, and I'm late. I forgot about that entirely. Do forgive me." He turned and reached out his hand to take mine. He then had to pause and shift his sketchbook to his other hand, which made him drop his butterfly net again. When he bent to pick it up, I saw past his glasses and barely stifled a gasp. His ice-blue eyes flecked with gray and rimmed in dark blue were the same as those of the bandit from the train.

IN WHICH
I LAND AMONGST
MAGISTERS

Lord Henry didn't seem to notice my dismay. If he recognized me from the train, he gave no sign whatsoever. He was so calm, in fact, that I immediately began to doubt myself. He picked up his net, placed it and the sketchbook on the sofa, then took my hand and said, "I'm delighted to meet you, Miss Newton. Did your journey go smoothly?"

I recalled that the bandit had wished me a smooth journey. Was this question meant as a hint—or a warning? I felt like he was testing me. "It went smoothly enough," I said, fighting to keep my voice even.

"I'm very glad to hear that." He gathered up the butterfly net and sketchbook and said, "I should put my gear away. I will leave you ladies to tea and return momentarily to chat with Miss Newton."

Mrs. Talbot gave a slight curtsy and said, "Yes, my lord."

He shook his head. "Now, Mrs. Talbot, what do I keep telling you about that?"

"Yes, sir." Her stiff tone indicated that she felt it wrong to be so casual with her employer, even if he was young enough to be her son.

He grinned. "That's better." He headed out, grabbing a few tea sandwiches as he left, but paused in the doorway and turned back. "Miss Newton, I have a question for you."

"Yes, sir?" My heart beat so hard I was afraid he could hear it. Would he ask about the train?

"Do you like bugs?"

That wasn't the question I'd anticipated, but thanks to my discussion with Mrs. Talbot, I wasn't taken aback. "I have yet to make fast friends with one."

His lips twitched like he was fighting a smile. "Are you afraid of them?"

I looked him square in the eyes and said firmly, "No, not at all." If he wanted to take that to mean I wasn't afraid of him either, he was welcome to do so.

He nodded with satisfaction. "Good. Good." Without another word he wandered off, again with that distracted air.

"What did you think of Lord Henry?" Mrs. Talbot asked, resuming her seat.

I wasn't quite sure how to answer. "He seems too young to have three children, or children that old," I said at last.

"They're not his. He's their guardian—their father's younger brother. Their mother died when the youngest was born, and when their father died a year ago, Lord Henry moved into the home to look after them."

I doubted a man responsible for three orphans would go about such risky business as banditry when he clearly had no need of funds. I must have been mistaken. There were probably dozens of men in the city with similar eyes. I was surprised to realize I felt slightly disappointed. If I had to be a governess, working for a bandit would make my life much more exciting. Now I supposed I had to hope for something like a madwoman in the attic, or perhaps a ghost.

Lord Henry returned a moment later. He sat in the chair next to Mrs. Talbot's and said, "Now, Mrs. Talbot, if you don't mind, I'd like to speak with Miss Newton alone."

She hesitated, and he said, "We're considering hiring her to chaperone Flora and Rollo. If you can't trust her alone with me, how can we trust her to supervise the children?" He gave me the slightest smile and added, "I assure you, her virtue is safe from me. You may stand in the hall if you wish to observe us." Mrs. Talbot reluctantly left the room, but she lurked in the hallway.

"Are you familiar with the sort of education that is customarily given to girls of my class?" he asked.

"Enough French to travel on the Continent, some drawing or painting, and enough music to perform for others?"

"Exactly. That is how Flora has been educated. In company, she smiles prettily and says little. I know of far too many men who would find that admirable in a wife, but that is not the sort of man I want her to marry. That's why although she doesn't need a governess, she does need some enlightenment. Do you have any ideas for how to achieve that?"

I finally felt like I was on familiar ground. "She should read the newspaper daily, at least one good magazine weekly, and classic literature regularly. I could then converse with her about those things so she would be prepared for social occasions." Although this was a proper interview, I felt like we were children playing house, talking about teaching someone barely younger than we were as though we were real adults.

He nodded enthusiastically and smiled. "Good, that makes sense. I would want you to do the same on a smaller scale with Rollo. He's getting a better education than she had, but I still feel it's lacking. With Olive, we have a chance to start her correctly. I've yet to find an adequate school for girls. I may resort to cutting her hair and dressing her as a boy so she can attend a decent school." He glanced at the open doorway and gave a friendly wave toward Mrs. Talbot. "I'm afraid my housekeeper doesn't approve, but I want to make it clear that although she managed the correspondence for filling the position, you would report directly to me, not to her."

He stood and extended a hand to assist me to my feet. "Now, would you like to meet the children?" He held his arm out to me, and I took it. He pointed out items of architectural interest as we made our way down the hall.

Inside a comfortable drawing room, a pretty, fair-haired girl played a grand piano while a lanky boy lay sprawled on the floor with schoolbooks in front of him. A little girl sat nearby with a book in her lap. The remnants of a tea were spread on a table in the middle of the room.

The smaller girl noticed us first. She jumped to her feet, crying out, "Uncle!" and ran to throw her arms around Lord Henry.

He tousled her brown curls and said, "Hello, Olive." He then addressed the others. "Flora, Rollo, this is Miss Newton."

The boy rose, came over to me, and bowed formally. "Roland Lyndon, Marquis of Westchester, at your service, miss," he said.

"But we call him Rollo," Lord Henry said. "We don't use titles at home."

Flora merely nodded at me as she kept playing. She was quite good, both technically and in musicality. There was real depth to her interpretation of the music. I could see why her uncle felt she had the potential to be more than just a decorative object.

"Hello," I said, feeling rather awkward. "It's a pleasure to meet all of you."

Olive flung her arms around my waist. If my corset hadn't already been cinched so tightly, she would have knocked the breath out of me. "Are you going to stay with us?" she asked. My heart went out to this child, who had already lost both parents at such a young age.

I squeezed her in response and said, "That is for your uncle to decide."

Lord Henry looked at me with surprise. "Oh, I thought you knew I was offering you the position. You do want it?"

I didn't know why I hesitated. I needed a job and a home, and this was my last option without starting my search anew. This was also the most beautiful house I'd ever seen and I'd already begun picturing myself living there. The only question was my nagging suspicion about Lord Henry. I studied his face again, and aside from his eyes, I saw nothing of the bandit. His way of walking, his mannerisms, even his voice were all different. The resemblance must have been my imagination.

"Why, yes, of course I do," I said at last.

"Then we should discuss details such as salary and schedule. Children, you can get to know Miss Newton better at dinner." He pried Olive's arms from around me, then patted her on the head before escorting me back to the morning room.

As we walked, he said, "We dine informally at home unless we're entertaining, and I do very little of that. You will join us, of course. That will be a good opportunity for the children to practice conversation. You'll keep to a normal school schedule on weekdays and will have Saturdays and Sundays free, aside from any social events where you would be needed as chaperone."

It was more generous than I could have imagined—almost too good to be true. When he told me my weekly salary, I wanted to pinch myself. Back in the morning room, he informed Mrs. Talbot that I had accepted the position. "Please show Miss Newton to her room," he instructed. He gave me a slight bow, squeezed my hand, and said, "Welcome to the family, Miss Newton," before leaving me alone with Mrs. Talbot.

I collected my bag, then Mrs. Talbot took me upstairs to a pleasant little room at the back of the house. It was simply furnished with a bed, wardrobe, desk, and dresser, and had its own bathroom. "I suppose we should send for your belongings," she said.

"I had my trunk held at Grand Central."

"I'll have the coachman retrieve it. Now, I'll leave you to get settled. We serve dinner at seven. I know that's early, but Lord Henry likes to include Olive, and she has an early bedtime. There's no need to dress. Lord Henry doesn't stand on ceremony." There was a distinct note of disapproval in her voice, and I wondered why she remained in his employ if she didn't like the way he did things.

When she was gone, I sank into the chair by the desk and allowed myself a long, deep sigh. I'd barely had time to remove my hat when Olive rushed into my room and flounced onto my bed. "I'm so glad you're staying," she said. "I didn't like the last governess, but I like you."

"You barely know me," I said, trying to hide my amusement.

"But I know these things." She dropped her voice to a dramatic whisper. "I have magical powers." She bounced off the bed. "Would you like to see the house? I could show you."

I was exhausted, but I didn't feel it was an invitation I could refuse. "I would like that very much."

She took my hand and dragged me into the hall. "The

schoolroom is here," she said, taking me across to a room over-looking the street. It was well equipped with books, a globe, some scientific apparatus, a desk, an easel, and an upright piano. "Uncle bought most of these things. He said our schoolroom before was woefully inadequate." She sounded like she must be mimicking her uncle without necessarily understanding the meaning.

Then she pulled me back across the hall to another bedroom, decorated in pink and white. "This is my room. We're neighbors. If I have nightmares, you will hear me."

"Do you often have nightmares?"

"Only sometimes. I dream about the airship crash that killed Papa. Uncle says it's only my imagination, since I wasn't there and don't know what it looked like for real, and my imagination probably makes it look even worse." She sounded out the word "imagination" slowly, making sure she got it right. "If I cry out, you will come to me, won't you?" she pleaded.

"I will," I assured her. "I sometimes have nightmares myself."

She pressed my hand and said earnestly, "If you cry out, I'll come to you."

She pointed out Rollo's and Flora's rooms, then led me downstairs to the library, which was something out of my wildest book-loving dreams. "There aren't many books in here I can read yet," Olive said. "My books are all in the schoolroom, but Uncle says that someday this will be my favorite room in the whole house." I got the impression that whatever Uncle said was accepted as gospel by Olive.

"Yes, I imagine it will be, if I do my job properly," I said. It was already my favorite room. My fingers itched to run along all those spines and see what wonders I might discover.

I reluctantly let Olive lead me out of the library to tour the rest of the mansion. We saw the dining room being set for dinner, the drawing room used for formal occasions, and many more rooms whose purpose I couldn't keep straight in my head. All of them were splendidly furnished and filled with artwork worthy of a museum. I could hardly believe that I would be living in a place like this. And to think I'd started the day terrified of what my future might hold.

Along the way, we passed a closed door. "That's Uncle's study," Olive informed me. "We're not allowed in there. The maids can't even go in there. Not that they want to. They don't like all those bugs. There's even a giant hairy spider." She said it with enough relish that I doubted she shared the maids' fears. "He has many valuable specimens, and some of them are so fragile that opening the door the wrong way disturbs them." She recited this as though it had been repeated to her many times. I wondered how many dragonfly wings had crumbled to dust because of Olive bursting in on her uncle.

When we returned to my room, Mrs. Talbot was there instructing a pair of footmen where to place my trunk. "Run along, Olive," she said when she saw us. "Give Miss Newton a chance to rest."

"Thank you for the tour, Olive," I said. She waved goodbye as she ran to her room.

"Would you like one of the maids to help you unpack?" Mrs. Talbot asked.

"No, thank you. I don't have much."

She dismissed the footmen, then said, "If you don't mind, I thought I should go over what you can expect tomorrow."

"Of course." I gestured her toward the chair and sat across from her on the edge of the bed.

"In the morning, you'll escort Rollo to school, leaving in time to arrive at nine. Olive usually goes along for the walk. You'll have lessons with Olive until lunchtime, after which the music teacher and drawing master arrive. The drawing master works with one girl while the music teacher works with the other, and then they switch. You'll be free during those lessons until it's time for you to meet Rollo at school."

"Surely Rollo is old enough to walk to and from school on his own," I said.

From her reaction, I might have thought I'd suggested that he run off to sea as a cabin boy on a pirate ship. "Oh no, that would not do at all. The children must be chaperoned at all times in public."

"Are they in danger?" I asked breathlessly, thinking I would do little good as a bodyguard.

"Not that kind of danger." She sighed. "Young people being what they are, we must take great caution that no unsuitable alliances or flirtations form."

"Are you worried about Rollo meeting shopgirls?"

She frowned. "You must not know the ways of the magisters.

To keep the magical blood pure, they must not mix with the non-magical."

My heart racing and a knot forming in my stomach, I asked, "What happens if a magister does . . ." I trailed off, searching for a euphemism, then settled for the one she'd used: ". . . mix with a nonmagical person?"

She looked even more horrified at that thought than she had when I suggested Rollo could walk to school on his own. Pressing her hand against her chest as if to quiet her heart, she said, "That would be unspeakable—an abomination!"

My stays seemed to constrict drastically around my chest, cutting off my breathing. There was a roaring in my ears, and my vision swam. It had never occurred to me that my very existence might be considered an abomination.

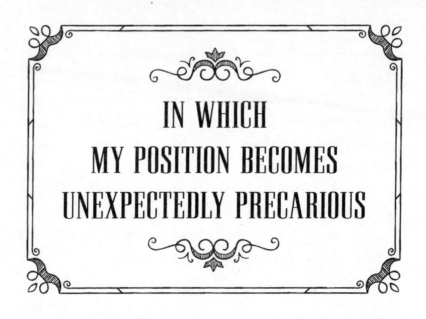

IN WHICH MY POSITION BECOMES UNEXPECTEDLY PRECARIOUS

Mrs. Talbot must have continued speaking, but I heard nothing over the roaring in my ears until she grasped my hand. "Miss Newton!" she said firmly enough to snap me out of my fugue. "You've gone absolutely ashen. Should I get the smelling salts?"

I came back to my senses enough to wave her away. "No, no, I'm quite all right. I'm afraid the events of the day caught up with me all at once." I gave her a smile that felt weak, shaky, and entirely unconvincing. "Please forgive me."

She patted my hand reassuringly. "You should rest until dinner, and I'll see to it that Olive leaves you alone." She slipped out of the room, easing the door shut behind her.

As soon as she left, I clasped my hands over my mouth to stifle a pained whimper, lest Olive hear my cry. I'd discovered

I had magical abilities when I was about Olive's age and tried to will a rosebud to open into a flower the way the magical princess in my storybook did, imagining a full blossom and channeling the power from the ether—and it worked. I tried other magical tricks I'd read about in fairy tales, like making feathers fly, conjuring balls of light, and sending scattered buttons into a jar, and I could do all of them. I had never seen anyone else in my family do these things, so I had kept it a secret.

A fanciful child with my head full of stories, I decided I was a princess in exile being kept safely in a secret hiding place until the time came for me to restore my kingdom. That seemed to explain so much about my family. My father was stern and remote with me, the way he wasn't with my siblings when they visited, because he wasn't really my father. He was my tutor, doing his duty to prepare me to one day rule my kingdom wisely. My mother must have been my nurse—in the stories, nurses always seemed to develop motherly feelings toward their charges.

When I was old enough to learn about biology, I discerned the likely truth. Although I had powers no one else in the family had and was very unlike my sister and brothers, I could see traces of my mother in myself. We had the same roundish face, wide-set eyes, and stubborn chin. It seemed as though my mother had been unfaithful to her husband with some magister, and I was the result. That explained my family even better than my princess fantasy—the large age gap between me and my siblings, the chilly distance between my parents, and the way my father was barely able to stand the sight of me when he wasn't teaching me.

I'd read many novels about nonmagical governesses falling in love with and eventually marrying their magister employers, and then there were all the fairy stories about nonmagical girls captivating magister princes. None of these had mentioned that such relationships were forbidden, even though that would have made far more interesting reading. Although I knew better than to think that novels were an accurate reflection of reality, I felt betrayed. Someone who read as much as I did shouldn't have been caught so unawares. But there had been few magisters at Yale because most of them went to England for their education, so I had learned everything I knew about them from novels, which I now realized had left out a critical fact. I had to wonder if these books perhaps reflected a magister fantasy about breaking with convention.

To think I'd worried that Lord Henry was secretly a bandit who knew I'd witnessed his crime when my real danger was that he might discover I was a magical half-breed. I wondered what would become of me if I were discovered, but there was no innocent way to ask. I told myself that I had nothing to fear as long as I exhibited no sign of having magical powers. I'd spent a lifetime keeping that secret, so it was second nature for me.

Lord Henry proved to be in earnest about dinner being informal. He and the children wore the same clothing they'd worn earlier. Olive greeted me as though she hadn't seen me for days, and Rollo stood politely until I was seated. Flora wore a distracted look similar to her uncle's, though I doubted she was thinking about insects. As soon as the soup had been served, Rollo blurted, "Uncle Henry, did you hear about the steam engine on Fifth Avenue today? I saw it out the window."

I nearly dropped my spoon in my soup. Could he have seen me alighting from the bus? No, it had let me off several blocks away.

"Really?" Lord Henry asked.

"Yes! It was like a big horse with wheels," Rollo excitedly described it with his hands waving, "but all in metal, and it chugged great puffs of smoke. Do you think steam power might replace magic?"

"I don't know," his uncle said. "I doubt we magisters would use steam for power, but it might replace horses."

"This was better than horses," Rollo enthused. "And it had a loud whistle."

"Our carriage has a bell," Olive said. "That's better than a whistle. It goes *ding, ding, ding.*"

"The whistle's louder," her brother argued.

"Louder isn't better."

"Yes, it is!"

"It's definitely not better at the dinner table," Lord Henry put in with a grin as he flicked his nephew on the ear. If my interview earlier had felt like a child's game, now I felt like I was sitting at a nursery table while the real adults were elsewhere.

"I wonder if they'll come back again," Rollo said. "I want to ride that bus. It must be exciting." I bit the inside of my lip to keep myself from smiling at the memory. It *had* been exciting.

"The Rebel Mechanics are treasonous," Lord Henry said mildly, but with an air of wistfulness, as though he was saying what a guardian should, even though he was just as interested as Rollo. "They're not the sort you should be associating with."

"I heard they're also experimenting with electricity," Rollo said, undaunted, as the footmen cleared the soup course and brought out the roast.

"Do you think it will be too cool tomorrow for my pink chiffon?" Flora asked, apparently not having heard a word of the conversation. "Or I could wear the lavender. I should call on the Merriweathers, and Jocelyn Merriweather looks awful in lavender, even though it's her favorite color. I look so much better in it than she does, so if we're both wearing lavender, it will be as though I've insulted her without saying a word." She smiled to herself. "Yes, I will definitely wear the lavender."

Lord Henry turned to her in dismay. "This is how you talk about your friends? I'd hate to be your enemy."

She heaved a deep sigh. "Honestly, Henry, I don't understand how anyone could be so socially inept. She's not *really* my friend. She's merely someone I call upon."

"If you don't like her, why do you call on her?" Rollo asked.

"Paying calls is a duty, not a pleasure." She directed her gaze heavenward, as though trying to conjure a halo of martyrdom around herself.

Lord Henry and Rollo both snorted with laughter, and Olive quickly joined in, imitating them. "Then I wonder what you'd do if I were to forbid you paying calls. You'd sulk for a week," Lord Henry said. "You'd run out of gossip entirely, and you couldn't show off your gowns."

Her eyes widened in panic. "You're not going to forbid me, are you?"

"Do it, Uncle Henry!" Rollo urged. Olive merely giggled.

Lord Henry's eyes twinkled, but he schooled his features into a stern expression—with visible effort—and said, "You may pay no calls."

"Henry, you wouldn't!" Flora yelped, throwing her napkin on the table and rising from her seat as her brother and sister sputtered with laughter.

Before Flora could complete her dramatic exit, Lord Henry grinned and said, "Tomorrow, that is. I'll be teaching you magic in the afternoon, after your music and drawing lessons."

"He got you there, Flora," Rollo chortled.

Flora flounced back to her seat. "That wasn't at all fair, Henry. You're *supposed* to be the adult in this house." Then she added hesitantly, "I may still pay calls on other days?"

"If I am not teaching you magic, you may," Lord Henry said. "But only if you want to."

I watched this entire exchange with fascination. I'd never had such conversations at dinner with my family, not only because my father never would have allowed it but also because all my siblings had left home before I left the nursery table to dine with the adults. Was this the way families without shameful secrets were? Behind the bickering, I got a sense of deep affection among the Lyndons, and I felt a pang of envy.

As if reading my mind, Lord Henry said, "We should all have behaved better for Miss Newton's first dinner with us. She must think we've escaped from the zoo."

"You three, perhaps," Flora said with a sniff. "*I've* been perfectly civilized."

"Why don't you tell us something of yourself, Miss Newton?" Lord Henry asked.

I took a sip of water to buy myself time to think. "My father is a professor and taught me the way he taught his students, starting when I was very young. I've done some tutoring and teaching myself. And now, here I am," I said, unsure what else I could say.

"But why did you decide to come here and be a governess?" Flora asked. "Couldn't you find a husband? Or is that why you're here?"

"Flora!" her uncle chided.

I looked directly at Flora and said, "My mother passed away recently after a yearlong illness, through which I nursed her. I needed a change of environment after that." Flora's haughty expression melted into a guilty wince.

Lord Henry jumped in to salvage the awkward moment, saying, "Miss Newton is quite well-read. Perhaps if you spend time with her, you'll learn to talk about something other than what color dress you'll be wearing."

Flora's glare chilled me. I could tell she had no desire to chat with me about anything and she resented the implication that I was in any way superior to her. "Well, *obviously* she won't be able to chat with me about dresses," she said with a toss of her hair. I had to admit she was right. I'd worn my most professional-looking gray dress, but even my fanciest party frock would look mousy next to Flora's day dress.

Lord Henry didn't seem to realize that she'd insulted me, and I supposed that in his world there was nothing wrong with not being able to discuss dresses. "There are many more worthy topics of conversation," he said. "I'm sure you'll soon realize that."

Not likely, said Flora's sidelong glance at me, and I hoped my performance wouldn't be evaluated based on my success with her.

As we left the dining room after the meal, Lord Henry stopped me. "I'm sure you've had a very long day. You're free for the rest of the evening. Breakfast is served in the breakfast room beginning at seven—I'm an early riser—and Rollo must be at school by nine. Mrs. Talbot will give you directions so you don't have to rely on him." He added with a crooked smile, "He'd probably lead you to the airfield or the docks and claim it was his school."

The next morning, I found the breakfast room with only a few wrong turns. Lord Henry was already there, sitting alone at the table. He glanced up from his newspaper as I entered and greeted me with a smile. "Good morning, Miss Newton. I trust you slept well. Your room is comfortable?"

"Yes, very, thank you."

"Breakfast is on the sideboard. Would you care for coffee or tea?"

"Tea, please."

He gestured to a footman, who left and then reappeared a moment later with a pot of tea and a cup on a tray, along with a small rack of toast. Rollo soon entered the room, yawning loudly. He wore a school uniform with a wide white collar, and his hair was slicked tight against his head. He filled his plate with food, then sat beside his uncle, appropriating a section of the newspaper that Lord Henry had already read and put aside. Rollo hadn't read much before he shouted, "Ye gods!"

"Rollo, language," his uncle corrected without raising his eyes from the newspaper.

"But, Uncle Henry, the Masked Bandits struck again yesterday!"

I couldn't resist looking at Lord Henry to see his reaction. He didn't show the slightest sign that this story affected him. His eyes didn't widen, narrow, or blink, and his face didn't redden or pale. No muscles twitched or tightened. He merely kept reading as he took a sip of tea and said, "Really?" in a tone of polite disinterest.

"Yes! They robbed a train!" Rollo frowned as he read some more, then his eyebrows rose. "Hey, it was the train from New

Haven. Miss Newton, didn't you come from New Haven? Was that your train?"

"I suppose it could have been," I said, trying to imitate Lord Henry's disinterested tone while surreptitiously watching him from beneath my eyelashes. "But it was a very big train, with many cars."

"Oh." Rollo sounded so disappointed that I was tempted to tell him about my adventure.

"There's an article about a new model of airship," Lord Henry said. "It's on page three." He knew exactly how to distract his nephew. Rollo eagerly turned to that page and became lost in the newspaper. Once Olive came skipping into the room, she took over the conversational burden, chattering amiably about any number of seemingly unrelated topics, to which her elders responded with nods and vague noises.

Lord Henry checked his watch, then said, "Rollo, you'd best leave for school. I'll save the newspaper for you." He nodded at the footman, who tugged on the bellpull on the wall.

Mrs. Talbot appeared and handed me a neatly drawn map. "This is the way to Rollo's school. It isn't far."

"I can show her," Olive said. "I know the way."

Rollo whirled to face his uncle. "I have to have the *governess* walk me to school?"

"You know very well that you don't go out without a chaperone," Lord Henry said.

"But you've been coming with me." I now understood Rollo's dismay. Walking to school with his uncle must have felt like a manly outing, but walking with the governess would make him feel like a child again.

Lord Henry's face softened slightly, so he must have understood as well. "I may still, when my schedule permits, but it is Miss Newton's job, and you will go with her." His voice grew slightly sharper with the last phrase, making it an order.

Rollo sighed dejectedly, and I hurried to say, "Olive and I will be taking a morning walk before we begin lessons. Would you be so kind as to escort us as far as your school?"

Rollo gave me a frown before saying, "I would be honored." Lord Henry mumbled a goodbye without looking up from his newspaper. Olive took my hand as we left the house, and Rollo held his elbow out for me to take.

I felt so very grownup and responsible in my first official task as governess. Then I wondered if there was something I should be doing. I supposed I should be getting better acquainted with my charges. "What is your favorite subject in school?" I asked Rollo.

"Mathematics. I want to be an engineer, but Father said that was no occupation for a gentleman. It's a trade, and a marquis isn't supposed to pursue a trade." His eyes lit up. "Maybe the Rebel Mechanics really will start a revolution, and then I won't be noble anymore and I can do anything I want!"

"I'm telling Uncle!" Olive said. "You're not supposed to talk like that!"

"Olive, no one likes a tattletale," I scolded gently. "I am present, and I will decide what needs to be told. I don't think Rollo meant anything by it."

After we saw Rollo safely into the care of his headmaster, Olive and I headed home, taking a different route along a more commercial street. That pleased her immensely, as she enjoyed looking in the shop windows, and I was glad of the excuse to do so myself. With such shops selling so many wonderful things, I could see how Flora could have an entire conversation about clothing.

"I got a doll for Christmas from this store," Olive informed me in a running commentary as we walked. "Flora buys her gloves here. She got a hat here once, but she didn't like it, and she told everyone else how awful it was, so nobody else bought hats here, and now it's not a hat shop anymore. It's a shoe shop. I don't know if their shoes are good, though. I don't think we've ever bought anything there. Do you like shopping, Miss Newton?"

"I haven't done much of it."

"Don't go with Flora. It's *boring* because she won't make up her mind and she has to look at *everything*. Maybe you could take me shopping."

"We'll see."

Apparently taking my noncommittal answer as an affirmative, she began skipping and singing, "We're going shopping! We're going shopping!"

Although I had worked as a tutor, I hadn't the least notion of the extent of a governess's duties. Was I responsible for Olive's deportment, and what were the boundaries of acceptable behavior? Should I consider skipping and singing harmless childish high spirits or unladylike actions that must be corrected?

I was still wrestling with this dilemma when I heard a voice calling my name. I turned to see a newspaper boy standing on the corner. "Nat!" I said with a smile. It was reassuring to see a familiar face.

"Good morning to you, Verity," he said. With a glance at Olive, he added, "I take it you got the job."

"Yes, I did. Olive, this is my friend Nat. Nat, this is Lady Olive Lyndon, my pupil." I realized that it might be improper to introduce Olive to a nonmagical boy, but since she was only six, I decided not to worry. Olive gave a pretty curtsy and bobbed her head so that her ringlets bounced.

"You'll want to read the newspaper this morning, Verity," Nat said with a wink. I felt I owed him at least the price of a newspaper after he'd helped me the day before, so I fished a penny out of my pocket and handed it to him. He presented a copy of the *World* to me with a bow. My father had subscribed to the *Herald*, and that had been the newspaper at the breakfast table that morning. Given Nat's association with the rebels, I assumed that the *World* must take a more radical editorial approach. Feeling a little uneasy about how acceptable such a paper might be, I folded it with the headlines inside and tucked it under my arm.

Nat's eyes widened, and he hissed, "Cross the street, Verity."

There was so much fear and tension in his face and voice that I didn't hesitate or ask questions. I clutched Olive's hand and darted with her across the street. Once we were safely on the opposite side, I looked back to see a pair of policemen approaching Nat. One of them grabbed a newspaper out of his hands, read the front page, then rolled it up and smacked him on the head with it.

"What's this, then?" the policeman snarled. "Selling sedition, are you, boy? This paper doesn't have the royal stamp on it, so it's not legal to sell. Did you know that?"

"I don't know anything about stamps," Nat cried. "I just sell papers."

The policeman backhanded him across the face, then sent him sprawling with a rough shove. I was so outraged to see a child treated this way that I ran back across the street to go to his aid, entirely forgetting that I still held Olive's hand.

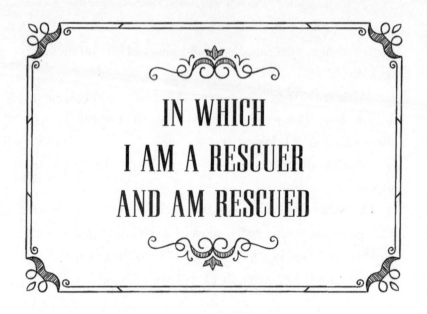

IN WHICH
I AM A RESCUER
AND AM RESCUED

"**Leave that boy alone!**" I shouted as I ran. "**He's not** responsible for what's in the newspaper."

When the policemen turned their attention to me, I belatedly realized that I'd dragged Olive into the confrontation. She stood beside me, staring wide-eyed at the proceedings. "And who might you be, miss?" one of the policemen growled at me as, behind him, Nat climbed to his feet and brushed himself off.

I didn't want to associate my employer's name with my impetuousness, but that became a moot point when Olive said, "She's my governess and I'm Lady Olive Lyndon. You were being mean to that boy, and that's *wrong*. Uncle says if you hit people who are weaker than you are, you're a *bully*."

I had to bite my tongue to keep a straight face, and Nat looked as though he might burst from holding back laughter. The policemen were stunned into silence, which Olive then filled by adding, "And I have magical powers." The situation was so ridiculous that the tension eased.

The policeman who'd addressed me gave Olive a courteous bow and said, "My apologies, your ladyship." To Nat, he said, "I'll have to confiscate your papers." He and his partner picked up the stack of newspapers at Nat's feet and, with one last glare at the boy, headed off.

"Thanks, Verity, you're a real piston," Nat said.

"No, she's not. She's a governess," Olive informed him.

"I'm sorry about your newspapers," I said.

He shrugged. "I can get more." He added with a grin, "This happens all the time when you're selling an unauthorized publication."

"What's 'unauthorized'?" Olive asked.

"It means the government hasn't approved it," I explained. "Come along now, Olive. Good day, Nat."

"Good day to you, Verity, and Olive, my heroine." He gave her a formal bow.

"What's a heroine?" Olive asked, resuming her skipping as we crossed the street.

"It means you're a very brave young lady who stands up for what's right."

"Oh, Uncle will like that." I groaned inwardly. I didn't want Lord Henry to know that I'd brought his niece into conflict with the police on my first day, but the way Olive talked, he might not hear half of what she said, and if I asked her not to tell, it would look even worse if the story came out. "Why did that boy call you Verity?" she asked.

"That's my name."

"I thought your name was Miss Newton."

"My Christian name is Verity, like your name is Olive. It's Latin for 'truth.'" My name was rather ironic, given my origins. I suspected my name had been my father's cruel joke on my mother.

"Verity, Verity, Verity," she chanted as she skipped. "Will I learn Latin?"

"Yes, you will."

"All of Uncle's bugs have Latin names." She giggled. "You have a Latin name, so maybe you're one of Uncle's bugs!"

Lord Henry nearly ran into us on the front steps when we returned to the house. He had his nose in a book, and an older man behind him caught him by the back of his coat in time to prevent a collision. Lord Henry didn't seem to notice. The man with him nodded a "good day" to us before he released Lord Henry's coat.

"That's Matthews, Uncle's valet," Olive informed me. "Rollo says his job is to make sure Uncle remembers to eat, sleep, and get dressed and to keep him from walking into walls." I got the feeling that one should never say anything within earshot of Olive that one didn't want repeated.

As far as I could tell, Flora still wasn't out of bed, but Lord Henry hadn't mentioned any routine for her other than my engaging her in conversation, which we could do later, and her afternoon music and drawing lessons, so I decided not to worry about her. Up in the schoolroom, I set Olive to working on her handwriting by copying a page from the science text. While she worked, I unfolded the newspaper I'd bought from Nat. Now I understood why every newspaper I'd seen before had the royal seal stamped on it. This one definitely took a different editorial approach than the newspapers I'd read. The main story on the front page was about the steam engine winning a race against a magical carriage. The story went on to describe the implications of bringing mass transportation into a restricted area. The article was vividly written, with a perspective that could only have come from someone on that bus. The author's name was Elizabeth Smith—the Lizzie who'd sat next to me, I guessed.

The other articles covered injustices in the city, the impact of taxes, and suppression of technological progress. I'd thought I was well-informed, but I had been entirely unaware of many of these issues. The only story this newspaper seemed to have in common with the paper Lord Henry and Rollo had discussed at breakfast was the Masked Bandits' robbery, only this paper seemed far more in favor of it. Editorial cartoons depicted magisters wearing wizards' robes and pointy hats covered in stars, and these magisters lived in remote castles, ruling from on high. I had to put down the newspaper when Olive brought her work to me. "Very nice, Olive," I told her. "Now let's do some math."

The morning passed quickly. Olive was an apt pupil who was eager to please. I had already seen how readily she memorized anything she heard, and that applied to her schoolwork as well. I seldom had to tell her anything twice. She also had an inquisitive mind and asked thoughtful questions. I understood why Lord Henry was reluctant to send her to the typical school for girls of her class. Flora finally emerged from her room for lunch and very pointedly refused to make conversation with me. After several attempts, I gave up and focused on Olive.

I got a respite after lunch when the music and art teachers arrived. It was a fine September day, so I put on my hat and gloves and crossed the street to the park. I'd read about New York's Central Park but hadn't realized it was so vast. I had only to walk a short while before I was able to forget I was in the middle of a city, in spite of the occasional magical carriage passing by. It was easy to imagine that I was out on a country lane. I might be a grand lady with a great estate or the daughter of a prosperous farmer, someone who didn't have to worry about securing or maintaining employment, who knew her place in the world instead of being a misfit in any place.

I was so caught up in my reverie that I was taken entirely by surprise when someone grabbed me bodily and lifted me off my feet. I couldn't find the air to scream, and I couldn't seem to move my arms and legs to fight back. Then a vehicle raced past, right through the spot on the lane where I'd been standing. It was a magical open-topped roadster, so it made little noise other than a soft hum and the crunch of wheels on gravel. The driver, who was dressed like a fashionable dandy, didn't slow at all and appeared entirely unaware that he'd nearly run down a pedestrian.

He wore his hat pulled low, and a pair of driving goggles obscured his face, but I got a glimpse of reddish hair before the roadster disappeared from view.

"Why, it's Verity!" a female voice near me said. I blinked in confusion, unsure why anyone in the park should know who I was. Then I recognized Lizzie rushing to my side. "Verity, are you all right?" she asked, her brow creased with concern.

The man holding me asked, "Are you able to stand on your own, miss?"

I turned to look at him, and when my eyes met his, I forgot everything else: my recent near miss, Lizzie, the park. All I saw was his green eyes boring into my soul. From the way he looked at me, I guessed that he'd been struck the same way. We were frozen together in that moment.

While I was incapable of speech and had even forgotten that I'd been asked a question, Lizzie answered for me. "Let's get her over to that bench, Alec. *My* legs are shaking, and I wasn't the one almost run down." They walked me between them to a nearby bench, where they settled me. I only realized I must have had tears springing to my eyes when the man handed me his handkerchief. Lizzie then said, "Alec, go get her some lemonade. She's had quite a shock."

I was unable to find my voice in time to protest before Alec darted off across the park to a refreshment stand. I dabbed at my eyes with a shaking hand, then clutched the handkerchief and tried to will myself into overcoming the combined shock of the near accident and the rapturous moment I'd just experienced.

Lizzie sat beside me on the bench and squeezed my hand. "It's fortunate that we came along when we did and that Alec has such excellent reflexes." Her voice sharpened. "Those magpies think the city belongs to them. They don't look out for anyone else. I don't know how many times I've nearly been run down by magpie dandies out for a spin in their fancy little roadsters."

My wits finally returned, and I remembered that I was in the company of a rebel. But she didn't look like a radical. She could have been any girl out for a stroll in the park. She wasn't even wearing the red ribbon and gear of the Rebel Mechanics. "I saw your article about the race," I said, finding my voice. "At least, I presumed you wrote it."

"Yes, 'Smith' is my nom de plume—or nom de guerre, as the case may be. It wouldn't be safe to use my real name when reporting on such topics and for such a newspaper."

"Being a journalist must be very exciting." When I had to find a way to support myself, I hadn't even considered journalism, although I could write quite well. I supposed there were far too many books about well-bred, educated young women being governesses and too few about young women being reporters.

Alec returned with two glasses of lemonade, one of which he handed to me with a bow, and the other to Lizzie. "Verity, I'd like you to meet Alec Emfinger," she said. "He's our genius who created the steam engine. Alec, this is Verity. She was one of your passengers yesterday. Oh dear, I don't know your surname, Verity. That's what happens when I let my brother make introductions."

So Alec was my savior. I hadn't seen him without his goggles yesterday. I had to fight to find my voice. "I'm Verity Newton," I said, answering Lizzie without taking my eyes off Alec. I added to him, "Thank you for saving my life."

He doffed his hat, revealing neatly trimmed fair hair, and gave me a slight bow. "The pleasure is all mine, Miss Newton. I'm glad I came along at the right time." He looked like he was about nineteen, and he reminded me of the university students I'd known in New Haven. He certainly didn't look like the radicals pictured in newspaper cartoons. None of them looked at all heroic or noble the way he did.

"Verity, you must tell me, did you get the position?" Lizzie asked, placing her hand lightly on my arm.

I dragged my gaze away from Alec to answer her. "Yes, I did. And I must thank you both for the ride. I might not have been on time for the interview otherwise."

"Which household employed you?"

I tensed, unsure I should tell the rebels where I worked, but not answering would be rude. "I'm working for the Lyndon family," I said.

"The marquis?" Alec asked.

"No, the marquis died in an airship accident a little more than a year ago," Lizzie said. "Don't you remember? You said that ship had a design flaw, something about the balloon material, and you expected a disaster. You gloated for days after it happened."

"The current marquis is one of my charges," I said. "My employer is the children's uncle. He's their guardian."

Alec sat on my other side, and his proximity sent a warm flush through my body. "You landed well, then," he said. "That's one of the highest families in the colonies."

"And not just because of the title," Lizzie added. "Do you know who the children's grandfather is?"

"It hasn't been mentioned," I said.

"Their mother was the daughter of Samuel DeLancey, the royal governor."

"Really? I had no idea."

"You didn't know this before you applied for the position?"

"No. I only wanted to find a position in a good home."

Lizzie nodded. "I understand. Women like us can't afford to be choosy when we must make our own way in the world. You're fortunate to have found such an excellent position. I may even be a little envious."

"But you're a newspaper reporter!"

"You're a governess for one of the highest families in the American colonies. I suppose they also want you to act as chaperone?"

"Yes."

"So you'll be going to balls and parties and meeting the most important people in the colonies, maybe even people visiting from England."

My job suddenly seemed a lot more interesting. "I hadn't thought of it that way."

Alec chuckled, and I turned to see him grinning at me. He had a nice smile that transformed his face from studious to boyish. "Aye, you've landed well. And to think you arrived in this new life on my machine. I'm honored to have been allowed to help." His voice was soft and husky, and he gazed at me with the same intensity as before. For a moment, I felt like the two of us were alone in the park, but then I remembered Lizzie. They'd been walking in the park together—was he her beau? She didn't appear to take offense at the way he focused so intently on me.

I smiled back at him, sure my cheeks must be flaming. "It's better than any magical pumpkin coach."

He winked. "Don't remind the magpies of that story. Next thing you know, they'll be turning pumpkins to coaches left and right, and I can't compete with that."

"Oh, but it was wonderful, better than magic," I insisted. Then I remembered how the ride had ended and felt bad for not having asked sooner. "Did the police catch you?"

"No, they didn't," he said, beaming. "You don't have to worry about us. We've got a number of hiding places. By the time they caught up with us beyond the magpie zone, Bessie was safe and an ordinary team of horses was pulling the bus. Everyone on Fifth Avenue must have imagined a speeding bus pulled by a steam engine."

"It really is a wonderful machine," I said.

"That's merely a small one," he said. He gestured animatedly as he spoke, his voice rising with fervor. "A larger one could pull a train. Or power a boat. A smaller one might drive a carriage. Steam power could run factories. I know a man who uses a steam engine to generate electrical power for light and to run machinery, even to send messages over long distances. With machines, we can do anything magic can do." He was so passionate about the subject and so close to me that I found my breath quickening in response.

Lizzie leaned across me and patted him on the knee. "Now, Alec, I'm sure Verity doesn't have all day." To me, she added, "He can go on for hours about his machines. You should hear him when he gets together with his university friends."

"My machines may win our freedom," he insisted. "If we don't need magic, then we don't need magisters, and then we don't need the aristocracy or Britain. They can cut off our power, like they did a century ago in the last rebellion, and it won't affect us at all. The factories can still run and goods can be delivered without magisters."

"See what I mean?" Lizzie said with a raised eyebrow.

I smiled at her, but it felt strained. These could be very dangerous people to know. Lord Henry might have had *Ideas*, but I doubted he'd want someone associated with the rebels teaching his wards, and it was entirely possible that he was within earshot, crawling through the bushes on a search for insect specimens.

Suddenly uncomfortable with my companions and the conversation, I checked my watch without really looking at it and said, "I should get back to the house. It was a pleasure meeting you properly, Mr. Emfinger."

Lizzie shot him a glare, to which he responded with a slight shrug. He turned to me and touched the brim of his hat. "Like-wise. I'm sure I'll see you around town, Verity."

"Thank you again for saving my life. And for the lemonade."

"Don't mention it at all," Alec said, standing and offering me a hand up. He gave my hand a lingering squeeze, adding with a smile, "On second thought, feel free to mention my heroics as often as you like."

Lizzie shook her head and sighed with long-suffering patience as she stood and took my glass from me. "Don't encourage him, or he'll be quite impossible."

"Have you ever considered that she might like impossible?" he asked her, smiling and winking at me. He was almost as dash-ing as the masked bandit had been—and possibly even more dangerous.

Before I could do anything impulsive and improper, I stam-mered another goodbye and hurried away. Despite wanting to, I forced myself not to look over my shoulder at Alec. If I had been the sort of girl who kept a diary that was more than a list of books I'd read and my thoughts on them, I'd have run home to record this encounter. I was crossing the street to the Lyndon home when I realized I still clutched Alec's handkerchief. I tucked it carefully into my pocket before climbing the front steps.

I entered the house to the sound of a piano. Flora must have been having her lesson. Her lush, passionate music perfectly suited my mood. I couldn't hold back a wistful sigh as I remem-bered the feeling of Alec's arms around me, the lightning bolt that had struck when I looked into his eyes. I jumped guiltily when I sensed someone behind me and turned just in time to step out of the way before Lord Henry stumbled into me. He was intent on the net he held with a large, vividly colored butterfly caught in it and didn't seem to see me. He also didn't seem to see the statue in his path.

With some trepidation about being so forward with my employer, I grabbed his arm and gave him a sharp pull, just before he fell into the arms of a naked marble woman. He blinked at me over the top of his glasses, then pushed them up his nose with his forearm. "Oh dear, you seem to have rescued me from a rather improper embrace, Miss Newton," he said with a rueful smile. "I'm afraid my glasses slipped, and I'm quite blind without them." I thought that if he'd been the one with me in the park, he'd have fallen headlong into the carriage's path and we'd both have been killed. "And now I'd better take care of this specimen." He started for the stairs, paused, then turned back to me. "Once you get Rollo this afternoon, you'll be free until dinner. I'll be teaching the children their magic lessons."

After I had Rollo safely home and in no danger of being seduced by a nonmagical girl or—more likely—running away to join the Rebel Mechanics, I went to my room. I hardly knew what to do with myself in all this spare time. I supposed it was the perfect opportunity to read my novel.

I settled onto my bed with my book, but I couldn't concentrate on the story. My mind kept returning to that afternoon in the park. I took Alec's handkerchief out of my pocket and held it to my nose to see if I could detect any trace of his scent, since that was an element missing from my memory. Unfortunately, it didn't smell like anything that reminded me of him, but I hid it in the drawer of my nightstand anyway. Even if I never saw him again, I'd have that memento of my adventure.

I tried to return to my book, but my thoughts still strayed. I finally gave up and closed my eyes to relive the moment—his arms around me, his eyes meeting mine, then later him smiling at me and his eyes flashing with passion when he discussed his cause.

I was jolted out of my thoughts when a wave of power washed over me, heightening every one of my senses and setting my nerves on fire. If I hadn't been lying down, I might have fallen. I shivered and burned as if with fever, and the sensation came in intense waves.

The magic lessons must have begun. I had never been around anyone else who could use magic, so I'd never known what it felt like. But the sensation was familiar, and I realized I'd felt something similar during the train robbery, only I'd attributed my reaction to the excitement of the situation and dismissed the idea that magisters would rob trains. If this was the way I reacted to magic being used nearby, then keeping my secret in a magical household would be impossible.

IN WHICH
I RECEIVE MULTIPLE
INVITATIONS

The sense of magic gradually became less shocking
and painful as I became accustomed to it, but I doubted I could
avoid reacting visibly when it was used. Surely magisters could
control or block the sensations, or else they'd go mad. I knew
very little about my magical heritage, but how was I to learn? I
couldn't ask to observe Lord Henry's lessons with the children
if I couldn't mask my reaction, and a commoner like me couldn't
ask for instruction from a magister without revealing that I had
forbidden powers.

When I entered the dining room later that evening, Olive and
Rollo were in high spirits, while Flora made a great effort to appear bored. No one commented that I was pale or looked ill, even
though I felt like I'd been put through a clothes wringer.

After grace, Lord Henry started the conversation by saying,
"Olive, would you like to tell Miss Newton what you learned?"

"I lit a candle, all by myself!" she said, beaming.

"We have lights," Flora sighed wearily. "I don't see why we need to learn to light candles. We don't even *use* candles."

"It's not about lighting a candle. It's about channeling and controlling the power," her uncle said. "The candle is merely an exercise."

"It's not as though we need to know how to *use* magic," Flora said with a toss of her hair. "We have magical devices to do things for us. Nobody who's anybody actually has to *perform* magic. That's so old-fashioned."

That was welcome news to me. If aristocratic magisters seldom used magic, then I might not suffer too terribly. But Lord Henry's eyes hardened and his jaw firmed, so that he lost his usual vague look. "Anyone can use a magical device—a servant can drive a magical carriage—but you have *power*. You've been given an incredible gift, and you will learn how to use it," he said, spitting the words out so crisply that little Olive shied away from him. "The rest of the aristocracy has become lazy, resting on their ancestors' achievements and willing to pay for magical power provided by magisters beneath us, but *we* will use our gifts." I wished I could ask him more about that. I'd assumed that all magisters were upper-crust, but it sounded as though some of them worked to provide the magic that powered their devices, which put them below the nobility but still above the nonmagical.

"I like using magic!" Olive piped up. "I'll be better at magic than you are, Flora. Look, can you do this?" She closed her eyes and concentrated very intently, then moved her hand like she was lifting something invisible. Her spoon rose a few inches off the table. It wasn't powerful magic, but it was performed so close to me that I felt the power surge through me in a violent wave. I couldn't suppress my reaction, so I grabbed my water glass, took a sip, and then began coughing as though the water had gone down the wrong way. That gave me an excuse to convulse and have tears in my eyes.

Flora unwittingly deflected attention from me by continuing the argument. "A high-born lady doesn't need magic," she insisted.

"Without it, there's no difference between you and the daughter of some nonmagister military hero or wealthy capitalist who couldn't marry into nobility," Rollo countered.

"But it's my *birth* that matters, not my magic. My father was a marquis and my grandfather is a duke, so I can marry a nobleman."

With a wicked grin at his sister, Rollo said, "Someday, some high-born lord will ask you to prove you can at least light a candle so he'll know you're not a commoner in disguise, and when you can't, he won't marry you. No one will."

"Men will want to marry me because of my position," Flora said.

Before the argument could escalate, Lord Henry said, "Did anyone read anything interesting today?"

"One of my friends at school had a newspaper that told all about the steam engine racing a magical carriage," Rollo said. "But it wasn't in the *Herald*. They missed the story entirely."

"And what about you, Flora?"

She gave a deep sigh and asked, *"Must I?"*

"If you don't want to participate in the conversation, you don't have to. I'm sure Miss Newton has something interesting to say."

I scrambled for some topic to discuss, but Flora shot me a chilling glare and then went into a summary of the *Herald*'s society pages: a list of who was holding balls in the coming weeks, who was expected to attend, which couples had announced engagements, and which families had gone to the Continent. When she finished, she smiled smugly, daring her uncle to comment.

Lord Henry's eyes widened in dismay. "Surely that's not your idea of conversation," he said. "Miss Newton, what do you talk about with your friends?"

His question caught me off-guard. The truth was, I didn't have many friends, not real ones. But I wouldn't admit that to Flora, who looked at me with a sly smile that said she knew I wasn't a very popular girl in any social circle. "Most of my friends were students at the university, so we talked about the books they were reading for class," I said, omitting the fact that these talks had been tutoring sessions. "We discussed the philosophies or principles from the books."

"I'd never be invited to another party if I had *that* kind of conversation," Flora protested to her uncle.

"I can't imagine any man wants to hear a list of the clothing you've bought lately," Lord Henry argued. *"I'd* rather discuss books with Miss Newton."

Flora gave me an appraising glance that clearly found me

wanting as a companion, then turned back to Lord Henry. Batting her eyelashes innocently, she said, "Well, if you insist on discussing something else, I have to say that they really must do something about that gang of bandits."

"Why do you say so?" I asked, trying to sound only casually interested.

"People should be able to travel without having their journeys interrupted by such unpleasantness. They don't even take much money. It doesn't seem as though it's the amount of money that matters to these bandits, but rather to whom the money belongs."

She had surpassed my knowledge of the event, which was limited to having experienced it. I'd seen them take the royal courier's bag that he'd said contained dispatches, but I didn't know what else they'd stolen before they reached my car. The guards had already been chasing them, so they must have committed a robbery before then, and they'd had those heavy sacks. But then why did they bother taking the courier's bag? "To whom does the money belong?" I asked, pretending that I knew already and was merely quizzing her.

"It always belongs to the government. In yesterday's robbery, they took tax money being delivered to the royal bank here in New York." She held her head high and gave me a smug smile, as if to point out that not only was she wealthy and beautiful, but she was as clever as I was when she wanted to be. There was no way in which she wasn't superior to me. It would have stung more if I hadn't been distracted by thinking about what she'd said.

"That is very interesting," Lord Henry said. "I look forward to hearing what you have to share with us tomorrow night." He paused, then said, "I saw the most exquisite swallowtail today."

"Why would it swallow its tail?" Olive asked with a giggle.

Rollo nudged her shoulder playfully. "It's a butterfly that has a tail like a swallow—the bird—right, Uncle Henry?"

The current events discussion thus became a lecture on butterflies. The two younger children participated, but Flora just sat there. I pretended to follow the conversation, smiling and nodding at what appeared to be appropriate points, while my mind was on what Flora had said about the bandits. Stealing from the government and taking royal dispatches suggested motives beyond mere greed, and that somewhat changed my perception.

Lord Henry stopped me as we left the dining room after the meal, letting the others go on ahead. "I think that went well enough, don't you?"

"You—you do?" I stammered.

He grinned boyishly. "That was the first time Flora has ever talked about anything but clothing or paying calls at the dinner table. I knew she wasn't as vapid as she pretends to be. Excellent work for your first day on the job, Miss Newton."

"I really can't take credit for that."

"But you are a good example to her." He bowed slightly to me. "Have a pleasant evening, Miss Newton."

I dragged myself wearily up the stairs to my room. This had only been one day, and not a particularly busy one, and yet I felt utterly drained. There wasn't as much physical exertion as there had been when I was nursing my mother, but I felt like I had to constantly remain alert. Although it was early in the evening, I could think of nothing but going to sleep. I was already pulling the pins out of my hair as I entered my room.

I threw back the covers on my bed and picked up the pillow to retrieve my nightgown from beneath it, then stumbled backward in horror. Fortunately, I was too tired to scream. I hadn't believed myself to be afraid of spiders, but then I'd never encountered one like this. It was nearly the size of my palm and covered in black fur. Now I understood why some of the previous governesses had fled.

When the spider didn't move after several minutes of me staring at it, I realized that it wasn't alive. It must have been one of Lord Henry's specimens, and I suspected Rollo was the culprit. Although Flora would probably take great delight in tormenting me, I couldn't imagine her willingly handling a giant spider.

The key would be not to react in a way that would reward Rollo, and I was glad I hadn't screamed. I took a sheet of writing paper from my desk, slid it under the spider, then carefully slid my hand under the paper, cradling the spider in my palm. I marched to Lord Henry's study and knocked on the door. When he opened it just far enough to peer at me, I held the spider out to him, saying, "I believe your friend got lost and ended up in the wrong room." As soon as he took it from me, I turned to go.

He called after me, "Miss Newton!" I stopped and slowly turned around. "I am terribly sorry about this, and I will punish Rollo."

"Don't," I said, shaking my head. "I would prefer that he think I didn't notice."

"You're not going to leave?" He sounded surprisingly concerned at the prospect.

"Over a little prank? Of course not."

It wasn't until I returned to my room that a glance in the mirror reminded me I'd taken my hair down already and had confronted my employer in that state of disarray. It hardly seemed to matter compared to everything else that had happened that day. Between dragging my youngest charge into conflict with the police, being narrowly rescued by a rebel, discovering the danger of being surrounded by magic, and earning what was likely to be the lifelong enmity of my oldest charge, it had been quite a first day on the job.

The next morning, I derived some satisfaction from the way Rollo studied me as though he was waiting for a reaction. He flinched every time his uncle spoke to him at breakfast and was overly polite to me on the way to school. He hesitated before entering the school, then blurted, "Flora made me do it."

"What did Flora make you do?" I asked.

"The spider in your bed. I didn't want to, but she thought it would be funny, and she said she'd tell Uncle Henry . . . well, there was something she said she'd tell him that I would rather he not know. But I wasn't being mean to you."

"I hardly noticed it," I said, and then I turned to Olive and added, "and we don't need to discuss this further with anyone. It will be our secret."

At home I found an unexpected letter in the morning post. It was from Lizzie, apologizing if Alec's radical talk had made me uncomfortable. "You must forgive him," she wrote. "Machines are his passion, and all he can see is the good they could do." She went on to invite me for afternoon refreshments. There was no time to decline the invitation, so once the girls began their music and art lessons, I put on my hat and went out.

Lizzie had given me the address of a coffee shop on Third Avenue. Although it was only four blocks from the Lyndon home, it might as well have been in an entirely different city. The streets were dirty and noisy, full of horse-drawn carriages and omnibuses, and there were many more people on the sidewalks. "Oh, good, you came!" she cried when I entered the shop, taking both my hands in hers and squeezing them fiercely. "I was worried you'd never want anything more to do with me. You fled so quickly yesterday."

"I was a little taken aback," I admitted.

"I am very sorry for that. Sometimes I wish I could muzzle those boys." She hooked her elbow through mine and led me to a table. "I do want us to be friends. You'll need friends outside magpie land, and I could do with some intelligent conversation that's not about machines."

She sounded so contrite that I wanted to reassure her. "I would like that," I said.

She brightened instantly. "Oh, good!" We sat down, and a

waiter soon came over. "I'll have coffee with milk, and we'll have some butter cakes," she said to him. "Verity?"

"I'll have a cup of tea."

The waiter stiffened and snarled, "We do not offer tea in this establishment."

"She's new here," Lizzie said to him. "She must not know."

"Do you offer lemonade?" I asked nervously. I didn't frequent coffee shops, but I didn't think it common to be criticized so harshly for one's choice of beverage.

"Lemonade it is. One moment, please," he said.

"This shop is sympathetic to our cause, and patriots don't drink tea," Lizzie explained when he was gone.

"Why ever not?" I asked.

"Because all tea in the American colonies must go through England so that we have to pay English taxes on it. We aren't allowed to import it directly from China or India. It's only a small form of protest, but every little thing that strikes back at them helps us."

"I never heard anything about that."

"You've been reading the wrong newspapers. Do you think the officially sanctioned papers would acknowledge that any subject of the Crown is less than perfectly content?" She laughed and shook her head. "And I promised we wouldn't discuss politics after we drove you away yesterday."

"You didn't drive me away," I insisted. "I had to get back to work. I hope I didn't offend Alec." It was the first time I'd said his name aloud, and my cheeks grew so warm I knew I must be blushing furiously.

"He's very difficult to offend." She smiled and added, "I believe he was quite taken with you."

My face grew even warmer. "Really?" I said in a squeak.

She laughed. "You like him?"

I was afraid to answer because I didn't want to appear overly eager. "I barely know him, but he did save my life, and he seems very clever."

She grinned. "Then I shall have to play matchmaker. It's high time Alec looked at something other than an engine."

A thought struck me, dampening my spirits. "I don't know if I'm allowed to have gentleman callers. Governesses aren't usually encouraged to court."

She winked. "He doesn't have to call on you, and it isn't anyone's business who you meet in your free time."

The waiter brought our refreshments, then Lizzie said, "Now, tell me about yourself. What brings you to New York to be a governess?"

I didn't want to tell her the version of the story I'd given Lord Henry. It sounded so very dull. "I had a good education and wanted to put it to some use other than becoming a professor's wife, so I decided to strike out on my own."

"And you landed among us your first day in the city! I suppose that was hardly what you expected."

"Not at all," I admitted.

"What is it like working in a magister house?"

"I've never lived among such wealth, but Lord Henry is very kind."

She snorted derisively. "For a magister, I'm sure he is. But that just means he's almost human."

My mouth went dry in spite of the sip of lemonade I'd just taken. "*Almost* human?"

"The magisters are what's wrong with the colonies, what's wrong with the Empire. They act as though they're some higher race with every right to subjugate us mere humans."

"Really?" I asked. That didn't fit my impression of Lord Henry at all.

"Why do you think it's so important that their children be chaperoned everywhere? They're terrified that if enough of them made improper liaisons, there might be common people with magical powers, and that would chip away at the basis of their rule. Not that it would make much difference. I imagine that anyone who got power would end up becoming like them."

I fought not to wince at what she'd think of me if she knew my heritage. If the magisters thought I was an abomination because I was a commoner with power and the Mechanics thought I wasn't entirely human because I had magical blood, then who might accept me? At least the Mechanics were unlikely to discover my secret. Being nonmagical, they wouldn't sense magic if I used it around them. "The family seems human enough to me," I said. "You'd hardly know they were magical."

"They have money, and plenty of it. That comes because of the power they control." She laughed and shook her head. "And there I go talking politics again. I've forgotten how to have a normal conversation. What do people talk about when they're not ranting about the inequities of the system and the role of machines in evening the balance?"

"I usually talk about books." It turned out that Lizzie was a great reader, too, and she enjoyed pulp novels as much as I did. It was the first time I'd been able to talk about these books with anyone else, and the rest of our visit passed far too quickly.

As we left the coffee shop, Lizzie said, "We shall have to get together again soon. Oh! I know just the thing. Do you have any obligations Saturday night?"

"As far as I know, there's nothing I have to attend with the children."

"Some of my friends are having a party, and I think you'd enjoy it."

"It isn't a political gathering, is it?"

"Of course not. It's just some music and dancing." She added with a meaningful grin, "I'm sure Alec will be there."

"It sounds like it would be great fun," I said, trying to appear calm and collected even though my heart was doing flips inside my chest.

"Excellent! I'll meet you on the corner near your employer's house at eight. I promise it won't be anything like the magister parties where you'll play chaperone."

Saturday evening, I put on my nicest gown. It was probably far too formal for the Mechanics' party, but it was the one gown I owned that didn't make me look like a governess, and I didn't want to look like a governess that night. The flounces were per-haps out of style, but I thought the bright teal silk was a becom-ing color for me. Lord Henry was heading down the stairs at the same time I was, a butterfly net over his shoulder and bin-oculars around his neck, and he gave me a second look after nod-ding absently in greeting. "Ah, going out for the evening, I take it," he said.

Hoping he wouldn't suddenly need me to work, I said, "Some friends have invited me to a party."

He didn't question how I had friends so soon after coming to the city. He merely said, "Have a good time, then." He sounded even more preoccupied than usual. After nodding farewell at the foot of the front steps, he crossed the street to the park. I watched him go, wondering why he was going out with a butterfly net at this hour, but then I forgot about him when I saw Lizzie waving at me from the corner.

When I reached her, she took my arm. "I was worried you'd change your mind."

"I've been looking forward to this," I assured her as we headed down the street. I felt very free and independent, going out for the evening with no parent or any other chaperone, like a proper career girl in the city.

At Third Avenue, we caught a horse-drawn omnibus head-ing downtown. I had to remind myself not to gape as I stared out the window while the bus trundled slowly down the street. The streets ran like canyons between towering storefronts and tenement buildings, and the lower we went in the city, the more crowded it became.

When the bus stopped in a particularly busy area, Lizzie said, "This is us." We stepped down to the curb and were immediately swallowed by chaos. Lizzie steered me through the crowds to a restaurant where a small group of young men and women were gathered around two tables pushed together. As a professor's daughter, I instantly recognized university students, though these were somewhat more down-at-the-heel than I was accustomed to seeing at Yale. A few of them wore the eccentric attire of the Mechanics. As I'd feared, I was dressed far more formally than any of them. I looked like a girl attending a tea dance, not a young woman out on the town with her friends.

This wasn't what I'd expected when Lizzie invited me to a party. A couple of them had drinks in front of them, but there was no food, and there wasn't room for dancing in the small restaurant. I tried to hide my disappointment as I took the seat Colin held for me. "Ah, the beautiful Miss Verity, gracing our humble gathering with her presence," he said, and I couldn't help but smile. A quick scan of the faces gathered around the tables made my smile fade because Alec wasn't there.

"Are we all here?" Lizzie asked.

"No, Higgins is on his way with a spark," said a boy about my age wearing a brightly striped waistcoat.

"He does have a way of finding them," one of the girls said with a giggle.

"Everyone, I'd like you to meet my friend Verity," Lizzie said. "She just came to the city this week, and she's working as a governess in the Lyndon house." They greeted me, but none gave their names in return, which I found very odd and rather rude.

Colin draped his arm around my shoulders. "Verity was brave enough to ride on our test run on her first day in the city," he said.

"She deserves a medal of valor for that," one of the men said, raising his glass to me.

The door opened, and in came a short, stocky young man with an equally stocky girl who looked as though she did physical labor. "Sorry we're late," he said. "This is Gwendolyn. She works in the laundry at the West Battery fort." The others greeted her, but as with me, they didn't introduce themselves.

Colin pushed his chair back from the table and said, "So we're ready, then." The others also stood, and I joined them, unsure of what was happening.

Lizzie hooked her arm through mine and whispered, "Don't worry, you'll see soon enough," as Colin led us through a narrow hallway beside the kitchen to the rear of the restaurant. We went down a flight of stairs into a basement, where a door opened into a dark passage. "Just follow me," Lizzie instructed, and I allowed her to lead me into the darkness.

The passage made many twists and turns before we came at last to another door that opened into a well-lit basement. The others headed for the stairs, but I held Lizzie back. "You said this wasn't a political meeting," I said.

"It isn't!"

"Then why all this secrecy?"

"It's the best way to keep out uninvited guests." She tugged on my arm, but I stood my ground.

"Lizzie, I expect my friends to be honest with me."

She sighed, glanced toward the stairs, then turned back to me. "Very well, then. Yes, most of the people at the party are members of the Rebel Mechanics, but this isn't an official meeting. We're merely having the party at the Mechanics' headquarters for convenience. But because the headquarters is secret, we can't very well issue invitations with the address. So the nonmembers have to enter a different way."

"It is merely a party, nothing more?"

"Some of the members will show off their inventions—they're having a little competition—but that has nothing to do with politics, I swear. It's just what happens when these people get together. Now, do you still want to come? I'll understand if you don't, and I'll take you home, no hard feelings."

Loud music and the sound of laughter wafted down the stairs from above, and I felt torn. Could being at this party be considered treason? Then again, if the location was so secret that not even all the party guests knew where it was, would the authorities know about it? I'd feel terrible making Lizzie leave to take me home, and it did sound like fun. Besides, if I left, I probably wouldn't ever see Alec again.

Feeling as though I was making a momentous decision, I squared my shoulders and said, "I believe there's a party upstairs."

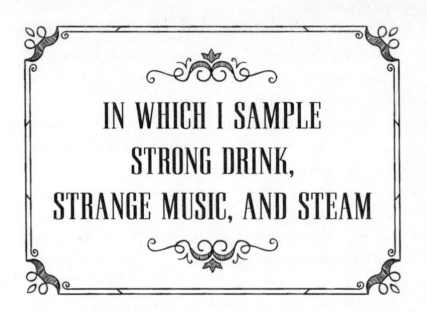

IN WHICH I SAMPLE STRONG DRINK, STRANGE MUSIC, AND STEAM

We entered the room at the top of the stairs, and all my senses were assaulted at once. I smelled smoke and dust and spicy food and spicier drink. Color, light, scent, and sound all competed for my attention, making it impossible to notice any one thing.

I finally regained enough equilibrium to distinguish individual elements. The cavernous space looked like it was an old theater. The light came from great glass globes hanging from wires draped across the ceiling. Red banners with large gears sewn on them hung among the globes. It wasn't a brass band I heard, but rather a small band playing lively dance music on a stage near where I stood. There were the usual fiddler and drummer, but there was another sound layered beneath that, a jaunty tone that sounded like a particularly breathy and brassy church organ. The sound came from a set of pipes on a cart next to the stage. I'd seen a steam calliope in a circus parade, but never thought one would be used as part of a dance band.

Most of the guests wore the Mechanics' unorthodox mix of attire. Their colorful clothing was garish in the bright lights. In the center of the room, couples spun wildly in time to the unusual music. Around the perimeter, groups of men and women tinkered with or showed off their inventions. Tables laden with food, punch bowls, and ale kegs lined a nearby wall. An odd contraption made up of tubes, clockwork gears, and strangely shaped bits of glass spewed vapor and flame and made loud clattering noises.

While I was still assessing the situation, someone rushed at me, grabbed me around the waist, and lifted me off my feet. "Verity, my lass! I thought we'd lost you in the tunnels!"

"Put her down, Colin," Lizzie scolded, and I was most grateful when my feet returned to the floor.

"You look positively parched," he said to me. "Lucky for you, I know just the thing for that ailment." He took my hand and led me toward the strange device. "The lady will have one, if you please," he told the man operating it.

The man, who wore a physician's white smock and a pair of laboratory safety goggles, said, "The lady will have to try her luck." He handed me a small brass gear and pointed to a metal dish on the end of the contraption. "Get this in there and you get yourself a drink."

Colin leaned over my shoulder. "Go on, Verity, you can do it."

"Didn't I see a punch bowl?" I asked.

The white-smocked man puffed out his chest and went red in the face. "You'd rather have punch than my fantabulous elixir?"

"It's not a case of preferences, sir," I hurried to say. "I merely doubt my ability to earn it."

He raised his goggles and winked. "I might be persuaded to give you a second try if you miss on the first one." He licked his lips to indicate how I would have to persuade him.

No drink was worth that, I decided, so I had better make the first shot count. As I tossed the gear, I mentally nudged the ether to surround the gear and guide it into the metal dish, the way I used to move buttons into a jar. "The lady has earned herself a drink!" Colin shouted, thumping me on the back.

When the gear hit the dish, it set the whole device in motion. Other gears turned, and an amber liquid flowed through the glass tubes. Flames shot up from a string of nozzles surrounding the tubes. The amber liquid poured into a jar, where another ingredient dropped in, then the jar shook before tipping over to spill into a funnel that led into another set of tubes that passed through more flames. Finally, the liquid poured down a chute and into a battered tin cup, which the man in the white smock handed to me with a flourish. "Your beverage, miss." It seemed an unnecessarily complicated way to dispense libations, but I supposed it was in keeping with the spirit of the occasion.

One sip of the drink sent a blast of heat throughout my body. At first, I thought it was because the liquid was so hot, but after I'd drunk nearly the entire cup, I realized that some of the warming sensation came from a generous portion of alcohol.

"Thank you for bringing your sister a drink," Lizzie said acidly to Colin, one eyebrow arched, when we rejoined her.

"You know the rules, Liz. You have to make the shot for yourself. But if you need me to escort you over there, I would be happy to oblige."

A young woman in a shockingly short skirt that showed the tops of her calf-high boots skipped over and grabbed Colin's arm. He shrugged helplessly as she dragged him away before Lizzie could retort. "He really is hopeless," Lizzie said with a shake of her head. "Come on, you should meet everyone."

She led me around the room, making introductions. She still didn't tell me anyone's name, but the people were warm and friendly. Most of Lizzie's friends had brought friends who didn't seem to be members of the group, and they came from all walks of life. Some were factory girls, others worked in government offices, and some were laundresses or seamstresses. Most were Irish, some were Chinese, some appeared to be of African ancestry, and a few were German. The one thing we all had in common was that we worked for magisters. Then again, it seemed as though everyone in the city worked for magisters, either directly or indirectly.

While I met everyone, I couldn't help but glance around looking for Alec. Surely he wouldn't miss the party, or was he away inventing some new machine?

Colin came off the dance floor, red-faced and sweating. "What, you're not letting her dance, Liz?" he asked. "Come on, Verity, let's have some fun." The drink had gone to my head, making me feel fuzzy and fizzy, so I went eagerly with him, letting him spin me around to the beat of that strange music. I could barely keep up with him. Tickles on my cheeks and forehead told me my hair was coming loose, and I felt sweat running down the middle of my back, under my corset. Even so, I was having more fun than I could recall in years—or possibly ever.

Colin suddenly jerked and yelped. His style wasn't conventional, but I didn't mistake this for a dance step. He reached up and pulled something out of the air, then quickly released it after yelping again. It was a small model of an airship, with steam and smoke pouring from beneath it. Muttering under his breath, Colin batted it ahead of him as he stalked toward the edge of the room. I hurried to keep up with him.

"And what, pray tell, is this supposed to be, Everett?" he asked an ebony-skinned man in a red tailcoat. "An airship that hits people in the head is no airship at all."

"I can't help it if you're a bloody giant, Col," Everett said. Then he sighed deeply. "It's the steam engine. Even in miniature, it's too heavy to get enough lift. I've already got a ship, but I don't have a power supply. Magic may be the only reasonable way to power an airship."

"What about electricity?" Colin asked. "Tom's created a storage battery, and it's not too heavy."

"Would it hold enough power to get us anywhere?"

"Talk to Tom. Maybe there's something he can do. But in the meantime, watch where you fly these things. That's gonna bruise, and I can't afford to mar my good looks." With that, he twirled me back onto the dance floor.

The next dance was just as energetic, and before it was over, I was gasping for breath. Colin guided me over to a refreshment table and handed me a cup of punch. This drink was cold, with chips of ice in it, and I downed the whole cup in a couple of swallows while Colin spoke to some of the men. Only when it was gone did I gasp as the harsh bite of the alcohol hit me. This was more than I was accustomed to, but as long as I didn't return home inebriated, there was no one to tell me I wasn't allowed to consume alcohol.

I was just about to suggest we return to the dance floor when I heard someone call my name and turned to see Alec approaching. He had his coat off and his shirtsleeves rolled up to his elbows. A pair of goggles with an array of fold-down magnifying lenses was shoved back on his forehead. There was a smear of soot across one cheekbone. Even disheveled as he was, I found him more appealing than in all the daydreams I'd had after our earlier meeting. Although I'd planned to act casual when seeing him, the punch had gone to my head, and I rushed toward him, smiling broadly. "I was wondering where you were," I said, louder than I intended.

"I've been working on the lights," he said, gesturing to the glowing globes above. "They're powered by a steam dynamo. It's been fussy tonight. She must feel like she's missing the party while she's stuck down in the basement."

I tilted my head back to look at the lights and would have

toppled over if Alec hadn't caught me. I knew I should have stepped away as soon as he steadied me, but I didn't really want to, so I stayed securely in the crook of his arm. "They're much better than gaslight."

"We think so. Someday they could replace gaslight for those who can't get magical lights. That is, if the magisters will allow a power other than magic." He looked at me with a smile that made me glad he was holding me upright. "But you came here for a party, not a political lecture. Would you care to dance?"

"I'd love to," I said. I'd caught my breath from my earlier exertions, but I was still greatly relieved when the band played a stately waltz. I'd waltzed with men before, but this was different. He held me closer than had been proper at New Haven tea dances, but the real difference was my memories of him whisking me out of the way of certain death and how my heart had raced then while I was in his arms. It raced again now.

"Are you enjoying yourself?"

I glanced up to see him looking down at me. Did my thoughts of him show on my face? I stiffened in his arms, suddenly self-conscious. "Yes, I'm having a very good time."

"I'm glad you came," he said with a smile. "I would have been disappointed if you hadn't."

His attention flustered me. I had all sorts of clever things planned to say, but my tongue had become so thick and heavy that I couldn't move it. Just when I opened my mouth to say something witty and flirtatious, the music abruptly stopped and the room went silent. Every head in the room turned, and I followed their gaze. A woman dressed all in black, with a veil hanging in front of her face nearly to her waist, stood at the front of the room. The crowd parted for her as she moved toward the demonstrations.

Gradually, the noise level rose from dead silence to a low murmur as conversation resumed. "Who is she?" I whispered to Alec. "Wasn't she on the bus?"

"She's our patroness. She's come to select the project she'll fund. My steam engine won last year, which was why she was on board for the race." He took my hand. "Come on, I want to see how she reacts."

Lizzie intercepted us. "I was wondering if you could help me," she said to me after a glance at Alec.

"How?" I asked.

"I'm covering this event for the newspaper, and I need another set of eyes to make sure I don't miss anything. You mentioned that journalism sounded exciting. Are you interested?"

"I don't know anything about being a reporter."

"Just write about what you see. You've read a newspaper, so you know how it goes. I could submit it for you. We'd have to come up with a pen name for you, of course. I wouldn't want to jeopardize your current position."

I imagined myself as an intrepid reporter and liked the image. I knew I didn't intend to be a governess the rest of my life. "I can try," I said.

"Here, you'll need this," she said, pinning the Mechanics' gear-and-ribbon insignia onto my bodice. "Don't worry, this doesn't make you a member, but it will make people more willing to talk to you." Then she handed me a notebook and pencil.

Alec and I followed the woman in black as she moved from exhibit to exhibit, watching silently as the inventors showed off their creations and explained the benefits while I frantically scribbled notes. "She's polished brass, that one is," Everett said with an admiring smile after the woman moved on from his airship demonstration.

Once she'd circled the room, she conferred with a tall man in a top hat, who stepped over to a device that looked like a giant trumpet and spoke into it. His voice echoed throughout the vast hall as he said, "The winner is Everett, who will receive a grant to help him finish devising a nonmagical means to power an airship." The crowd cheered, and the Mechanics slapped Everett on the back as the band resumed playing.

"Care for another dance?" Alec asked. I shifted the notebook into my left hand and rested it on his shoulder as he swept me onto the floor. We'd barely made a circuit when the music stopped again. The dancers grumbled, but then there was a shout from above.

Everyone looked up to the old theater's balcony to see a man waving a long streamer of paper. "They're searching the area again! Everyone out!"

Chaos ensued as people ran left and right, gathering machines and running with them toward the exits. Others pulled banners off the balcony railing. I saw the rest of the newcomers being herded back to the basement, the way we'd come in, and I started to follow them, but Alec grabbed my hand and hustled me to a doorway beside the stage. "I know another way out," he explained.

Down in the basement, where a steam engine that looked like it had been built from the building's furnace chugged away, Alec shut and barred the door before pulling the goggles off his forehead and donning a coat that hung on the back of a chair. "This is our dynamo that powers the lights," he explained as he moved a ladder beneath an open window. "I hope they don't seize it. I'll go up first to make sure it's safe, then you climb up after me."

He clambered up the ladder and out through the ground-level window. A moment later he gestured to me. I gathered my skirts and climbed as quickly as I could. When I reached the top, Alec pulled me through the window and lifted me to my feet.

We were in what must have been an alley behind the theater. Alec pulled a large handkerchief out of his pocket and said, "I'm sorry, but you aren't yet a member."

I realized he was going to blindfold me. I didn't feel I had the option to protest, so I let him wrap the handkerchief around my eyes and tie it. He guided me down the alley, his arm around my waist. We made two or three turns, and soon I heard street noise. He stopped and untied my blindfold, then unpinned his Mechanics' insignia and put it in his pocket with the handkerchief. Following his lead, I removed the insignia Lizzie had given me, putting it in my pocket. I tucked the notebook under my arm as Alec peered out of the alley. He nodded, offered me his arm, and we stepped onto the sidewalk, blending in with the Saturday night crowds. "Try not to look nervous," he whispered.

"You're merely out for the evening. There's no reason to worry that anyone's following you." I nodded stiffly and forced myself to look ahead instead of darting glances over my shoulder. The blindfold had been entirely unnecessary, as I had no idea where I was even with it removed.

A distant clang of bells and the shriek of whistles could have been the police closing in on the theater, or it could have been a normal Saturday night in New York City. There seemed to be an alarming number of red-coated soldiers on the street. Were they also part of the raid? I'd always before seen soldiers as a sign of Imperial security and stability, but now they looked threatening.

After we'd walked several blocks, Alec pulled me into a narrow gap between buildings. He took a coil of wire out of his waistcoat pocket and clamped one end to a cable dangling into the alley down the side of the building. At the other end of Alec's wire was a small disk that he held against his ear. He listened for a moment, then tapped on a tiny lever attached to his wire before disconnecting the apparatus and returning it to his pocket.

"Looks like everyone got out safely with all their machines. As far as the police knew, it was just an empty theater. But that was a close call. We'll have to be more careful in the future," he said. Then he explained, gesturing at the cable, "It's a telegraph. It sends electrical signals down wires so we can communicate using a code. The cables go from building to building, hidden around clotheslines, and there are wires all over that we can tap into. The moment there's a sign of danger from any lookout, the signal travels as fast as light, and we get the warning in plenty of time."

We were very close together in the tight space, and although there had been a chill in the air, I felt rather warm. I couldn't help but sigh in disappointment when he said, "I'd better get you home. I'm sorry the party turned out this way for you."

We caught the Third Avenue bus heading uptown, and the long ride gave me time to think. After we got off the bus, as Alec escorted me the last few blocks to my home, I ventured, "Lizzie told me it wasn't a political gathering."

"Did you see us doing anything political? They're the ones who make it political. We can't even have a party without being harassed." He gave my hand a reassuring squeeze.

"If it wasn't political, then why were the police looking for your headquarters?"

"They want to find and shut down our inventions so everyone will stay dependent on magical power."

"Building machines is illegal?"

"There's no law against it, but they come up with other excuses to come after us, like accusing us of sedition or treason. Not that they yet have any evidence of that, no matter how many times they search the area."

"That's not at all fair! Those machines could do good!"

We stopped on a dark corner, and he turned to face me. "So you see why I tend to burst out in political speeches. I can create wonderful things, but they want to stop me because I'm not a magister."

I resumed walking, lost in thought. There was so much I hadn't considered, that I hadn't known. The colonial government had always seemed benign, aside from levying higher and higher taxes. But harassing innocent people merely because they could do amazing things without magic was monstrous.

Alec must have realized I had a lot to think about because he remained silent the rest of the way. He wished me a good night once we reached the end of my block, and then he stood on the corner and watched until I was safely indoors.

I was still thinking about everything I'd discovered when I encountered Lord Henry on the stairs. "Oh, Miss Newton, you're back," he said. "Did you have a good evening?"

I had, before the police raid, so I smiled and said, "Yes, thank you." Then I tensed, worried that he might smell alcohol on my breath. Our flight and the journey uptown had cleared my head so I no longer felt tipsy, but I didn't want my employer to dismiss me for drunkenness.

He didn't appear to notice anything amiss. "Good, good," he said with a vague nod. He paused, frowned as if in thought, then seemed to come to a decision. "Now, might I ask a small favor of you? Matthews is off on an errand for me, and I hate to disturb Mrs. Talbot."

"Of course, I'd be happy to help."

"I would most appreciate it. Come this way." He led me toward his study, then he turned back, frowning. "I hope you don't have a problem with blood."

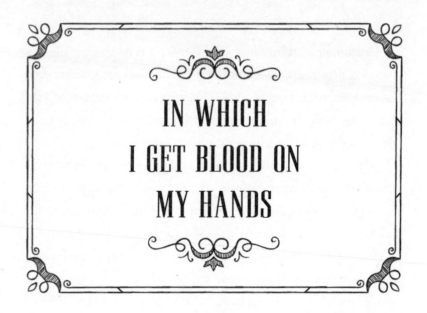

IN WHICH
I GET BLOOD ON
MY HANDS

"A problem with blood?" I repeated dumbly, standing dead still in the hallway.

"You don't faint or become ill? You certainly don't seem the type."

"But . . . *blood*?"

"I need your assistance with a minor medical matter. I would take care of it myself, but it's so awkward working with just one hand."

All thoughts of the evening's earlier excitement fled as I faced a new crisis. He opened the study door with his left hand and gestured me inside before closing it behind us. A wave of his left hand made the lights brighter while sending so strong a magical tingle through my body that I had to bite my lip to keep myself from gasping out loud.

"I need help getting this coat off first," he said, sounding as calm as if he were asking for the sugar at the breakfast table rather than help in undressing. I suddenly felt very conscious of being alone in the room with him. He extracted his left arm from the sleeve, then had trouble with the right. I dropped Lizzie's notebook on the desk that sat beside the door so I could peel off the right sleeve for him, and I gasped at what I saw beneath.

The whole right sleeve of his white shirt was red. I noticed then that my hands had become bloody from handling his coat. The fabric was a dark wool that hadn't shown the stain, but it was damp with blood and there was a jagged tear in the upper arm. I had never seen quite so much blood all at once, and although I have a strong constitution, I felt queasy.

He must have heard my gasp, for he hurried to say, "It's nothing, really. I was merely observing nocturnal insects when I caught my arm on some jagged protuberance. It was most inconvenient."

"You'd—you'd better sit down," I stammered, putting his coat aside. He lowered himself into the desk chair. I fought for and found my inner resolve and firmed my voice to ask, "Do you have medical supplies?"

"In a box in that lower right drawer." I followed his directions and found a box clearly marked with a red cross. "While my hobby is not generally dangerous, I am accident-prone, so it pays to be prepared," he added. I noticed that he was very pale, and beads of sweat were forming on his upper lip and forehead. He'd managed a breezy tone, but he was in pain.

I gingerly touched his sleeve to try to see the wound through the torn cloth, and he said, "There are scissors in the kit. Just cut off the sleeve. The shirt's ruined anyway." In giving instructions, his voice lost its customary vague quality.

I snipped around the sleeve, trying not to look at the blood. But then that meant I found myself staring resolutely at the skin my scissors revealed. The sight of his flesh was almost as unsettling as all the blood, though in a different way. I wasn't sure where to look. I turned my attention to his wrist, where I removed the cuff link so I could pull the damaged sleeve off his arm. The cloth had already stuck to the drying blood, so I had to touch him to remove it. The way he flinched at my touch made me wonder if he was as aware of the strange intimacy of our situation as I was.

My stomach heaved when I saw the wound. It was a bloody groove across his upper arm. "Are you all right?" he asked, looking at me with deep concern.

"You need to see a physician," I said. "I can't do anything for this."

"It's not as bad as it looks. You just need to clean the wound. I'll direct you." There was an unexpected pleading tone to his voice, and he looked very young and nearly as afraid as I felt. When I hesitated, he added, "Please, Miss Newton."

I took a couple of deep breaths to steel myself, then followed his instructions. When he winced or gasped in pain, I pulled back, but he urged me on. Finally, I had the wound bandaged.

He inspected my work and said, "Well done. You make an excellent nurse."

"I hope so," I said, frowning at him in worry. He still looked awful, all pale and sweaty. Without thinking, because I'd done this sort of thing so often for my mother during her illness, I took the handkerchief from my pocket and blotted the sweat from his face. He closed his eyes and gave a little sigh, and then I realized what I was doing and withdrew my hand. I'd used Alec's handkerchief, which I'd brought to the party with the intention of returning to him but had entirely forgotten in all the excitement, and it seemed a betrayal of him to use it to tend to a magister. I shoved it back into my pocket.

"Might I ask you one more favor tonight?" Lord Henry said.

I was afraid of what else he might want me to do, but I still said, "Of course."

"I could use a cup of cocoa. If no one's in the kitchen, ring the bell to summon a maid. Get enough for two and bring it back here."

He sounded so commanding that I had to obey. The kitchen was deserted, but rather than wake a maid I made the cocoa myself. When I returned to the study with a tray, I found Lord Henry dressed in a clean shirt. If I hadn't known to look for it, I wouldn't have noticed the lump of bandage under his sleeve.

"Oh, bless you, you're a treasure," he said as I poured the cocoa into cups and handed him one. He was still very pale.

Concerned, I said, "You should see a physician. You don't want that wound to fester."

"Matthews is an expert at tending to these things, so don't worry yourself. Now, did you enjoy your party?" He sounded more like his usual absentminded-scientist self again.

"Yes, quite a bit." This seemed an odd conversation to have so soon after I'd bandaged his arm. It was so disconcertingly normal, though I supposed there was nothing normal about being closeted with my wounded employer in his study late on a Saturday night. If I'd been a different class of girl, this would have been enough to compromise me, and he would have been required to marry me. My face grew warm at the idea, and I couldn't meet his eyes when he smiled at me, for fear he could read my thoughts.

Instead, I took the opportunity to look away from him and examine the forbidden room. It was much as Olive had described, full of jars of bugs and spiders, with boards covered in butterflies on the walls. Books were piled on every horizontal surface. Sketches of specimens were pinned haphazardly around the room, and if Lord Henry had drawn them, he had considerable artistic talent.

"Are you enjoying your work thus far?" he asked, startling me out of my observation.

"Yes, very much," I said. "Olive is a delightful pupil, and Rollo shows great promise. Flora is . . . " I trailed off, not sure what to say about her.

He grinned. "Yes, quite. Flora is a challenge. Oh, and that reminds me." He turned in his chair and sifted through some papers on his desk, coming up with an invitation card. "Flora and Rollo have been invited to a dinner party Wednesday, and you'll need to chaperone them. I don't like Rollo going out on a school night, but his grandfather the governor issued the invitation, so I don't have much choice." He handed the card to me.

His name was included on the invitation, and when I glanced up at him, a smile flickered across his lips before he said with deadpan solemnity, "Unfortunately, I have a feeling I will be quite ill that evening and will have to send Flora and Rollo with my regrets."

Perhaps it was the lingering effect of the punch that loosened my tongue, but before I was aware I'd spoken, I said, "You don't get on well with the governor?"

He moved his cup into his right hand, then with his left he reached up to rub his eyes wearily under his glasses. "He didn't agree with my brother's choice of guardian for the children. As I recall, he said something about a boy barely out of knee britches being entirely unsuitable. I don't disagree with him, but I learned from a very early age not to argue with my brother. If anyone could win a fight from beyond the grave, it would be Robert. And I felt I owed it to my brother to carry out his wishes. I was like Olive, losing my parents when I was young, so Robert and Lily were like parents to me." He fought back a yawn, then said, "I've kept you up far too late, Miss Newton, but I thank you again for your assistance."

I stood and picked up the tray. "I'm happy to help, sir."

He struggled up from his chair and moved to open the door

for me, pausing with his hand on the doorknob. "You won't mind not mentioning this to the children or Mrs. Talbot? I wouldn't want them worrying about me when I'm on my excursions."

"I can't imagine why I should need to mention it."

"Good, thank you, Miss Newton. I bless the day you came to us."

"I feel very fortunate, as well." I was just about to step through the doorway when I remembered Lizzie's notebook. A jolt of panic shot through me. It was full of incriminating evidence that linked me to the Rebel Mechanics. If I'd left it and if he'd opened it, I could have been in terrible trouble. I balanced the tray against my hip so I could free a hand to retrieve the book and place it on the tray before I left the study. If he thought it odd that I'd brought a notebook from a party, he said nothing. I couldn't help but smile as it occurred to me that it would seem perfectly normal to him. Only the contents would shock him.

When I got to my room after returning the tray to the kitchen, I took the handkerchief out of my pocket and clutched it briefly before folding it and putting it back in the nightstand drawer. In the same pocket, I found the small gear on its red ribbon. I held it on my palm for a moment, letting it reawaken all the memories from earlier in the evening, when I'd danced with Alec and then run through alleys with him. I gave it a quick little kiss, then stuck it inside Lizzie's notebook, wrapped the book in a pair of woolen stockings, and tucked them at the back of a drawer behind all my undergarments. Lord Henry might have been eccentric, but I doubted a magister would be pleased about those items being in his home.

The next afternoon, Olive hung on my arm as we left the dining room after Sunday lunch. "Will you play with me, Miss Newton?" she asked.

Her uncle answered for me. "This is Miss Newton's free day. I'll read you a story."

I did have plans for the afternoon, but the child looked so heartbroken that I said, "I may take a walk in the park later. Perhaps you can join me."

She gave me a hug and went off happily with Lord Henry. Once I was alone in my room, I took Lizzie's notebook out of my drawer, got some notepaper and a pen out of my desk, and set about writing an article from my notes on the Mechanics' competition. After seeing how the colonial government wanted to suppress the machines, I felt it was crucial to notify the public about them. When I had something that satisfied me, with many cross-throughs and scribbled inserts in the margins, I made a clean copy, then folded my drafts into the notebook and tucked it back in its hiding place.

Now I needed to get the article to Lizzie. I doubted the mail would be safe or timely enough. I thought I might find her in the park, since we'd met there before. Then I remembered that I'd invited Olive on my walk. She was not an ideal companion for a clandestine meeting. I'd have to find a way to distract her long enough to hand over the article. I folded the pages and put them in the crown of my hat, then put on my hat and gloves. Returning Lizzie's notebook would have to wait for a meeting without an audience.

I found Olive reading one of her picture books to her uncle, who still looked rather pale. He was drowsing, barely conscious of what she read to him. "Olive, would you care to join me in the park?" I asked, hoping that she'd decline the invitation.

Instead, she closed the book and jumped off the sofa. Lord Henry blinked awake, then said, "Be home before dark."

"Uncle Henry, we won't be out *that* late," she chided. He smiled before his eyes fluttered closed again.

As I went out with Olive, I wondered how I'd find Lizzie in such a vast space as the park. We wandered the pathways, with Olive chattering nonstop and darting off the path every so often to pick up a leaf or an acorn. Soon, her pockets were full of treasures to take home to her uncle, but I had yet to see any sign of Lizzie. We made a full circuit of the Conservatory Water, stopping to watch small boys sailing their toy boats. I couldn't help but imagine how the Mechanics would propel such boats.

I was beginning to lose hope when I saw Alec on the other side of the pool. My heart leaped but I tried to appear calm as I took Olive's hand and ambled casually around the pool.

As we approached him, he tipped his hat to me and said, "Miss Newton! How delightful to see you again."

"Mr. Emfinger!" I greeted him. "How are you today?" I

indicated Olive. "This is my pupil Olive. Olive, this is my friend Mr. Emfinger."

Alec bent to shake Olive's hand. "It is a pleasure to meet you, Olive."

"Likewise," Olive said in a perfect imitation of her older sister. She broke the illusion by bursting into giggles. "That's what Flora always says," she tittered. "She thinks she's a proper lady."

"Flora is Olive's older sister," I explained to Alec.

Alec smiled and said, "I thought you sounded like a proper lady. You must be quite grownup." While Alec bantered with Olive, I desperately tried to think of a way to pass over my article.

Salvation came in the form of a balloon vendor setting up shop nearby and drawing a crowd of children by twisting long, narrow balloons into animal shapes before tying them to magical ribbon tethers that allowed them to float. Olive's eyes went wide when she saw him, and she tugged on my skirt. "Miss Newton, may I? I have my own money."

I tried to sound reluctant rather than gleeful when I said, "Very well, but just one."

As soon as she joined the crowd of children, I took off my hat and removed the article, pressing it into Alec's hand. "I wrote this from my notes," I told him as I resecured my hat. "Can you take it to Lizzie? I still have her notebook, but I couldn't think of a way to carry it without Olive asking questions."

"Keep it," he said as he slid the article into his breast pocket. "Perhaps you'll find a chance to use it again. I'm glad you decided to write the article." His eyes met mine with a hint of the intensity from our previous meeting in the park, and I felt a thrill to know I'd pleased him.

I glanced around to make sure where Olive was, then whispered, "I felt I ought to do *something*. The way the government treats you is such an injustice."

He continued gazing at me, and the connection was so intense that I almost couldn't bear it, but I also couldn't bear to look away. "You can help by continuing to do what you've done here. If you learn something you think people need to know, write about it. And not just about the Mechanics. You see more of the magister world than any of us. You could write about that."

I gasped and took an unconscious step away from him, breaking the eye contact. "I can't do that! I'm no rebel."

He moved closer to me. "It's not against the law to write for the newspaper. It's the publisher who's in danger. It would mean so much to us, though. You're the only one who can do this. No one else we know has the access you do. You could even meet the governor himself."

"Actually, I'm going to a party at his home Wednesday evening." I said it without thinking, then instantly regretted it. I should have been more circumspect, but I supposed I'd wanted to impress him.

He took my arm, gripping it tightly in his eagerness. "That's exactly what we need. You could describe the way he lives while so many live in poverty, unable to afford magical devices but with no alternatives available."

Olive saved me from having to answer by skipping over with a pink balloon poodle bobbing over her head. "See what I have, Miss Newton? I'm going to call her Guinevere. What do you think, Mr. Emfinger?"

Alec released my arm and stepped back. "I think that's a lovely name, Olive. And now I must be going. It was so good to see you again, Miss Newton, and a pleasure to meet you, Olive."

I barely heard Olive's chatter on our way back to the house, I was so torn inside my mind. I did believe there was injustice, and I wanted to please Alec, but I doubted that my reporting on the governor's home would do much for the cause. It would more likely jeopardize my position, which I couldn't risk losing. Why did he have to ask such an impossible thing of me?

Monday morning's newspaper contained a story about how the Masked Bandits had nearly been caught in an attempted burglary at the tax agent's office on Saturday night. Guards had been waiting for them and the bandits had fled with no money, but the guards believed that at least one of them had been injured in the fight. I wondered for a moment if that could possibly have had something to do with Lord Henry's wound, but as I studied him across the breakfast table from over the top of the newspaper, I still couldn't bring myself to believe the eccentric and absentminded amateur scientist capable of committing such daring crimes.

As Olive and I walked our usual route back home from

Rollo's school that morning, Olive said, "Look, Miss Newton, there's your friend!"

Nat stood on a street corner only a couple of blocks away from his previous position with a stack of papers. He waved to us. "Hey, Olive and Verity!" he called out. "Verity, you'll want a copy of today's issue. There's an important story."

Curious, I handed him a coin and took a paper. Olive stood on her tiptoes to look at the front page. "Those words are big," she complained. "What does it say?"

" 'Mechanics' Exposition,' " I read. "It means that people were showing off machines they built."

"Rollo would like that."

"I'm sure he would." The author's name was "Liberty Jones," but it was the article I'd written. I'd never seen my own words in print like that before, and I couldn't hold back a smile.

Nat winked and said, "That article's selling a lot of papers for me today. Liberty Jones must be a great writer."

"It's likely the subject matter," I said, struggling for modesty. "Thank you for the newspaper, Nat. Come along, Olive."

The thrill of having my article published didn't change my mind about using my position to report on the magisters. I did waver somewhat, though, when the afternoon post brought a letter from Lizzie, with a banknote in payment for my article enclosed. I supposed that made me a professional journalist.

And, quite possibly in the government's eyes, a rebel.

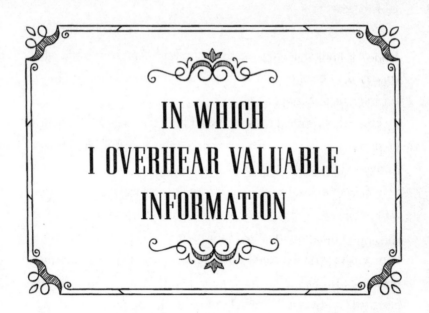

IN WHICH
I OVERHEAR VALUABLE
INFORMATION

I was correcting one of Olive's papers late Tuesday afternoon when a surge struck me and I remembered that Lord Henry was teaching magic again. I groaned as I fought to get my breathing under control. I needed to be able to manage my reactions to magic, and that was even more important now that I was going to the governor's house, whether as a journalist or as a chaperone.

Then it occurred to me that while so much magic was in use during the lessons, they might not notice a little more. This was my opportunity to learn how to shield myself. I headed straight for the library, where I hoped to find a basic treatise on the subject.

It wasn't easy to concentrate with waves of magic making me reel. Every so often, I had to lean my forehead against the bookcase and take deep, steadying breaths. At last, I found what appeared to be the right book. I carried it to a table and hid it behind a history book.

I quickly skimmed the text. What I knew of magic, I'd learned by instinct or imitated from novels, so this was the first authoritative information I'd read. It seemed that the ability to use magic was a talent for channeling and directing power from the ether. "Spells" were merely step-by-step procedures for doing this, and once someone had internalized the process, it was no longer necessary to consciously follow each step. I was rather pleased with myself for having learned this on my own. Hand gestures and contact were helpful for directing power in certain circumstances. Gestures were also among the tools used to help students learn to channel power, and they became a habit even for magisters who no longer needed them.

Finally, I found a chapter that pertained to my predicament. According to the author, magisters were affected when others excited the ether nearby, but the excited ether could be deflected to diminish these effects. Following the instructions, I visualized a bubble around myself, the magically excited ether flowing around it. But then a wave of magic more powerful than ever nearly knocked me out of my seat. Gathering my wits, I made another attempt. This time, the tingle eased. I was still aware of the presence of magic, but it didn't distress me so badly. I allowed myself a smile of triumph, and then another wave hit me as my concentration faltered.

"Oh, this will never do," I said, sighing. A shield was of little use if it took constant effort to maintain it. However, after another half hour of practice, I was able to deflect the excited ether and maintain the shield without intense concentration. To test myself, I tried reading further in the book while continuing to deflect the magic. I knew I was successful when I became so engrossed that I forgot entirely about the shield, and yet I wasn't overwhelmed by any surges of power. I didn't think it would be long before maintaining the shield became second nature to me.

The library door opened and I jumped guiltily, unable to stifle a startled squeak. My reaction wasn't nearly so severe as the cry that came from the intruder. I thought Mrs. Talbot might fall from shock as she froze in the doorway. Then she laughed nervously. "Why, Miss Newton, you startled me," she said. "I didn't expect to find anyone here."

Glad I'd hidden the magic book, I said, "I'm looking for discussion topics for the children."

"My, but you are diligent," she said, her voice sounding steadier. "I came to find some light reading, but I don't want to disturb your work." Before I could protest—which I was not planning to do—she backed away and closed the door.

I let out my breath in a huge sigh of relief, then reshelved the books. It was only as I entered my room that I realized I hadn't dropped my shield during that scare with Mrs. Talbot. I could face a magical dinner party.

* * *

I remained determined to play no role other than chaperone when Rollo, Flora, and I boarded the family's carriage to go to the governor's home Wednesday night. It was my first ride in a magical carriage, and despite my appreciation of Alec's steam engine, I had to admit that I far preferred the magical ride, which was much quieter and smoother. Rollo obliged me with a complete recitation of the carriage's specifications, none of which I understood.

The governor's estate stood on a hill overlooking the Hudson River at the northern tip of the island. I wasn't sure how I would be received as a chaperone or what I would be expected to do. Once the children were in their grandfather's home, I presumed they would be considered safe. However, the butler informed me as he ushered us inside that my services would be required for the social portion of the evening, as His Excellency had invited a variety of people to this affair. I took that to mean that there would be nonmagisters present, and the governor couldn't be expected to monitor the children while attending to his guests. I didn't think either Flora or Rollo was in any great danger of an improper liaison. Flora would sneer at any man she considered beneath her, and Rollo was far more interested in machines than in girls.

I followed my charges into the drawing room, where the guests mingled before dinner. A tall, husky man with graying muttonchop sideburns stood in the middle of the room, and it was he to whom the children went, so I presumed he was Samuel DeLancey, Duke of New York, and royal governor of the

American colonies. He kissed Flora's cheek and ruffled Rollo's hair in a fond, if somewhat halfhearted, greeting.

I kept to the edge of the room, where I could watch the children without being in the way. The governor looked up from Rollo and saw me, then frowned quizzically before bending to ask Flora a question. I couldn't hear what he said, but her voice carried, saying, "That's our new governess, Miss Newton," in a tone that implied she didn't consider the information to be of much importance.

The governor gave me another sharp look. Recalling what Lord Henry had said about the governor not approving of him, I suspected that Lord Henry's choice of employee was being evaluated and found wanting. My suspicions appeared to be confirmed when the governor said, "And where is your uncle?"

"Uncle Henry is unwell and sends his regrets," Rollo said.

The governor made a loud "Harrumph!" in response to the excuse.

Liveried footmen served drinks to the guests, but not to me or to the sharp-faced woman standing near the wall on the other side of the room. The sharp-faced woman stared at a pretty girl chatting animatedly with a bored-looking Flora. Another family stood in a cluster at the other end of the room. The father wore a military uniform covered with gold braid, sashes, and medals, and his wife was dressed in the height of fashion. They had two sons around my age. I didn't notice anyone near them who acted like a chaperone, so I decided they must be the perceived nonmagical threat for this party. The boys were handsome and dressed well enough to imply extreme wealth. Even without magic, they might be tempting to a young lady. Flora and her friend hadn't seemed to notice them, though.

The governor brought Flora and Rollo across the room to introduce them to the young men's parents. Out of a sense of duty (and no small amount of curiosity), I followed as unobtrusively as possible, arriving in time to hear the father introduced as General Hubert Montgomery, commander of British troops in the American colonies. The two boys were very gallant to Flora, though I got the impression she would have snubbed them entirely if her grandfather hadn't been present. Rollo was far friendlier.

As I watched my charges, I felt a tap on my elbow. I turned to see a young maid. "Excuse me, miss," she said, "but you are the chaperone for the Lyndons, are you not?"

"I am," I confirmed.

"Lady Elinor has asked to see Lord Roland and Lady Flora."

"I beg your pardon?" I said.

"Lady Elinor is their aunt," the maid explained. "She's an invalid, so she won't be coming down. She'd like to see the children, though."

"Oh, well, of course," I said. "One moment." I edged closer to the group and waited for a break in conversation before saying, "Excuse me, but Lady Elinor would like to see Lady Flora and Lord Roland."

The governor turned to stare at me again, his eyes narrowing beneath bushy brows, and I feared I'd done the wrong thing.

But then he smiled and nodded. "Of course. How could I forget? Run along, children, and see your aunt before dinner is served."

The maid led us up the stairs and knocked on a bedroom door before opening it and gesturing for us to go inside. A woman's voice from within said, "That will be all for now, thank you, Mary."

The room seemed dark at first, but then I realized that was because it was so vast, larger than any bedroom I'd ever seen, so the light from the bedside lamps barely reached the doorway. Rollo ran forward and sat on the edge of the imposing four-poster bed, leaning to hug its occupant. Flora followed more sedately and bent to kiss her aunt's cheek. Feeling like an intruder on this family scene, I stayed in the doorway, but the woman's voice called out, "Is that the new governess? Come inside, please. I'd like to meet you."

I moved farther into the room and around to the head of the great bed. A woman of perhaps twenty-five lay there, propped up against a pile of pillows. Aside from having the sort of pallor that suggested she never saw the sun, she didn't look that unhealthy to me. She was thin but didn't have the gaunt, drawn look that came with extended illness. In fact, she was rather pretty, with wide-set green eyes and a mass of rich brown curls piled loosely on top of her head. She looked like a doll lying on a child's bed.

Rollo stood and said formally, "Aunt Elinor, may I present Miss Verity Newton, our new governess. Miss Newton, this is Lady Elinor DeLancey, our aunt."

I bobbed a quick curtsy, but before I could complete it, she waved her hand and said, "Bah, none of that, please." Her voice was rich and warm, with a tone that made her sound like she was constantly struggling to hold back laughter. "It is a pleasure to meet you, Verity."

"Likewise, my lady."

"Please, sit down." She gestured toward a chair next to the bed, and I moved to sit in it. She studied me for a long moment, looking as though she was trying to determine my personality based on the shape of my head and the contours of my face. Then she smiled. "Yes, you do look like the sort Henry would select. As long as you're not afraid of bugs, you might actually last. You aren't afraid of bugs, are you?"

"No, my lady."

Her mouth twitched as if she were struggling to suppress a fit of giggles. "Of course you aren't. I'd wager you're quite the bold one."

"No one has ever accused me of boldness, my lady."

"Hmmm," she said, with an enigmatic gleam in her eye.

"Uncle Henry says Miss Newton is a good example for Flora because she reads and talks about things other than clothes," Rollo said with great relish.

"Verity, I like you already," Elinor said. She gestured around the room at walls entirely covered in bookshelves that stretched from floor to ceiling. "You are welcome to borrow any of my books. Oh, I know! We can read the same book and then discuss it together—and you, too, Flora. I would appreciate the company."

"That's not necessary, Aunt Elinor—" Flora began, but Lady Elinor cut her off.

"Oh, but I insist. It will be great fun." She waved her hand, and a book flew off a shelf to land next to her on the bed. I could detect the use of magic, but because of my shield it wasn't strong enough to cause a visible reaction. I allowed myself a moment of triumph for having mastered that technique. She handed the book to me. "Give it to Flora once you're home. I don't want her accidentally leaving it in the drawing room here." Flora flushed and glanced away, and I knew that was exactly what she'd planned to do.

"Now," Elinor continued, "let's set a time to discuss it. I'm sure you can read this within a week, so let's say we'll meet to chat a week from Thursday at four. Verity, you have read this, haven't you?"

I glanced at the spine. It was *Jane Eyre*, a novel about a governess in the home of a mysterious magister. I wondered if Elinor had selected it because she thought it might make her niece more sympathetic to my situation, or if she merely thought the romance might appeal to Flora. "Yes, my lady, I have."

"Oh, please stop the 'my lady' nonsense. It's so tiresome." I smiled at the suspicion that she and Lord Henry must get along very well.

The maid returned to the room and said, "Dinner will be served in five minutes."

"Thank you, Mary," Elinor said. "Please escort Flora and Rollo to the dining room. Miss Newton will dine with me." She turned to me. "I hope you don't mind, but I suspect you'd prefer that to dining with the housekeeper and butler. Father will want chaperones around for any mingling, but not at the dinner table."

Flora and Rollo left with the maid, and soon a pair of maids bearing trays with covered dishes arrived. They unfolded a small table in front of my chair and arranged a bed tray for Lady Elinor before leaving us alone. I'd barely eaten two bites when she said, "Now, Verity, I want to know everything about you." Thus began a far more comprehensive interview than I'd gone through when I was being considered for employment. Lord Henry might have had more success in hiring governesses if he'd turned the task over to the children's aunt rather than to his housekeeper.

And yet I didn't feel at all unnerved by her questions because she sounded like she was truly interested and not judging me. Being bedridden, she must have been starved for company. I found myself liking her more and more as our conversation continued. It seemed as though only moments had passed before the maid appeared to tell me that the men were about to join the ladies in the drawing room.

"I suppose you must go do your duty," Lady Elinor said. "It's a pity because I've so enjoyed our chat, and you and I both know that our Flora would never be tempted by those Montgomery boys, no matter how handsome they might be. But appearances do matter. Tongues would surely wag."

I returned to my post, and as Lady Elinor had predicted, Flora was ignoring the handsome Montgomery boys, her back turned to them while she chatted with her friend and her friend's mother. Rollo and the boys appeared to be discussing the merits of various airships.

I focused my attention on the governor and General Montgomery, who sat so close together that their heads almost touched. They seemed to be trying to speak softly, but they were the sort of men who were accustomed to making themselves heard in a crowd and they had deep voices that carried well. I didn't have to strain to overhear their conversation.

"The police haven't been of much use?" the general asked.

"Oh, here and there they catch the odd rabble-rousing incident among the rebels," the governor said. "The trouble is, the police don't seem to care all that much. They must sympathize. They do tend to come from that class. And there's not much they can do as long as the Mechanics aren't technically breaking the law. I'm sure they're up to no good with those machines, but we can't arrest them for building them."

"You think the military is the answer?"

"I'm not sure what the answer is, but if we don't stop these rumblings now, it will be more difficult later. It can't hurt to remind the Mechanics who's in charge and the people what they'd be up against if they joined these Mechanics and rebelled. Just a little show of force."

The general nodded. "My men could use a training exercise. We've been patrolling the streets, as you asked, but we need to show a mass of red coats every so often. Sunday would be good because people will be out and about."

"No shots fired, mind you, even if you encounter the Mechanics," the governor said. Although he'd apparently received what he'd asked for, he was frowning now. "No violence, except in self-defense."

"Oh, you can count on that lot getting rowdy." The general chortled. "That's what happens with a load of ruffians. My men are sure to get some action."

"Hubert, these aren't the yokels they put down last century. These Mechanics are clever. Waving your guns may not impress them, and they aren't going to throw bricks." He snorted and cleared his throat with a loud, rasping sound. "That is, unless they've invented a steam-powered brick-throwing machine. Show off your drilled and disciplined troops and remind them of our military might, but we don't want a battle."

I'd never have told stories about the bedridden Lady Elinor or about the magister girls snubbing the general's sons. But if the governor was going to make a military show of force and if the general was eager for a fight, then the rebels needed to know. Whether or not I considered myself a rebel, people I cared for might be hurt.

Before I could be caught eavesdropping, I turned to check on Rollo and the boys and then Flora and her friend. Still, I heard the voices discussing when and where to make their display. Unable to take notes, I concentrated on committing the details to memory.

When we returned home, a drowsy-looking Lord Henry was

waiting for us. He asked his niece and nephew a few questions about the evening before sending them to bed, and then he hung back to walk up the stairs with me. I hoped he wasn't hurt again. I was in no mood to deal with blood tonight.

He nodded toward the book I held. "I see you met Elinor."

"Yes, I did. The book is for Flora to read. Lady Elinor wants us to come back and discuss it with her."

"That's a capital idea. Elinor could use the company, and with any luck, she'll influence Flora a little."

"Do you know Lady Elinor well?"

"We were children when my brother and her sister married. She forced me to dance with her at the wedding. Of course, that was before she became ill."

"Do you know—or mind saying—what her illness is?"

"To be perfectly honest, I think she became sick of Society during her debut season. Better to lock herself in her room with her books than to spend her life paying calls and going to balls. The doctors said something about fragile nerves. She gets a lot of headaches, apparently." He quirked an eyebrow and added, "Especially around people she doesn't like."

We reached the top of the stairs, and he bade me good night without further conversation. After checking that Olive was sound asleep, I went to my room, took Lizzie's notebook out of its hiding place, and frantically wrote down everything I'd heard from the general and the governor.

*   *   *

The next morning, I was barely able to focus on Olive's lessons and I let her get away with far more chatter than I usually allowed in the schoolroom. When the music teacher and drawing master arrived that afternoon, I almost ran over them in my haste to get out to the park. I hoped that someone would be looking for me the day after the party to see if I'd come through with a story. I walked my usual route and encountered Alec near the spot where he'd rescued me from the carriage. "I knew you'd come around," he said with a smile when he saw me.

Grabbing his arm more fiercely than I intended, I whispered, "I have no gossip for you about how richly the governor lives." He raised an eyebrow and opened his mouth to speak, but I rushed ahead. "However, I do need to warn you." Barely stopping to catch my breath, I spilled out everything I'd overheard from the governor and the general. "I thought I should let you know," I finished.

He patted me on the shoulder. "Easy, Verity. Come, you should sit down." He got me settled on the nearest bench and sat next to me, holding my hand. With a grin, he said, "That's intelligence, not news. My dearest Verity, you've just become the most valuable spy in our organization."

"A spy?" I squeaked, startled enough by what he said that I barely noticed him holding my hand. "I'm not a spy. I was just warning you so you'd know to stay out of their way."

"You've brought us intelligence from within the enemy camp. That makes you a spy."

If someone had told me when I left New Haven that I would

become a rebel spy, I would have found the idea preposterous. But it had come about in such small steps—accepting the ride, helping Nat, being rescued by Alec, becoming friends with Lizzie, going to the rebel party, escaping from the police, writing the article, and now reporting what I'd heard from the governor. Each step had seemed so easy and had led to the next, larger step. That was the way my pastor said sin worked, but I didn't think this was a sin. It couldn't be wrong to protect people I cared about.

"I'm not spying, not really," I whispered, but whether I was talking to myself or to Alec, I wasn't sure.

He grasped my hand and placed his other hand on top of it. "Verity, listen to me," he said. "I would never ask you to do anything dangerous, but your position gives you access to important people, and that means you may overhear things that could help us or keep us out of trouble. You haven't been sworn to secrecy, have you?"

"No," I admitted.

"Then it's their fault if they talk in front of you as though you weren't there."

I nodded, feeling increasingly aware of his hands clasping mine. He stood and pulled me to my feet. "And now, I believe you are a governess with a free hour. Shall we take a stroll in the park? We can discuss my plans for a steam-powered brick-throwing machine. I would hate to disappoint the governor." He tucked my hand into the crook of his elbow, and we set off down the park path, laughing as we came up with ideas for silly machines he could invent. By the time I returned home, I'd nearly forgotten that I'd unwittingly become a rebel spy.

The next afternoon, Mr. Chastain, the butler, brought me a letter that had come in the post. It was from Lizzie. She made no reference to the information I'd given Alec or the fact that I hadn't written an article about the governor's lavish lifestyle. She merely invited me to come along on an outing the Mechanics were planning that Sunday and to spend Saturday night with her so we could get an early start. They were going to use the steam engine to take poor children from the slums to the park on the Battery for a picnic and a demonstration of some machines.

That was the day and place the general had planned to begin the show of military force.

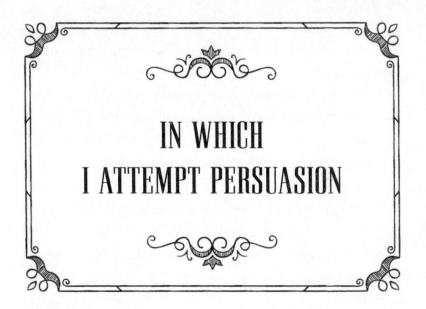

IN WHICH
I ATTEMPT PERSUASION

I rushed to the park to look for Lizzie or Alec the moment I was free on Friday afternoon, but they were nowhere to be found. I went to the coffee shop where Lizzie and I had met, and the proprietor acted as though he'd never heard of her. I thought the Mechanics were mad to taunt the British with their outing, and they were putting children's lives at risk, but I had no way to reach them. My only hope was to meet Lizzie at the appointed time and try to make them see reason then.

After dinner that evening, I played the piano in the schoolroom in an attempt to quiet the turmoil in my brain. I played as though it was a dexterity drill, my fingers precisely plinking out the notes. I was so focused on the music and on the arguments swirling around in my head that I didn't notice I had an audience until I glanced up and saw Lord Henry leaning against the piano. All ten of my fingers simultaneously hit their respective keys, sounding a dissonant chord.

"Perhaps we don't need the music teacher, after all," he said cheerfully. "I had no idea you were so talented, Miss Newton."

"I wouldn't presume to teach Flora," I said, leaning back from the keyboard and placing my hands in my lap. "She could probably teach me. I play notes. I don't make music."

"I thought it sounded wonderful, very fiery. Is something troubling you, Miss Newton?"

"Troubling me?" Although I tried to sound innocent, I feared my quavering voice gave me away. "Whatever gave you that impression?"

He nodded toward the piano. "I recognize the habit. I had music lessons as a boy, but now the only time I ever play is when I'm troubled. Occupying one's hands and one's concentration frees the mind to truly think."

I looked up at him, studying his guileless face and the innocent blue eyes behind the scholarly glasses, trying to read what he might really be saying. Did he know something about my activities, or was he merely being perspicacious? "Yes, that's it exactly," I said, trying to match his guilelessness. "In this case, however, the trouble is not mine. A friend has asked my advice, and I wanted to think before I spoke to her."

His brow furrowed. "Is your friend in trouble?"

Not yet, I thought. Out loud, I said, "Her dilemma involves the attentions of a young man." I thought that would keep someone like Lord Henry from prying further.

It appeared to work. "Oh, yes, I see," he said. "I'm sure you'll give very wise advice." Still, though, he kept his focus on me in a way that indicated he wasn't sure he'd heard the whole story—or the truth.

"Incidentally," I said before he could formulate another question, "are you opposed to my being away from the house overnight? My friend has asked me to stay with her Saturday. We're working on a charity project Sunday morning, and we need an early start." I gave him a conspiratorial smile and added, "And I think she wants to talk about her young man before she sees him again."

"What sort of charity project is it?"

"She works with children in the tenements. She and some friends are preparing a Sunday lunch for them."

"What an excellent endeavor!" I feared for a moment that he would ask if he could come along, but he merely said, "Of course you may go. Your time is yours outside the usual school hours and any other events where your presence is required."

"Thank you, sir," I said, returning my hands to the keyboard in what I hoped he would take as a signal that I still needed to think.

He reached into his breast pocket, pulled out a wallet, and took out several bills. "My contribution to your charity," he said, placing them on top of the piano.

"That's very generous of you, sir," I said, so touched that I felt guilty for not telling him the complete truth about the project.

He blushed a little as he glanced downward and said, "Get the children a good lunch and some treats," before leaving.

Saturday afternoon, I packed some overnight things in my bag, hiding Lizzie's notebook and the Mechanics' insignia at the bottom.

As she'd promised in her letter, Lizzie was waiting for me at the nearest bus stop. "What's wrong?" she asked when she saw me.

I hadn't realized my emotions were so evident. "I'm worried," I admitted. "I can't believe you're planning to do something so mad."

"Did you come to help us or to talk us out of it?"

"To be honest? Talk you out of it, if I can."

"Oh, Verity, there's nothing to worry about. We know what we're doing." That didn't reassure me much, but I didn't turn back.

We took the bus to the same part of town where we'd gone the night of the party. Lizzie led me through the bustling streets to a narrow redbrick town house that was a relic of the time when this neighborhood was fashionable. Now the paint on the black shutters and the white front door was peeling, and posters with the Rebel Mechanics' symbol were pasted to the brick walls. She opened the front door, and we entered a foyer with a scuffed wooden floor. I got a glimpse of a shabbily genteel parlor before Lizzie led me up the stairs.

"I've got a couch in my room that should make a decent bed for you," she said as she opened a door on the second floor at the rear of the house. The room was slightly larger than mine in the Lyndon house, but without its own bathroom. There was a narrow iron bedstead, a small writing desk, a washstand with ewer and basin, and a couch. Lizzie's clothes hung from hooks on the wall and rag rugs dotted the floor.

I imagined that these were the sort of accommodations I could expect if I had to live on my own, and I thought I might find a boardinghouse like this tolerable. More than tolerable, actually. I'd be totally free, with no one to answer to. "You can put your bag over there on the couch," Lizzie directed. "And now, we're meeting the boys for dinner." She gave me a wry smirk. "You can test your persuasive abilities on them."

"Do you think it will do any good?"

She laughed. "Not a chance, unless you manage to get Alec under your spell."

"How likely do you think that is?" I asked, my pulse quickening alarmingly.

She took a long time to answer, frowning quizzically at me. "I don't know," she said eventually. "I haven't seen him like this before. But you'd also have to convince Colin, and although he's a great flirt, the cause is his only true mistress."

We went back downstairs, where Lizzie stuck her head into the parlor and addressed the young women who sat there. "I'm going out for dinner tonight, so tell Moll not to set a place for me."

We went to the restaurant where we'd met before the Mechanics' party, but this time Lizzie asked for menus after we sat down. "We may as well order now because I have no idea when they'll arrive," she said. "Once Alec gets started on something, he'll never leave the lab, and Colin's not reliable enough to serve as timekeeper."

"And a lovely evening to you all!" a voice boomed from the entrance.

Lizzie smiled and shook her head. "It's just like him to prove me wrong."

Colin sauntered over to us, waving to everyone else in the establishment. His entrance was so noisy and dramatic that it took me a moment to realize that Alec had followed in his wake. Alec's eyes met mine, and he gave a smile that I felt was meant just for me as he approached our table. "I'm glad you came," he said when he reached us.

"She's planning to talk us out of it," Lizzie said.

"Oh, are you, now?" Colin pulled out a chair and folded his lanky body into it. "That'll be a challenge." He waved the waiter over to our table. "Luigi, a bottle of your finest house red for our table, please." The waiter left, then returned and poured ruby-red liquid into glasses and distributed them around the table. Colin picked up one, took a sip, and said, "Ah, last week was a very good week for the grapes." He then raised his glass high in the air. "A toast to our great endeavor." We all clinked our glasses together, then drank. The wine was sweet and fruity, but left a bitter aftertaste.

After we'd placed our orders, Alec fixed me with a steady gaze and an amused smile. "So, Verity, you're going to talk us out of our plan, are you?"

"Well—I—um," I stammered, feeling much less confident than when I set out. I broke eye contact with him and pulled myself together. "I'm worried. You didn't hear the way they talked. It's too dangerous for children."

"You're right, it could be dangerous," Alec agreed solemnly, "but it's more dangerous without the children. There's already unrest in the colonies. Nobody likes the new taxes or the new laws, but most people don't do anything about it other than complain to each other. If royal troops harmed colonial children, it would be like lighting a powder keg."

Aghast, I asked, "Is that what you want? For children to be hurt so people will become angry enough to revolt?"

He shook his head as he reached for my hand and gripped it fiercely. "No! Not at all. But they don't want it either, so they won't confront us with children there."

"You've got to admire the irony," Colin said, tilting his chair back and stretching his long legs under the table. "They'll be using weapons and uniforms to remind the colonists that they rule them. We'll be using our machines to brighten the lives of poor wee children who so seldom get the slightest breath of fresh air or sliver of sunlight in their dark world. Whose 'show' will win people's hearts and earn loyalty? They'll have to try some other way when this fails."

"We'll have to hope Verity can overhear that bit of information, too," Lizzie said with a grin.

"I hope you're not counting on that!" I said, dismayed. "It was pure chance that I overheard what I did. It's unlikely that I should have another opportunity."

"Your chances are better than any of ours," Alec said somberly. Still holding my hand, he rubbed his thumb back and forth across my knuckles, which made it difficult for me to think properly. "And you don't have to worry about the children. We've got plans for any eventuality."

"If you've got plans for trouble, then that must mean you're expecting it," I pointed out.

"We're merely being cautious."

"Don't you know that if you plan for something, it'll never happen?" Colin asked. "We plan for trouble, and we'll have ourselves a pleasant picnic."

"I only told you about the show of force so you could stay out of the way and be safe," I said. "If this is what you do with my information, then I'll have to be more careful about what I tell you."

"Oh, but you wouldn't do that, would you, lass?" Colin said with a grin. "You know how important you are to us." He refilled his glass and raised it. "To Verity! Our secret weapon, the daring lady spy of magpie land." They all drank to me, and while it gave me some pleasure to be honored that way—no one had ever drunk to me before—I feared my information was only leading them into danger.

"Schoolchildren one day will sing songs about you," Colin said after draining his glass. "We can all live and be free, thanks to a lass named Verity," he sang heartily.

"Though we hope the songs will be better than that," Lizzie said.

"That was purely off the cuff, sister of mine," he said defensively. "Give me time, and I'll write a proper ballad. Our Verity deserves nothing less."

Alec wrapped my hand in both of his. "You'll see, it will be fine. The British may even call it all off once they see the children."

Our meals arrived, and our group grew as others came into the restaurant and joined us. We stayed until very late, eating, drinking wine, laughing, and talking. I was shy at first around so many strangers who were entirely unlike anyone I'd ever met, but as the evening wore on, I joined in the boisterous joking and even engaged in a political discussion. Alec remained particularly attentive, as though he was making sure the other boys knew I was spoken for. He rested his arm around the back of my chair and sometimes even my shoulders. Every so often, he'd touch my hand or my arm when making a point.

When the restaurant's owner finally shooed us out into the night so he could close, Alec walked Lizzie and me back to the boardinghouse. Lizzie hurried inside after giving me a knowing wink, and Alec paused at the foot of the front steps to say good night to me. "We won't take any unnecessary risks tomorrow," he assured me, resting his hand on my waist. I could barely feel his touch through all the layers of clothing, but knowing that he was touching me made my skin grow warm in that spot. "This is too important to get wrong."

"I still wish you wouldn't challenge them so directly. I don't want you to get hurt."

"Verity, we can't have a revolution—we can't change things—without challenging them." His face softened as he added gently, "But I am touched that you care for my safety." He stroked my cheek, and then he leaned over and kissed me on the mouth.

I'd never kissed a boy before. That wasn't the sort of thing a proper lady would do without an engagement ring, at the very least, but my prospects of being a proper lady were slim. I returned the kiss, tentatively at first, but then with more vigor as my entire body came to life.

I was left breathless when Alec pulled away. Keeping his hands on my shoulders, he said, "I'll see you in the morning, Verity." After a light kiss on my forehead, he released me. He waited until I'd opened the front door, and I gave him a shy wave as I slipped inside. I practically floated up the stairs to Lizzie's room.

"You two took long enough to say good night," she teased when I entered.

"We had things to discuss," I said, hoping I didn't blush badly enough to give myself away.

"Oh, I'm sure it was a very deep discussion."

Now I knew my cheeks had to be flaming. What must she think of me? "Was it that obvious?"

"Only to someone who was watching the two of you all evening. I do believe our Alec is smitten. He'll probably name his next engine after you. The question is, are you as smitten as he is?"

I sat on the couch and hugged a pillow to my chest. "Oh, yes, very much so." It was nice to have someone I could confide in. I might have burst if I'd had to keep this all to myself.

"I suppose that means you've decided to join us tomorrow," she said.

Only then did I realize that I'd never actually made a firm decision. I'd been swept along with all the fervor of Alec's cause and his kisses, but now I didn't think I could turn back.

In spite of the late night, we were up early the next morning to get supplies for the outing. Lizzie stopped in front of a bakery and took a list and a few bills out of her purse. "It may take a loaves-and-fishes miracle to get enough food for a proper picnic," she said with a frown.

I handed her the money Lord Henry had given me. "This will help."

"Verity, you don't have to give us money."

"It's not mine. Lord Henry gave it to me for the children." Anticipating the protest her horrified expression told me was coming, I added, "And no, I didn't tell him where I was going or exactly what I was doing, but I needed to give him a reason I'd be away for the weekend, and I thought that a charity project with slum children would meet with no objection. He insisted on contributing to the cause."

She counted the money and let out a low whistle. "He was very generous. We can get fruit and sweets."

"Not all magisters are evil oppressors. It's not the magic that makes them bad."

"He still lives far better than anyone in this part of town, and it's the magic that allows him that life without toil. Magic corrupts." As she whirled to enter the shop, I winced at the reminder that she might not accept me if she knew what I really was.

After we'd finished shopping, Lizzie stopped at a street corner and faced me, her expression very serious. "I need to know if you're in this with us."

"I said I wouldn't stop you, and I'm here with you now."

"That's not what I meant. Are you choosing to be one of us, to be a full member of the movement? Can we trust you absolutely?"

"Well, of course," I said, somewhat annoyed at being questioned. "I've been writing for you and passing on information. Even when I don't entirely agree, I'd never betray you."

She regarded me a moment longer, then nodded. "Very well, then. That's what I needed to know. Come on." She resumed walking and led me to an old opera house with a faded sign announcing it as the home of the university theatrical society. "You'll need to pin on your insignia to get through the door," Lizzie told me, and I realized she'd taken me directly to the Mechanics' headquarters, which meant they now considered me a member. So *that* was what that odd little scene had been about. She'd been making sure of me before trusting me with this last bit of information. There would be no going back now.

The door guard waved me inside with a slight bow of

deference. Apparently it was no secret that I had brought the prized intelligence that had sparked this plot. I sent up a silent prayer that things would go according to plan. The auditorium wasn't nearly as festive as it had been the night of the party. The banners were gone, and rows of chairs faced the stage so that the place looked like an ordinary theater.

I joined Lizzie and a group of other women in making sandwiches and packing picnic baskets. We'd just finished the last basket when a shrill whistle sounded, and we went outside with our baskets to find Bessie the steam engine with two omnibuses hitched behind her. Alec was in his usual place on the engine itself, next to the driver, and I blew him a kiss, which he returned with a smile. I suddenly felt much better about this outing. We'd be doing a good deed while I got to spend time with my sweetheart—I presumed I could safely call him that after the kisses we'd shared.

Colin once again played conductor, helping the ladies onto the bus with a tip of his bowler hat. Once we were all on board, the engine moved more sedately than it had on that fateful trip my first day in the city, perhaps because of its greater load and perhaps because they didn't want to attract trouble.

While we journeyed farther downtown, Colin lectured us on the plan, shouting to make himself heard over the chugging of the engine. "Give the soldiers no reason to feel threatened by you, no excuse to fire on you. Only the girls and children are to approach the soldiers. We don't want any bloodshed today, and they won't either. Is that understood?" As soon as everyone had acknowledged him, Colin grinned broadly and led us in a rousing chorus of "Yankee Doodle."

The engine stopped on a lower block of the Bowery, and Alec sounded the steam whistle. Children playing on the sidewalks stopped their games, and adults conversing or haggling turned to stare. Others gradually emerged from the tenement buildings and alleys to gawk at the great machine. I'd expected them to be awestruck, as I had been on my first encounter with it, but they looked at the engine, the buses, and us with suspicion, if not outright hostility. While some of the smaller children cowered behind their mothers' skirts, the older ones moved closer to the engine, and without the boyish enthusiasm Rollo would have shown. To them, we seemed to be unwelcome invaders.

"Don't look now, but I believe we're surrounded," Colin muttered.

I knew then that none of us had planned for the *real* trouble we'd face in this endeavor.

IN WHICH WE FACE YOUNG CRIMINALS AND TRAITORS

"They know why we're here, don't they?" I asked Lizzie.

"I told a few people, and I thought they'd spread the word," she replied without taking her eyes off the crowd surrounding us. "They're here, so they must know, right?"

"Whether they want us to be here is another story," Colin said.

Alec tapped on the front window, and Colin opened it. "I suppose we should do this," Alec said, sounding less sure of himself now. He'd talked bravely about facing down the British troops, but the slum children were something different entirely.

I had pictured proud, sad-eyed people dressed in meticulously maintained rags who would weep with gratitude for our generosity. These people's rags were filthy and unkempt. Their eyes were neither sad nor proud. A few looked sullen, others blank. Many of the adults—and some of the children—appeared to be intoxicated, even at that hour on a Sunday morning. They probably didn't know or care about the struggles between the Mechanics and the British because they'd come out the same, either way. They were no more likely to use machinery than magic.

Colin straightened his hat, took a deep breath, and stood in the doorway. "All children are invited to join us on a magnificent excursion, at no cost to you!" he shouted. "Take a ride on our steam-driven omnibus for a picnic on the Battery, where you'll see amazing machines in action!"

Somebody threw a rock at the engine, narrowly missing the driver but hitting the machine with an echoing clang. "Hey!" Alec shouted, then he pulled a lever, sending a burst of steam billowing into the air. That drove the troublemakers back.

A few children stepped up, and some of the parents gave their children a hard shove toward the buses, but most still hung back. Other parents grabbed their children and held them close or pushed them into doorways. "We'll return them," Colin blurted, sounding affronted. A few more children edged forward, but we still didn't have enough to fill both buses. "We have sweets!" Colin shouted in desperation, and a mob of children materialized as if from thin air to rush, shouting, toward us.

Colin instinctively jumped away from the door. "We appear to be under attack," he said wryly. Putting on his conductor persona, he said with a welcoming grin, "Right this way, ladies and gentlemen, one at a time." But the children, who had likely never ridden any conveyance with a conductor, nearly trampled him in their eagerness to find the sweets.

When we had everyone on board, there were so many children that the smaller ones had to sit in the bigger ones' laps, and there were even a couple of older boys riding on the engine. Finally, with one last great blast of the whistle, we were off. We'd barely gone three blocks before the children were out of their seats, running up and down the aisle. The bus threatened to tip over when a particularly interesting sight on one side brought all of them over to see it.

Colin rushed up the aisle to push children back into their seats. "Stay down!" he shouted. A few of the children appeared properly cowed, but the rest ignored him entirely. It took him, Lizzie, and me several minutes to get everyone down again because no sooner had we seated one child than another got up.

To distract the children, Colin attempted to start a sing-along, but the children didn't know any of his songs. "You're a great bunch of Philistines, you are," he grumbled good-naturedly. "Well, it's high time you got some culture." He proceeded to teach them his version of "Yankee Doodle," and the children must have liked mocking the magisters because eventually they joined in the chorus.

We reached the Battery, and the stone walls of the fort came into view. It had been built to protect the harbor, but now it served more as a reminder of British might on colonial shores. As if to mitigate that impression, the Battery next to the fort was open as a public park when it wasn't being used for military ceremonies.

There was no sign of the military outside the gates of the fort, but other Mechanics were already there in force. The calliope, which was on wheels and had its own engine, sat in the park playing merrily. Nearby, a steam engine smaller than Bessie was hitched to a wagon loaded with hay. Some of the devices from the exposition were there, including miniature trains and airships.

When the bus stopped, it took all of Colin's effort to make the children get off one at a time. Once they were off, he took a red handkerchief out of his pocket and wiped his face. "Bringing this lot here might count as an act of war," he said with a rueful grin. "The soldiers'll barricade themselves in the fort if they know what's good for 'em."

Alec jumped down from the engine and pushed his goggles back on his forehead. "Do you feel better about what we're doing here now?" he asked me.

"I was worried about the soldiers," I said, eyeing the children at play. "Now I have to agree with Colin. The soldiers may be the least of our worries."

Alec put a protective arm around me. "Don't worry, I'll keep you safe from the hooligans."

"Verity, this isn't a romantic outing for two," Lizzie called, and I stepped guiltily away from Alec before going to help carry out the baskets for the picnic. We soon had to call in reinforcements because it took several guards to keep children from stealing food while we readied the picnic. As skinny as these children were, I suspected some of them hadn't eaten in days.

Rather than fight off the children until after they'd done some of the activities, we decided to serve lunch right away, handing out one apple and one sandwich to each child. They pressed toward us en masse, and it took all the Mechanics to guide the unruly boys into something resembling a line.

I was too busy serving food to pay much attention to the children, but one boy gave me pause. "I've already given you a sandwich," I told him.

"You ain't never," he said.

"I recognize you," I insisted. His hair was redder than Colin's, so he stood out.

"That was my twin brother."

"Wearing the same clothes?"

"Ma makes us dress alike."

"With the same stains?"

"We get into the same trouble."

"With crumbs on your shirt?"

"Oh, fudge!" he said, kicking at the ground before he stepped out of the line.

I couldn't help but laugh, and from the looks of him, I knew he could use a good meal or three. "Once everyone's eaten, you can get seconds if there's anything left," I assured him. When everyone had been served, I brought him the largest sandwich left in the basket and another apple, and from his reaction you'd have thought I'd handed him the crown jewels. "I thought you were just sayin' that," he said. "I never thought you'd really give me more."

"See, good things come when you have good manners," I said, but he was too busy devouring the sandwich to notice. He shoved the apple into his pocket and ran off to join the others.

Once the children's bellies were full, the Mechanics had better luck interesting them in the machines. Lizzie and I caught our breath from serving lunch while we watched the children play. "When should we distribute the s-w-e-e-t-s?" I asked, hoping no children in earshot were literate enough to understand the spelling.

"Not until the end of the day. That's the only leverage we've got over these hellions," she said, brushing a stray strand of hair off her forehead.

I spent the next hour or so rushing from one commotion to another, as did every other member of our group. When I saw that the miniature model train wasn't running, it turned out that the red-haired "twin" had taken the engine apart to see how it worked while the Mechanic in charge of it was breaking up a fight between two other boys. I reached down and grabbed his arm. "If you're so interested in engines, you may as well be put to work." I jerked him to his feet. "Come on." I then dragged him over to the hayride. "Alec!" I shouted, waving my free hand at him. When he jumped off the engine and came over, I said, "You should apprentice this one."

Alec glared at the boy. "What's your name?"

"Mick."

"You like engines?"

"Well enough."

"Are you in school?"

Mick laughed. "What do you think?"

"Do you have a job?"

The boy shrugged. "Sometimes."

"Let's see what you can do." He shoved the boy toward the engine pulling the hayride, calling out, "Put this one to work on the tender." Then he turned back to me with a shy smile. I wondered if he was remembering our kiss from the night before the way I was. "Are you enjoying yourself, Verity?"

"I'm not sure 'enjoying' is the right word. But it appears you were right. The British are staying in the fort and leaving us alone."

"Of course I was right." He raised an eyebrow. "I can't believe you doubted me."

"I won't do it again," I promised.

"It's time you had some fun, too," he said, and before I realized what was happening, he'd caught me around the waist and boosted me up into the hay wagon, then he jumped on board and sat next to me with his arm around my shoulders. I leaned against him and laughed when one of the boys threw a handful of hay at him. Then I yelped when I got a faceful of hay, and it was Alec's turn to laugh. To get him back for laughing, I pushed him into the hay, but he pulled me with him, so I fell face-to-face on top of him. Suddenly, we weren't laughing anymore. I wasn't sure who started the kiss, but I pulled back hastily when the boys' catcalls reminded me where I was.

With the steam engine so close by, the shouts of the children, and the sound of all the other machines and the calliope music, I didn't notice the drumbeats at first. Eventually, I became aware of a steady rhythm slowly growing louder and louder. I turned to see that the gates of the fort had opened, and rank upon rank of red-coated soldiers were coming out, heading straight into the park, their weapons resting against their shoulders.

"On second thought, I might not be so sure of your infallibility," I said, tugging Alec's sleeve.

Alec turned to see the soldiers and went pale beneath the layer of soot and dust on his face. He jumped off the hay wagon and reached up to help me down. "Go," he said, giving me a slight shove. "Make sure everyone else knows."

I ran to where Lizzie was dancing in a circle with a group of girls. Behind me, I heard the hayride's engine stop as Alec shouted to the other men to help him get Bessie stoked up and ready to go. "Lizzie!" I called out as I ran, but she'd already noticed the soldiers.

"This doesn't mean anything," she said when I was close enough to speak. "We should continue what we're doing. We have a right to be here."

The soldiers didn't seem to see it the same way. They marched inexorably forward, even though there were children directly ahead of them. Surely they wouldn't trample the children, I thought, and then sighed in relief when the commander called the soldiers to a halt just before they reached them. The children, oblivious to any potential danger, cheered their approach. They thought the bright red coats, shiny brass buttons, and glistening rifle barrels were all great fun.

The soldiers did an about-face and marched in the opposite direction, then turned smartly and marched back and forth. The children cheered their every move, running alongside them. Some formed into their own ranks and mimicked the soldiers' maneuvers. I glanced back to Alec and saw that he and the others had completed preparations to transport the children home. Now they leaned against Bessie and chatted as though they didn't have a care in the world.

A man on a white horse came out of the fort and approached the drilling soldiers. He wore a uniform resplendent with gold braid and medals, and when he drew near enough, I recognized the general. I immediately turned away from him. "What is it, Verity?" Lizzie asked.

"It's General Montgomery, the one I overheard."

"We can't let him recognize you. Go back to Alec." I started to run, but she called, "No! Don't act like you're fleeing." I had to force myself to walk at a normal pace as I headed toward Alec and the machines.

I must have looked terrified, for Alec pulled me close in a comforting embrace. "There's no trouble," he assured me. "They obviously don't want violence."

"And I don't want the general to recognize me."

He moved to block me from the general's view. "No, we'd lose you as a spy."

"I might also lose my job," I snapped.

"Oh." He hesitated a moment, then said, "Well, that goes without saying, of course." I shouldn't have been surprised that the cause was his highest priority, but it still stung that my well-being was an afterthought.

From the shadow of the steam engine, we watched the soldiers drill for their appreciative audience of children. "The little traitors!" Alec remarked. "We bring them here and feed them, and they cheer for the British."

"I don't think they care about your politics," I said.

"They should. We're their only chance to be free."

"How much difference would freedom make for them, though?"

He looked at me in astonishment. "It's the first step. Without the magisters, things will be fairer for everyone."

So far, the soldiers seemed to be avoiding trouble. They were merely putting on a show. After a few more drills, they closed ranks and faced the park exit. The general raised his saber over his head and shouted an order before riding forward. The soldiers marched out of the park, heading uptown on Broadway.

Alec looked down at me with a grin. "So it appears I'm still infallible. They're more interested in showing their might throughout the city than in confronting us." When I didn't respond, he hugged me tighter. "Let's go look at those airship models. I want to see how the electric battery is working."

I let him lead me over to where a group of boys watched the miniature airships race, but my mind wasn't easy. I'd heard the way the general and the governor had talked, and I was fairly certain we hadn't yet seen the full show of force.

The boys watching the airship races suddenly began shouting and waving, and I saw a cluster of oblong shapes heading through the air toward us from the fort on Governor's Island, across the harbor. "Airships!" the boys cried out, and they stood gaping as the shapes grew larger. It wasn't long before the first ship had tethered at the West Battery fort near us. The boys cheered and ran to get a closer view, apparently thinking this was just another mechanical demonstration.

Soon, all the children had noticed the airships and were running to see them. I couldn't blame them for running. The ships were magnificent. It was incredible to imagine that something so large could fly.

The gangplank on the lead ship lowered, and red-coated soldiers marched down it in tight formation. In an odd burst of premonition, I knew what would happen next, but I didn't have the chance to cry out a warning.

IN WHICH
THINGS DO NOT GO
ACCORDING TO PLAN

The soldiers saw a ragged, unruly horde rushing at them and reacted instinctively, before they could tell that it was only a mass of children wanting to see the amazing magical airships. Two soldiers in the front rank fired into the crowd, and soon the cries of joy turned into screams of terror. The children turned and ran away, only to collide with those coming from behind who didn't yet know what had happened. In all the confusion, the soldiers still didn't realize these were merely children rather than a mob of assailants, and they continued firing.

I sagged against Alec in horror, whispering, "No!"

He pushed me upright, grabbed me by the shoulders, looked me in the eye, and said, "Verity! Get the children on the bus, now!"

I pulled myself together and hurried to collect the children who hadn't rushed toward the airships. Alec ran to Bessie while Lizzie and the other girls confronted the soldiers.

"Hold your fire!" I heard an officer shouting above the tumult.

"These are children! How dare you fire on children! They just wanted to see the airships!" Lizzie screeched at the top of her lungs.

There were other shouts and cries, and I glanced over my shoulder to see that some of the boys were throwing rocks and clumps of dirt at the soldiers. That made it nearly impossible for the officer to calm his troops, who must have felt like they truly were under attack. I lunged for the hand of a child running toward the commotion. When the child tried to pull away from me, I said, "Let's go to the bus. There's candy on the bus." I raised my voice and shouted, "There's candy on the bus! Come with me if you want some!"

That got the attention of most of the younger ones. To the older children, a row with the soldiers was more appealing. I herded all the children I could onto the bus just as another airship approached.

I turned back to see what was happening. Lizzie was still haranguing the soldiers, even as their commander tried in vain to make them stand down. More children ran toward the bus. Some of them were crying. Colin and a couple of the men carried the wounded. "See what you can do for them, Verity," Colin said as he placed a bleeding child on the floor of the bus. Then he ran back, shouting for his sister.

The second airship had landed, bringing with it even more

soldiers. Colin and Lizzie returned with the last of the children, and as Lizzie jumped on board the bus, Colin shouted to Alec, "Go!" He stood in the doorway of the bus, his goggles over his eyes and a pistol in his hand.

I ripped strips off my petticoats to bandage the wounded child in front of me. Lizzie tended another with a brisk efficiency. "How weak are those soldiers that they're terrified of children?" she sputtered in fury as she worked. "Shouldn't Imperial Regulars be made of sterner stuff than that? The kids only wanted to see the airships."

"Seeing that bunch running at them must have been frightening," I attempted to joke, even as my voice shook. More seriously, I added, "I don't think their commander was very pleased with them."

As we entered the maze of downtown streets, the bus slowed and Colin stepped aside from the door. One of the women came forward. "You know the message to send?" he asked her.

She nodded as she pulled a telegraph rig from her corset. "I'll send to all, urgent."

He bent to kiss her cheek. "Off you go, then," he said, patting her on the behind as she stepped off the bus and ran for an alley. Colin signaled to Alec, and the bus sped up again.

A voice piped up, "Miss, what about the candy?"

"Just a moment," I said. "We have to care for the injured." That wasn't easy with the bus careening down the streets. The mad race my first day in the city had been a stately procession in comparison.

"Go on and pass out the candy, Verity," Lizzie said. "I can deal with the rest."

The bus swayed so wildly that I could barely stay on my feet by hanging on to the hand straps as I made my way up the aisle to the stash. I distributed the candy, then waited until we were on a straightaway before passing the bag through the back window to a woman in the rear car.

As we approached the block where we'd picked up the children that morning, Alec sounded a long blast on the engine's whistle. Even before the bus stopped, Colin jumped off and climbed up behind Alec on the engine. A crowd formed as people drifted out of alleys and buildings or came from nearby streets to find out what the noise was.

From my position kneeling on the floor by the wounded, I could see Colin through the front windows of the bus. He took off his hat and waved it for emphasis as he spoke in a dramatic oratorical fashion that wouldn't have been out of place in a revivalist's pulpit. "My good friends and fellow citizens," he began. "We hoped to do some good today by using our machine to take your children out for an innocent picnic and a chance to play in fresh air and sunshine.

"But the British wouldn't allow that. British troops fired on your children!" He paused to allow the gasps of shock and outraged shouts to work their way through the crowd before continuing. "We're returning the healthy children to you. We'll take the wounded to our doctors. If your children are among the wounded, you may come with us."

He tapped on the window, and Lizzie told the uninjured children to go home. Anxious parents boarded the bus, though there were far fewer parents than wounded children.

Colin addressed what was left of the crowd. "Those cowards who fear children are marching up Broadway even now to remind us how mighty they are. After we tend the wounded, we'll meet them at Eighth Street to make them account for what they've done. Come with us now if you want to make your voice heard."

A few of the older boys boarded the bus, and several young women and a couple of young men followed them. I spotted Mick on the engine, waving a red kerchief over his head. The rest of the people scurried back into their buildings and alleyways. Colin jumped off the engine and boarded the bus as it began moving uptown again. "Humph," he snorted. "What a bunch of mindless sheep."

"Colin!" Lizzie chided, gesturing with her head toward the "mindless sheep" who were sitting with their wounded children—children who had been wounded for the Mechanics' political display.

The bus slowed again as we neared Lizzie's neighborhood. Lizzie grabbed my arm and said, "We must go—*now.*" Colin swung me off the bus after her, and I let her drag me down the street toward her boardinghouse.

Once inside her room, Lizzie shoved me into a chair, took a towel off a hook, poured water over it, and wiped my face. "What are you doing?" I asked.

"Getting you cleaned up."

"But why?"

She scrubbed the blood off my hands. "We need a reporter on the scene who can blend in as an ordinary citizen. You're our best bet for that." She leaned back to check her work, plucked a bit of hay out of my hair, and gave me a wry grin. "I doubt the soldiers will forget the mad redhead who harangued them. You're less memorable."

"Thank you very much," I said dryly.

"That's not what I meant, and you know it. You're respectable. No one would imagine you to be a troublemaker. You look every inch the governess—and don't you dare take offense at that."

She attempted to smooth my hair, but gave that up as a lost cause. "Your dress doesn't look too bad, and the blood doesn't show on the dark blue, so you shouldn't stand out as someone who was on the Battery today. Well, without that." She removed the Mechanics' insignia from my bodice, dropped it in my bag, then handed me the bag and said, "Now, head for Broadway and Eighth. Watch what happens and write an article tonight. We'll get it from you in the morning."

She went downstairs with me, pushed me toward Broadway, then ran uptown. Too exhausted to run, I settled for a brisk walk. It was only a block to Broadway, and there didn't seem to be anything happening yet.

The crowd grew denser as I approached Eighth Street, and the signs of protest became evident. Some people held sticks with

red paint–smeared white cloth tied to them. Others held placards printed with the words "The Blood of Our Children." The
ink was still wet, and men moved through the crowd, distributing
signs. Most of the protesters looked like the Mechanics I knew.
A few had tried to dress as though they represented the people
of the slums, but having seen the actual slum residents, I could
tell these were merely costumes.

Not everyone present was part of the protest. When someone asked, "What is this?" I realized that some of the bystand-
ers didn't even know what was happening.

"It's those damned Mechanics," a nearby man muttered.
"They're causing trouble again."

Soon, a rhythmic *click, click, click* echoed down the canyon of
the street, and a moment later the red-coated soldiers came into
view. The drums began playing a cadence, accompanied by the
shrill tone of dozens of fifes. I held my breath as I waited to see
what would happen when they reached this crowd. The mob was
looking for a fight, and if the troops were as well, then there
could be even more bloodshed.

But the crowd merely held their signs and bloody banners and
stood in accusing silence as the troops marched toward them.
When the soldiers neared Eighth Street, the crowd filled the
street, blocking the way. I had to fight to hold my position on
the sidewalk as people around me surged into the street. They
made no threatening moves but just stood there, staring down
the British.

General Montgomery, still on horseback, called a halt when
he was nearly half a block from the crowd. The soldiers stopped

behind him, but he rode forward until he was directly in front of the human barricade. "My good people," he shouted. "Please clear the street." The people didn't move, but they also didn't say anything. They simply stared at the general, who grew flustered. "You don't want trouble, do you?" he asked, his voice darkening. "We will not hesitate to use force."

"We have no doubt about that," a woman's voice called out from within the crowd. "If you'll shoot at children, you'll shoot at us."

A red flush rose from the general's high collar to his hairline. He glanced around, and his eyes widened as if he'd just then noticed the placards and the "bloody" cloth banners. He'd been with the first group of soldiers. Did he even know what had happened behind him?

He gestured to another officer on horseback, who took something that looked like a small hand mirror from a pouch on his saddle. He glanced at it, then the color drained from his face. It took him a moment to recover before he kicked his horse forward and showed the object to the general. The general's flushed face went stark white.

After that, he didn't ask again for the crowd to move, nor did he order his men forward. Some of the soldiers shifted uncomfortably in their ranks as they glanced at the crowd. These men probably had more in common with the people blocking their way than with the people giving them orders. I wondered if they realized that or if they truly believed in the British cause and the superiority of the magister class.

The British drums had stopped, but a new drumbeat entered

the uncomfortable silence. This sound was deeper than the click-ing of the British drums and much slower, like a dirge. As the sound came closer, the crowd in the street parted, and a funeral procession came through.

I couldn't stop myself from crying out in dismay when I saw that a child's body lay on the bier a group of Mechanics carried. I hadn't thought that any of the children had been mortally wounded, but I might have missed an internal injury. I fumbled for a handkerchief and clutched it against my mouth as I fought back tears.

The procession stopped directly in front of the general. He'd gone a horrible pasty color, with beads of sweat on his forehead that were visible even from where I stood within the crowd on the sidewalk.

A ragged, dirty woman with a shawl over her head emerged from the funeral party and approached the general. "How dare you?" she sobbed at the general in a heavy Irish brogue. "He was merely a child on a picnic, and your men fired upon him! Do you think we're no better than animals?"

The woman's voice was familiar. I stared at her for a long mo-ment, then was glad I had my handkerchief over my mouth be-cause I couldn't stop from gasping in shock as recognition struck me. It was Lizzie! I turned to look at the body on the bier and realized that it was Mick, doing an admirable job of playing dead. Several of the older boys from the tenements surrounded the bier, barely fighting back smiles as they hung their heads in mock grief.

My relief quickly turned to anger. While British troops had indeed fired on children, this was a lie. Had that been their plan all along, to stir up an incident that they could then magnify to gain even more sympathy? Had they expected me to fall for the act and report on it?

The general took off his hat and held it against his heart. "Madam," he said, inclining his head toward her, "you have my sincere condolences. I will investigate this incident thoroughly, and the men who broke discipline to fire upon children will be punished."

"They ought to be!" she snapped. "And what were ye doin' bringin' soldiers to the park on a Sunday?"

Angry murmurs spread throughout the crowd. The general stammered for a moment, then addressed Lizzie. "Madam, please accept this token of our remorse for your loss. It should provide a good funeral for your boy and something for yourself." His aide bent in his saddle to hand Lizzie several banknotes.

"But it won't bring my boy back!" she wailed. Colin—also dressed in slumlike rags—stepped out of the funeral party to put his arm around her and lead her back to the group.

The general said something to one of his men, who then shouted at the assembled troops, "About-face!" The soldiers snapped about briskly.

"You know whose fault this really is, don't you?" the general said to the people blocking the street. "It's the rebels'. We have no quarrel with the people of this city, but those Mechanics stir up trouble, and you're the ones who suffer for it. Someday the

Mechanics will pay for the damage they've done." Wheeling his horse around, he called out, "Sergeant! Block off the streets at Fourteenth. We don't want that rabble getting uptown."

The sergeant called men out of the ranks and sent them off, then ordered the remaining soldiers to march. The procession moved slowly down Broadway.

As the crowd started to disperse, Lizzie saw me and hurried over. "I hope you saw all that!" she called out.

Feeling sick from betrayal, I turned and tried to get away from her. The crowd was too dense for me to make it very far, and she easily caught up to me. "Verity, whatever's the matter?"

I didn't want to face her because I couldn't hold back the tears that stung my eyes. "That was all a lie," I said, my voice coming out in a sob instead of in the sharp retort I would have liked. "If your cause is so just, you shouldn't have to lie about it."

"Hush, Verity!" she hissed, dragging me out of the throng.

I resisted, snapping, "Why? You don't want everyone hearing about your lies?"

"It could have been true," she insisted when she'd propelled me into a relatively quiet doorway. She kept a firm grasp on my arm, preventing me from escaping. "For all we know, it is true, but the parents aren't bold enough to confront the general."

"One of the children died?"

"One *could* have. The military needed to see the possible consequences of their actions. Maybe they'll think twice before they act the next time. That little bit of theater may save countless lives in the future."

"Was that the plan all along, to provoke an attack and then stage that scene? You told me the children would be safe, that the troops wouldn't dare fire on them."

She shook her head urgently. "No, we didn't expect this at all. But when it did happen, we took advantage of it. We weren't deceiving you."

I jerked my arm out of her grasp. "Don't count on me deceiving anyone else. I won't report on this."

"We don't expect you to. It served its purpose of making the soldiers look bad in front of a crowd, which makes our cause look better." She took my arm again. "Now, come on, we're having a party, courtesy of the general."

"No, thank you," I said stiffly. "I need to get home. I have an article to write—a true one."

As I pulled away from her, she said, "Verity, please don't be angry." Her voice was rough with emotion, sounding like she was near tears herself, but I didn't let myself look back. I wasn't ready to forgive, and if I saw her cry I might relent.

I caught an uptown bus, but it only traveled a few blocks before stopping. "Looks like a roadblock," the conductor reported. I craned my neck to look out the front window and saw red-coated soldiers questioning and searching the passengers on vehicles ahead of us—only the horse-drawn ones, of course. Magical carriages were waved forward. I realized with a jolt of horror that I had my book full of notes about the Mechanics and the Mechanics' insignia in my bag.

Trying to look as casual as I could when my whole body was

shaking, I got up and said to the conductor, "I may as well get off here. I don't have far to walk."

Once off the bus, I headed up the sidewalk and saw that no one was getting past the roadblock. Even people who looked as respectable as I did were being stopped and searched. I headed down a side street as though that had been my aim all along, then stopped to consider my options. I wondered if I could bluff my way past the roadblock by invoking the name of my employer and acting like a governess on her day out. I feared I was too nervous to manage that.

I appeared to be trapped.

IN WHICH
THE FIGHT MOVES
UPTOWN

I whirled in surprise and terror when someone called my name. For a moment, I feared my role with the Mechanics had been discovered and the authorities had come after me, but then I recognized Nat running toward me. "Hey, Verity! There you are!"

"Did Lizzie send you?" I snarled.

"Nope. Alec did."

Had Alec been in on the deception? He hadn't been there, but had he known? "What does Alec want?" I asked.

"We're havin' a big party with the general's money, and he was afraid you got lost." His eyes narrowed as he apparently put together the tearstains on my face, the fact that I was fleeing, and my agitated state. "Is something wrong?"

"I—I need to go home," I stammered, the tears threatening to spill again. "B-but the roadblocks. I'll never make it through."

He patted me on the arm. "Easy, there, Verity. I can get you outta here. Don't you worry about that. Come on." He led me down a short flight of stairs to a basement door, which he opened, gesturing for me to follow him into the gloom. I felt my way through a narrow passage toward a square of light at the end, where Nat held open a door that led into a barren yard between buildings. We crossed the yard and entered another basement, then came up onto the sidewalk on a major street.

"There you are, on Fourteenth, past the roadblock," Nat said, brushing his hands together in satisfaction. "The roadblocks only keep out people like you who follow the rules. The ones they're guarding against know how to get past. Now, d'you need me to get you home, or can you make it from here?"

"I can make it on my own," I said, even though I wasn't sure. I knew the way, but my strength was failing.

He disappeared back into the basement, and I waited for a break in traffic to cross the busy street and head for the nearest bus stop. Fortunately, the bus I caught wasn't the one I'd just left. It was practically empty, so I had a seat to myself for the long ride. I was so lost in thought that I almost missed my stop.

The sun was setting and the streets were growing dark as I walked the last few blocks toward the Lyndon home, which now seemed like some distant dream. It couldn't really exist in the same world where the slum children lived and British troops shot at them, could it?

But it was real, and I wanted to weep for joy when I saw it.

Climbing the front steps took the last remnants of my strength, and I barely managed to stumble inside when Mr. Chastain opened the door for me.

"Miss Newton!" a voice cried out in alarm. Lord Henry rushed toward me down the main staircase.

I tried to tell him that I was perfectly fine, only a bit tired, but the words disappeared into the blackness that blocked out the rest of the world.

I must have been unconscious only a few seconds, for I opened my eyes to find myself in the same spot in the entry hall, slumped against Lord Henry's shoulder. "Oh dear, that was terribly silly of me," I said, trying to push away from him.

He didn't release me. "Whatever is the matter, Miss Newton?" he asked.

I couldn't begin to answer that question honestly, so I settled for a half-truth. "It was a very trying day, and I'm afraid in all the to-do of serving the children lunch and making sure they didn't steal it from each other, I completely forgot that I needed to eat, too."

His smile was warm and reassuring. "Then we must get you some dinner." Addressing the butler, he said, "Could you please have Matthews bring something for Miss Newton to my study? I believe I still have some tea to help restore her in the meantime."

I would have preferred making it up the stairs on my own,

but he kept a firm grip on me, and I was too weak to resist. After everything I'd been through, it was nice to lean against someone else for a moment.

He brought me to his study and seated me in the chair where he'd sat when I tended his wounded arm. There was a tea service on his desk, and he filled a teacup from the pot, poured a generous splash of something from a bottle on his desk, then waved his hand over it. He handed me the cup, making sure I had both hands firmly wrapped around it, and ordered, "Drink up. It will make you feel much better."

The tea was hot, strong, and extremely sweet, and it had another flavor that reminded me of the punch at the Mechanics' party. I squeezed my eyes shut and fought back a shudder at the memory of the Mechanics. He was right, though. I did feel much stronger as soon as it hit my stomach. "That was very restorative," I told him, handing the cup back. "Thank you for your assistance, but I'll be perfectly fine."

"You're not going anywhere until you get some color in your cheeks," he said firmly, but with a slight smile. "We can't have you scaring the children."

"Yes, sir," I said meekly.

It wasn't long before Matthews tapped on the door and entered, carrying a tray. "Cook sent up some soup and bread," he said, setting the tray on a low table next to the chair. "Will there be anything else, sir?"

"Not now, thank you." When he was gone, Lord Henry removed the cover from the tray and handed me a bowl. "Cook makes the best soup," he said, his voice soft and gentle, the way he spoke to Olive.

He turned his attention to other tasks within his study while I ate. By the time I'd finished the soup and bread—which had been liberally coated with butter and served with a tiny cup of honey on the side—I felt quite restored. But Lord Henry wasn't ready to let me leave.

"No, you still don't look like anything I want the children seeing," he said when I attempted to stand. There was a teasing tone to his voice, but he stood firm in not allowing me to go. He sat in front of me again, and his face and voice softened as he said, "I know how disturbing it can be to see the slums for the first time."

How could he have known one of the reasons for my distress? "It was worse than anything I imagined," I whispered, relieved to have the opportunity to talk about it. "To think that they live like that while we live like this." I gestured around the room, although the study was hardly the best example of opulence in this mansion.

"If it makes you feel better, I am no slumlord. When I became trustee of the estate, I made sure we didn't own any of those hellholes. I tried to purchase some of those properties, with an eye to improving them and asking a fairer rent, but they're so profitable that none of the owners cared to sell at a price I could spend on Rollo's behalf. I had to find other ways to help."

"You helped today. Your money bought a splendid lunch and candy." That candy may have saved the lives of some of those children. Without it, I might never have persuaded them to leave the fight and board the bus.

"Did the children enjoy themselves?"

I remembered them running and playing on the grass, and smiled. "Yes, I believe they did."

"Good! Now you're looking more yourself again. You gave me quite a fright when you arrived."

"Thank you for being so kind to me." This time I managed to stand without his help, or without him trying to keep me seated.

He rose with me. "I'm glad I could be of service."

I returned to my room to find my bag already there. I'd dropped it when I fainted, and one of the servants must have brought it up. With a rush of panic, I opened it, fearing that someone might have searched it, but everything was as I'd left it, my notebook and Mechanics' insignia still safely hidden.

I ran a bath and peeled off my clothes, then soaked until the water cooled. Dried and dressed in my nightgown, with my damp hair loose, I sat at my desk to write my article while the impressions were still fresh in my brain.

It was easy to depict the plight of the slum children and their delight at the day out. I had no trouble summoning outrage at the British troops who had shot at children who wanted nothing more than to see the airships, even though I sympathized with the fear they must have felt at seeing that mob rushing toward them. I was at a complete loss, though, for how to describe the confrontation with the general. I didn't want to report the lie as truth, but exposing the lie would only hurt the cause. I may have had doubts about some of the rebels' tactics, but I had become an even more fervent believer in the cause of liberty.

I was still chewing on the end of my pen, lost in thought, when I heard a terrible noise, followed by a scream that sounded like Olive. I shoved my notebook into the desk drawer and rushed into the hallway to see what was happening.

Olive ran to wrap her arms around me and bury her face against me. "What's that sound?" she sobbed. A rumbling noise came from the street, but I couldn't identify it.

Rollo came charging out of the schoolroom, shouting excitedly, "It's a riot!"

What I'd heard was the rumble of many voices from a distance. With my arm around Olive, I followed Rollo into the schoolroom. If I stood to the far side of the window, I could just see a dark mass with torches rushing toward us up Fifth Avenue.

Lord Henry entered then, still dressed but in his shirtsleeves, without coat, waistcoat, or necktie. "Uncle Henry, it's a riot!" Rollo said.

"A riot? Are you sure?" Lord Henry looked out the window, then turned to me. "Verity, take the children to the back of the house."

"But, Uncle Henry!" Rollo protested. "I want to see what's happening, and I'd be more scared not knowing. We're on an upper floor, and the house is warded, isn't it?"

Lord Henry placed his hand on the window frame. "Yes, it is warded," he murmured. Then he nodded. "Stay here." He left the room, returning a few minutes later with a shotgun. "Just in case," he said. "Chastain, Matthews, and the rest of the male staff are guarding the doors downstairs. The maids are safe up in their rooms." For a moment, he looked wryly amused. "And Flora is somehow still asleep. Mrs. Talbot is in with her."

The riot was close enough now that we could hear occasional words in the shouting instead of just a rumble. They cried out for blood to atone for the blood the British had shed that day. I jumped at the sound of breaking glass. Olive clung more tightly to me, and Henry put one arm around Rollo and the other around my shoulders, pulling us close to him.

I remembered then that I was dressed only in my nightgown and felt a different kind of warmth than when Alec had touched me the night before. This time, it wasn't my overly excited imagination, but rather Henry's body heat passing through the thin layer of fabric between his hand and my skin.

When the rioters reached the mansion next door, the sounds became bloodcurdling. Olive whimpered, and Henry grasped my shoulder so firmly that I feared he'd leave bruises. "Verity, perhaps you should take the children to the back," he whispered, but none of us moved.

The breaking and crashing sounds stopped, and the mob moved closer. Henry released Rollo and me and picked up the shotgun. I held my breath as the riot reached the Lyndon house. Henry had said the house was warded, but surely the other magisters warded their homes and yet they had been damaged. There was a metallic sound as Henry chambered a round, then he held the gun at the ready. "Verity, shut the door. Rollo, help her move the piano in front of it."

Olive moved from me to her uncle as Rollo and I obeyed Henry's commands. When we returned to the window, the riot was clearly visible, right in front of the house. In the poor lighting, I couldn't make out any faces that I recognized, but some of the rioters were dressed in the Mechanics' distinct style. Others looked like slum residents, but I couldn't tell if that's who they really were or if these were costumes like Lizzie and Colin had worn when confronting the general.

The leading edge of the mob had now passed our front walk, and they kept going. Someone threw something over the fence into the front garden, but there was no flame or sound of breaking glass. The next time we heard sounds of violence, it was from the neighboring house. The mob had completely passed us by.

It was a long time before we stirred from our spot in front of the window. When the mob was out of sight, Henry put down his gun and pulled us all to him again in a big hug. This time, his hand was lower on my back, at the curve of my waist. In that proximity, I could feel him trembling.

When we could no longer hear the mob or the sound of their violence, he gave a deep sigh, as though releasing a breath he'd been holding a long time, and said, "We should be safe now."

"But why didn't they hurt our house?" Olive asked.

He released his hold on me to reach down and ruffle her hair. "Probably because they know you live here, Olive. No one could hurt anyone as sweet as you." But he looked at me when he said it, frowning as though he didn't understand either.

"They probably couldn't get through our wards, right, Uncle Henry?" Rollo said.

"But wouldn't the others have wards, too?" I asked.

"A lot of these people don't know the magic to create them. There's no automated technology for that." Lord Henry's tone said exactly what he thought of magical people who didn't know how to perform magic.

"You're going to teach us to make wards, aren't you, Uncle Henry?" Rollo asked.

"That's very advanced magic. You'll learn it someday, but there is much you need to learn first."

"I'd use wards to keep you from doing mean things to my dolls," Olive said to her brother. She'd quit clinging to me and had more of her usual spirit in her voice.

"And I'd keep you out of my room," Rollo said.

Lord Henry broke up the argument by stepping between them and saying, "First, though, you must learn your other lessons. You both have school tomorrow."

"If they don't burn the school down or break all its windows," Rollo said, a trifle too eagerly.

"Let's plan as though everything will be perfectly normal in the morning. Just think, you'll have something to talk about with your friends." Lord Henry unlocked the piano's wheels and pushed it aside so he could open the door.

"And Flora slept through it!" Olive said.

"That's probably for the best," Lord Henry said with a crooked smile. "I'm not very good with fainting, hysterical ladies." I knew otherwise from earlier in the evening, but then my hysteria had been far less dramatic than Flora's likely would have been.

"She wouldn't have fainted unless there was a boy here she wanted to catch her," Olive said. "Or she'd have just said the riot was boring because it didn't come here."

"She'd have been insulted that they skipped us and she'd have gone out to demand our fair share," Rollo said.

"That's quite enough insulting your sister in her absence," Lord Henry said with an ill-concealed grin. I was smiling myself. It was a good sign if the children were already joking. "Now, off to bed with the both of you."

Rollo went right away, but Olive lingered. "I don't think I can sleep," she said plaintively.

"If you go choose a book and then get in bed, I predict that Miss Newton will come read you a story."

"I can read *her* a story," she said indignantly before flouncing off to her room.

When she was gone, Lord Henry turned to me, his smile fading and his shoulders sagging with weariness. I suddenly felt intensely conscious of standing before him in my nightgown, with my feet bare and my hair loose and wild. It was an extremely inappropriate way of facing my employer. I reassured myself that we had kept the lights off in the room, which made the nightgown less revealing. "I don't think they'll come back tonight," he said softly, "but we'll keep a watch, all the same."

The sound of a clanging bell sent us to the window to see the police and a fire crew arriving. "I hope no one was hurt," I said.

"I should go out to check the damage and see if anyone needs help," he said, still staring out the window. Then he turned to me. "Thank you for being so calm in the crisis tonight. That helped the children remain calm." He stared at me for a long moment more before saying, "Olive's probably wondering if she'll get that story."

"Maybe she's already fallen asleep."

"Olive? Not likely." Before I could leave, he took my hand. "Again, thank you. I believe I made a very good decision in hiring you, Miss Newton."

As I went to Olive's room, two things occurred to me: he'd called me by my Christian name during the crisis, apparently entirely unconsciously, and he hadn't been wearing his eyeglasses, even while having his shotgun at the ready, in spite of his claim that he was practically blind without them.

Now I knew for certain that Lord Henry's absentminded-scientist persona was nothing more than an act. Did that mean he really was the bandit, after all?

IN WHICH
I REASSESS MANY
THINGS

Olive fell asleep five pages into her story, but there was little sleep for me that night. I returned to my room to finish writing my article, but it was nearly impossible to concentrate with so many conflicting thoughts swirling around in my brain. Alec, who had acted so devoted to me, who had kissed me so ardently, had callously disregarded the possible consequences of my spying for the rebels. Lizzie and Colin, who'd seemed such true friends, had staged that deception. I still wasn't sure whether the rebels had lied to me about not expecting violence at the picnic. And now I was certain that Lord Henry was the masked bandit I'd encountered on the train.

But what should I do about my discovery? If I knew he was the leader of the Masked Bandits, wasn't it the duty of a good citizen to report him to the police? Criminal or not, I knew he was a good man. He was generous and kind, and he was spending his own youth caring for his brother's children. There had to be some reason for his secret life of crime. I reassured myself with the fact that the Masked Bandits apparently only stole from the government. Perhaps they were like Robin Hood, stealing for a worthy cause rather than for greed. I couldn't turn him in until I knew what he was really doing and why.

Then I had to wonder why I was so willing to justify Lord Henry's deception while I felt so betrayed by Lizzie's scheme. Both pretended to be something they weren't in order to achieve some goal. Lord Henry was living a lie, hiding his activities from everyone, while Lizzie had only lied to the general. She had admitted what she was doing to me, and it seemed to be a one-time-only event. Still, it felt different and I didn't understand why.

If I was honest with myself, I wasn't blameless either. I hadn't let Lord Henry or the Mechanics know that I had magical abilities that implied I was the result of an illegal liaison. I was working among the Mechanics while being something I knew they hated. Perhaps I had been too harsh on them.

The next morning, I arrived in the breakfast room as breakfast was being set out to find Lord Henry already there, seated at the table with his head bent over the newspaper. I held my breath and hovered in the doorway for a moment, tempted to turn back and wait until later to eat. I didn't know what to think of him anymore. Shockingly, it wasn't his criminal activities that first came to mind, but rather the recollection of his hand on my waist, with only my nightgown between us. I unconsciously moved my own hand up to my waist at the memory.

But this morning I was armored in my layers of undergarments, corset, and woolen dress, and my hair was safely knotted at the back of my head. He was fully dressed as well, and his spectacles were back in their accustomed position, making it easier for me to pretend that he was exactly what he appeared to be instead of so much more.

"Good morning, Lord Henry," I said as I forced myself to enter the room. When he looked up at me, I knew he'd slept even less than I had. Behind his glasses, his eyes were bloodshot with dark shadows underneath.

"Miss Newton," he said mildly, but there was a slight twitch of a muscle in his jaw that made me wonder what he thought of the night before.

When the servants finished arranging the breakfast dishes and brought us tea, I asked, "How bad was the damage last night?"

"Not as bad as I feared. A few broken windows, some red paint thrown against walls, and any wooden fences were burned, but it wasn't wholesale destruction. I suspect it was meant more as a demonstration than as a real attack. The neighbors thought it was the Irish from the slums, but this is a very long way for them to travel to throw a few rocks."

Olive's arrival put a halt to the conversation. She hugged her uncle, then came over to me. "Miss Newton, I am sincerely sorry for falling asleep last night when you were reading me a story," she said, her head bowed in contrition.

I patted her on the shoulder. "That's quite all right. I was reading you the story to help you sleep." She brightened instantly and took her seat to nibble at a slice of toast.

Henry met my eyes, and for a second I caught a glimpse of the man who lay behind the absentminded mask. The mask returned when Rollo entered, bright-eyed and eager. "Did they burn down the city?" he asked.

"It probably won't be in the newspaper until the afternoon edition," his uncle said, "but there was little damage around here."

"Oh." Rollo's shoulders sagged with disappointment as he turned to fill his plate from the sideboard.

"But until we know more," Lord Henry continued, "I'll walk you to school this morning. I'd rather not have Olive and Miss Newton that far from home on their own."

I barely swallowed my cry of dismay. I'd hoped to give my article to Nat on the way home from the school. "Do you really think it's that bad?" I asked, trying to sound as though the answer was immaterial to me. "They'll hardly riot in daylight."

"I'm probably being overly cautious," Lord Henry agreed. "But please indulge me this once." I couldn't argue with that, not without raising suspicions, but I needed to find a way to get out, however briefly.

Mrs. Talbot entered the breakfast room and said, "Sir, there's been a message from the school. Classes are canceled for today. There was some damage from last night's unfortunate events.

Repairs are being made, and classes should resume tomorrow at the usual time."

"Thank you, Mrs. Talbot," Lord Henry said with a nod, and she departed.

Rollo jumped out of his seat with a shout of triumph.

"If I weren't absolutely certain that you didn't leave the house last night, I'd suspect you of having done the damage yourself," Lord Henry said to his nephew. "However, your celebration is premature. You'll have lessons today with Miss Newton and Olive."

"That's not fair!" Rollo blurted. "Everyone else in my class will have a holiday."

"Then you'll be ahead of them." To me, Lord Henry added, "I think you should work on his reading and writing. Math and science aren't a problem, but his writing is barely literate. Perhaps some Latin drills, as well."

A steady *thunk, thunk* told me that a sulking Rollo was kicking his heels against his chair legs. Although I understood Lord Henry's reasoning, he hadn't done me any favors. It would tax my skills to work with two such different pupils, especially when one of them resented having to take lessons. It also made delivering my article even more difficult. At this rate, I'd never get away from the house.

Rollo came to my rescue. "Can't we at least go out and see what happened?" he begged.

Lord Henry hesitated, and before he could deny the request, I hurried to say, "I doubt he'll be able to concentrate while he's so curious. Perhaps I could make it his writing exercise. He could write an essay on the aftermath of the riot." Worried that I sounded overly eager, I added, "That is, if you don't think it's too dangerous. We would stay within sight of the house."

"I would like to read this essay when it's written," Lord Henry said.

Rollo bounced out of his seat. "So I can go out?"

"After you've finished eating and when Miss Newton is ready."

Rollo immediately set to wolfing down the rest of his breakfast with great enthusiasm, his sulk entirely forgotten.

Flora drifted into the room, dressed in a morning dress but with her hair still loose. "You're up early," her uncle remarked dryly.

"I had such a restful night, there was no need to linger in bed."

"A restful night?" Rollo asked with a snort, and Olive giggled.

Flora turned around from serving herself from the sideboard. "What's so funny about that?" she asked.

"You didn't hear anything odd last night?" Rollo asked, his eyes wide with disbelief.

"Was there anything to hear?"

"Only a huge riot that came up the avenue, with hundreds of people shouting and throwing rocks and setting fires." He waved his arms vigorously as he spoke.

"There was no such thing. Stop making up stories. That's so very childish."

"There *was* a riot," Lord Henry said. "Our house escaped unscathed, but our neighbors lost some windows."

"You're in on it, too," she accused.

"Really, there was a riot," I said. "You must sleep very soundly not to have heard it. Mrs. Talbot even went into your room to ensure your safety."

"Rollo's school is closed for the day because of the damage," Lord Henry added. "He'll be having lessons at home. I believe you already have your reading for the week."

"I do?"

"The book your aunt lent you?" At her blank look, he prompted, "You're supposed to go with Miss Newton to discuss it on Thursday."

"Oh, yes, that," she replied, her cheeks tinting delicately with pink.

"You forgot about it completely," Rollo chortled.

"I did not. I merely set aside time this week to read it."

The instant I put down my fork, Rollo was out of his seat like a shot. "Hat, gloves, and coat!" his uncle called after him. "It's cool this morning. Autumn has definitely come to us."

When I went up to my room to get my own hat, gloves, and coat, I folded my article into a narrow packet and tucked it into my left glove, against my palm. Now all I needed was to find someone to take it from me, for I feared I wouldn't get out again.

Rollo practically danced with impatience in the foyer while he waited for me to button Olive's coat. He tore down the front steps to the sidewalk, where he stopped and looked up and down the avenue. When Olive and I reached him, he complained, "There's hardly anything to see."

"That's what your uncle said. It appears they made a lot of noise but did little damage."

We walked down the sidewalk to the neighbor's house. The front windows on the lower level had been boarded over, and servants were scrubbing a great red stain off the white marble façade. Other servants picked trash out of the front garden. I found these blots on the perfection of the block shocking, but Rollo kicked at the ground in disappointment. "That's all?" he asked.

"One would think you sympathized with the rioters," I teased.

The white picket fence at the next mansion was charred. Tears trickled down Olive's cheeks. "That was such a pretty fence. I liked it. And the roses burned, too. They shouldn't have burned the roses."

"When people get that angry, they don't think about things like that," I said gently.

"Why were they angry?"

"We don't know yet."

"They won't come back, will they?" Olive asked, her lip trembling.

"I don't know that either."

Rollo and Olive got into an argument over the best way to get rid of invading rioters, in case they came back, and I took advantage of their distraction to look around for a possible newspaper contact. The only people in sight were servants and workmen cleaning up the mess. Could it be one of them? None of them appeared to be wearing the Mechanics' symbol, and none of them seemed to notice me.

At the end of the block, I led the children across the avenue to walk on the park side of the street back toward the house. They were now debating whether we should have thrown things at the rioters as they passed. "I bet they wouldn't have expected that," Rollo said.

"But then they'd have been mad at us, and they'd have hurt our house," Olive countered.

When we stood across from the Lyndon mansion, it was striking how untouched it appeared in contrast to its neighbors. Most of the damage to the nearby mansions was merely vandalism, but it still looked unseemly against the gleaming, virginal white of the Lyndon home.

"Why didn't they attack us?" Rollo wondered out loud.

"We may never know," I said. I was about to suggest that we return home for lessons when a glint of white against the dark stones of the park wall caught my eye. The Mechanics' gear symbol had been scrawled there in chalk. At first, I thought it was a signature claiming credit for the riot, but then I noticed a gap in the stones at the middle of the gear where the mortar was missing.

I'd read a novel once in which the spies left secret messages in a gap between stones in a wall. They'd called it a "drop." Was this my drop? The children were busy arguing about which house on the block was most badly damaged, so I slipped the folded paper out of my glove and tucked it into the niche before saying briskly, "Enough of that, you two. It's time to get to our lessons. Rollo, you may make all your arguments in your essay."

As we crossed the avenue, I hoped I hadn't misinterpreted the symbol. It would be dangerous for my article to fall into the wrong hands.

It proved to be my busiest day thus far in the Lyndons' home. I not only had to teach Rollo along with Olive, but we also got word shortly before lunch that neither the drawing master nor the music teacher would be coming that day. The police were restricting access to the magisters' district, and only residents were allowed to pass the barriers. While Rollo and Olive worked on their assignments, I concocted lesson plans for the afternoon.

Lord Henry was absent from lunch, and I had my hands full keeping the three children from turning their squabbling to physical violence. I barely caught Rollo before he flung a spoonful of soup onto Flora's skirt. Even Olive, who was usually so obedient, tried to roll peas across the table. "You're behaving like slum hoodlums," I finally snapped in frustration, startling Rollo and Olive into temporary silence while Flora smirked.

That afternoon, I moved lessons to the family parlor so I could make sure Flora was reading her book. She sighed dramatically a great deal while she read, but she was regularly turning pages. I assigned Rollo some Latin conjugations to do while I supervised Olive's piano practice on the parlor's grand piano.

I had the strangest feeling that I was being watched, and I glanced over my shoulder to see Lord Henry standing in the doorway, a folded newspaper under his arm. He caught my eye, gave me a grim nod, then put on a smile and strode into the room, saying cheerfully, "I think it's time for a break. You may go upstairs and do whatever you like for an hour."

"But I don't need a break!" Olive protested.

"I suspect Miss Newton does. If you want, you may continue your practice in the schoolroom."

When the children had gone, he said, "I hope I wasn't being presumptuous, but you appeared to be somewhat frazzled. This is more than is usually expected of you."

"It's been no trouble at all," I lied.

"And I wanted to show these to you," he said, heading to a table where he unfolded his newspaper. "They published extra editions for the afternoon to report on the riots." He leaned over to read the headlines, then grunted in disgust. "As I expected, the *Herald* has little to say on the matter, other than reporting the extent of the damage—and probably inflating the estimates." He pulled a second newspaper out from under the first, then glanced at me. "Don't tell anyone you saw me read this." It was the *World*.

He leaned over to scan the headlines, and then all the color drained from his face. "Oh, dear Lord," he whispered. "They couldn't!"

Even though I was fairly certain I already knew, I asked, "What is it?"

Still ashen, he shook his head in disbelief and said, "British troops fired on some slum children who were playing in the

Battery park. It doesn't appear that they were following orders, but it still says a lot about the way the British regard the colonists."

As he spoke, he jabbed his finger repeatedly at the article, as though it was the article's fault. I leaned over and saw that the author was "Liberty Jones." "That's—that's awful," I stammered, shaken by the thought that he was reading my words.

He moved on to the next article. "Apparently, the people of the slums were so outraged that they rioted uptown in magister districts. The authorities are baffled about the riots. No one knows how the rioters got past the barriers set up after the shootings and came this far without being noticed. When the police finally arrived to break it up, they found no rioters at all. They simply vanished. How can an entire mob appear out of nowhere, and then vanish?"

"That *is* odd," I murmured as I leaned over to read my article. I wanted to be certain they'd printed only what I wrote, with no lies added to it.

"It is the *World*," he said. "They can be inflammatory, but I can't imagine them making up something about the rioters coming and going mysteriously."

I let out a faint relieved sigh when I saw that the article was exactly as I had written it. My friends might not have been totally honest, but they hadn't betrayed my integrity. I looked up at Henry, who was still frowning at the newspaper. His reaction to the shootings and the riots sounded rather revolutionary for a magister—yet another thing about him that didn't fit.

Someone behind us cleared her throat, and both of us whirled guiltily. Mrs. Talbot stood in the doorway. "His Grace the Duke is here to see you, my lord. Are you at home to visitors?"

"Is he here to see me or the children?" Lord Henry asked.

"He specifically asked to speak with you, on a personal matter."

Lord Henry suddenly seemed very young, like a schoolboy dreading a meeting with his headmaster. "I suppose I have to talk to him. Have Chastain send him up."

"Up here, my lord? Not to the formal parlor?"

"He is family, isn't he? Yes, send him here." When she was gone, he said, "I feel so small in the formal parlor, and that's the last thing I need when I face him."

I remembered the newspapers and hurried to fold them up, the *World* inside the *Herald*. "Oh, good thinking, Ver—Miss Newton," he said with a gulp. "If he'd seen that . . . "

"I'll get these out of the way, then," I said. "I can go see how the children are doing."

He caught my arm. "No! Don't leave me alone with him!" He sounded desperate. "If there's a witness, he'll have to be careful what he says to me." With a crooked grin, he added, "Please be my chaperone."

I glanced down at the newspapers I held, then stuffed them behind a potted palm in the corner. A second later, the governor entered. Lord Henry put on a smile and moved to greet him, stumbling over the edge of the carpet. "Your Grace, what brings you here today?"

"Lyndon," the governor began, but then he turned as if noticing me for the first time.

"I believe you've already met our governess, Miss Newton," Lord Henry said. "We were just conferring on her plan for the children's lessons."

The governor frowned at me, then stared at Henry and waited. Lord Henry looked back at him guilelessly. It took all my self-control to school my face once I realized what was happening. The governor didn't want me there, but it was up to Lord Henry to dismiss his employee. After a long, silent battle between the two men, the governor gave an exasperated huff and said, "I'm sure you're aware of last night's events."

"Yes, we heard the mob go past the house. It was quite harrowing."

"Your house seems to have been spared."

"No doubt because they feared the repercussions of inciting your wrath, Your Grace." Henry somehow managed to say that with a perfectly straight face.

"I wanted to assure you that nothing like it will happen again. The city is now under martial law, and the queen is sending additional troops from England by airship. That should put an end to talk of rebellion."

IN WHICH I GAIN A NEW PERSPECTIVE ON THE CITY

I was glad the governor wasn't looking at me because my dismay had to be evident on my face. "Oh?" Lord Henry said with the mild interest he usually showed for Flora's talk of clothing. "Then I can tell the servants we don't have to keep an armed watch tonight. Will there be a curfew? I'm studying nocturnal species, and my research will be hampered if I can't go out at night."

The governor glanced heavenward, as though offering a silent prayer for patience. "The curfew won't apply to magisters, but I'd prefer you remain home with my grandchildren until the crisis has been contained. Or if that will interfere with your studies, I would be happy to send them to England, where I can ensure their safety."

"Surely that won't be necessary," Lord Henry said tightly.

"I'm confident those highly disciplined and brave British soldiers will be able to maintain the peace and protect us from the dangerous radicals. The children will be fine. Would you care to see them? I can have them come down."

"Not today, Lyndon. I only came to check on your household and let you know about the restrictions before they're announced. You'll be allowed anywhere, of course, but tradesmen may undergo particular scrutiny, so you'll need to plan accordingly."

"Just make sure that Flora's music teacher can get here, or she'll drive me quite mad," Lord Henry said with a smile.

"Consider my offer to send the children to England, Lyndon. Good day. I'll show myself out." With a brusque nod to me, the governor headed for the doorway. Then he paused and turned back. "Miss Newton, is it? I don't suppose your father is a Professor Newton at Yale?"

"He is, Your Grace."

He smiled ever so slightly and nodded. "I met your parents once, years ago, when I sponsored an academic symposium of colonial scholars where your father presented an important paper. I trust your parents are well?"

"My father is, but my mother is no longer with us."

"I am terribly sorry to hear that. My deepest condolences. Your mother was a lovely woman—the only person at that symposium whose conversation I understood." He looked so sad that I felt his sympathies were more than just a social nicety.

"Thank you, Your Grace."

The governor shot a glare at Lord Henry, as if daring him to comment, before striding through the doorway.

At the sound of the front door closing, Henry let out a long, slow breath. "That wasn't as bad as I feared," he said. Grinning, he added, "Thank you for shielding me in battle. I shall have to make use of you again, now that I know my nemesis has a connection with you."

"It appears to be only a slight connection, but I am happy to oblige whenever you need me, sir."

"You don't think I should send the children to England, do you? They would be safe—and if there is revolution, it will probably be ugly—but if I let them go, I might lose them forever."

"Flora might go willingly, but I doubt Rollo or Olive would forgive you for sending them away."

"I believe the chief struggle of being a parent must be learning to discern between one's own desires and the children's welfare. But I have kept you from your duties long enough, Miss Newton."

My thoughts churned as I headed to the schoolroom to make sure the children hadn't killed each other while they were unsupervised. I needed to inform the rebels about the new developments. They'd found the article in the park wall niche. I wondered if that would work again.

When all I heard from the schoolroom was Olive playing the piano, with no raised, angry voices, I ducked into my room and scribbled a quick note about the martial law and additional troops. The trick now was to find an excuse to go out and leave it in the wall. It was a pity this household didn't have a dog that needed to be walked.

I got my opportunity late in the day when Mrs. Talbot

informed me that Lord Henry wouldn't be at dinner that evening. I gave her a weary smile and said, "In that case, I may take a short walk before dinner to clear my head. I've already spent far too much time alone with all three of them today."

. She smiled sympathetically and patted me on the arm. "I'll have a glass of sherry sent to your room for after your walk. Don't you worry, dear, we'll have the music and drawing teachers here tomorrow if we have to send our carriage for them."

Life in our household returned to normal the next day. Rollo's school was back in session, Flora didn't come to breakfast, and Lord Henry was his usual absentminded self, spending most of the day in his study. There were few signs of damage remaining between the Lyndon mansion and Rollo's school. The only difference between this morning and any other was the absence of Nat selling newspapers. I suspected the *World* was even more restricted under martial law.

While I knew what the magisters were doing, I'd heard nothing of the Mechanics' plans in response. I didn't receive any letters from them, and I saw no sign of my friends when I walked in the park. The entire world could have been changing sixty blocks away, and I was not only not a part of it, I was entirely unaware of it. Worse, I didn't know where Alec was or if he was in danger. For all I knew, he'd built that brick-throwing machine and had been arrested or killed. Or else Lizzie had told him what I'd said to her, and he was angry or disappointed in me for not supporting his cause wholeheartedly.

Lord Henry was unusually quiet and distracted at dinner, and he snapped at the children's antics. That made me wonder if he and the bandits might have something planned. Attempting to look as innocent as I could, I stopped him on the way out of the dining room. "Are you quite all right, sir? You don't look as though you feel well."

He gave a groaning sigh. "Was I that awful a grouch? No, I'm sure I was. I'm sorry. You're right. I'm afraid I've got a headache coming on."

"You should go lie down. I'll sit with the children until bedtime and get Olive to bed."

He smiled wearily. "Thank you. I owe you a favor, Miss Newton."

"I hope you feel better soon."

While I sat with the children in the parlor, I listened for sounds of the front door opening, but then I realized he probably wouldn't go out so early after making the excuse of a headache. He'd slip out once he thought everyone was asleep. After I got Olive to bed and Rollo and Flora had gone to their own rooms, I remained fully dressed, though with my shoes off, as I turned out the light in my room and kept the door slightly ajar so I could listen for footsteps.

It was nearly eleven when I heard someone coming down the hallway. Holding my breath, I stood where I could peer through the crack in my door and watched Henry move with uncharacteristic grace and confidence toward the stairs. I counted to ten—long enough for him to get to the first landing—before easing my door open and tiptoeing after him.

I heard muffled voices in the foyer and ducked below the balustrade on the landing. Peeking between the railings, I saw Matthews meet Henry before the two of them left the house. I stood and started to hurry down the staircase, but stopped. What did I propose to do, catch him in the act and confront him? In my stocking feet, I realized, looking down. I could hardly chase him across the city like that. Reluctantly, I turned and trudged back up the stairs to get ready for bed.

Sleep didn't come easily. I couldn't stop myself from imagining horrific scenarios of my friends' fates—all of them, including Henry. Therefore, I sat bolt upright at the first tap on my bedroom window. I held my breath, waiting for another sound. I tried telling myself that it was just a tree branch tapping in the wind, but there was no tree that close to the house.

The sound returned, too rhythmic to be accidental. I slid out of bed and peered between the curtains, barely stifling a scream when I found myself face-to-face with someone outside my window. As I stumbled backward in horror, I inadvertently opened the curtains wider and then I recognized Alec. Opening the window, I blurted, "Alec! I was worried when I didn't hear from you after the riot." Then the obvious question occurred to me. "How did you know which window was mine?"

"The other windows on this level have fancier curtains, with two windows per room. One window with simple curtains seemed like a governess's room."

That made sense, I thought with a nod. And then the truly obvious question struck me. "How did you get up here?"

He was hanging on to a rope ladder dangling from something far above. I leaned out the window and looked upward to see a faint gray blur against the sky. After staring at it for a while, I realized it was an airship. "Would you like a ride on my magic carpet?" Alec whispered with a grin. "We're on a reconnaissance mission, and I thought another pair of eyes might help."

"Oh," I breathed, pulling back out of the window. "I shouldn't . . . I mustn't." But to fly above the city . . . how could I not?

"Dress warmly," Alec said, as if reading the decision from my mind, and then I remembered that I was in my nightgown. This really was the week for me to be seen in my nightclothes by men.

"One moment," I said, letting the curtains fall closed. I doubted I had time to get fully dressed, so I pulled on woolen stockings under my nightgown. Without garters, they sagged around my knees. I shoved my feet into my boots and laced them loosely. I put on my long coat over my nightgown and buttoned it all the way up. My hair was braided, and I decided that would have to do. I put on my gloves, and then I carried my desk chair over to the window and climbed onto it, shoving the curtains aside.

Alec reached through the window and guided me out onto the ladder. I held my breath as I made the terrifying transition from the security of the house to the swaying ladder so far off the ground. "Hold tight," he instructed, though that was hardly necessary, as I clung to the ladder for all I was worth. He scrambled up the ladder into the basket suspended beneath the airship. I hoped he didn't expect me to do the same because I wasn't sure I could. I couldn't stop a tiny yelp of shock when the ladder began to move. I looked up and saw that it was being reeled upward by a cranking device.

Now I was even higher off the ground, looking down at the roof of the mansion. Wind whipped around me, and I wrapped one arm and one leg around the ladder, in case my grip weakened. My head came up even with the bottom of the basket, and Alec was waiting there at a gate in the basket's wall. "Give me your hand, Verity," he said.

It went against every survival instinct I possessed to release my hold while I hung so high in the air, but I pried my fingers off the rope and reached for him. He caught me with both hands and helped me on board. While I sat on the floor of the basket and caught my breath, he pulled the tail of the ladder inside and then closed the gate. "Off we go, Everett," he said, and I turned to see the dark-skinned man I'd met at the exposition. He nodded to me before he pushed a lever, and then the ship moved forward, over the roof of the Lyndon home and toward the park.

Alec pulled goggles over his eyes, then handed a pair to me. "You'll need these," he said. When he helped me stand, I was grateful for the goggles. It was windy this high in the air, especially with the airship moving. I wouldn't have been able to keep my eyes open, and I wouldn't want to miss this view.

Alec guided me to the edge of the basket, and I cautiously leaned over to look below. We were above the park, which looked like a dark hole in the middle of the city. Tiny pools of light made curving dotted lines throughout the park where lampposts marked the roads and walking paths. We crossed the park at an angle, coming out on the southwest corner, heading downtown. The city lay below me like a model railroad set. "This is amazing!" I shouted to Alec over the roar of the wind.

"Isn't it?" He grinned boyishly, reminding me of Rollo in his enthusiasm.

Someone came down from the rigging and landed next to me in the basket. "Good evening to you, miss," he said. I might not have recognized Mick in clean clothes, a close-fitting leather coat, and a leather hood with goggles, but I couldn't mistake his voice.

"I'm glad you've recovered from your premature demise," I said dryly. He grinned and darted to the rear of the basket.

Alec shifted uncomfortably, and I suspected that if I could have seen his eyes, they would have been full of remorse. "About that," he said. "I know you were angry."

"But it was for the cause," I concluded. "And what about that riot?"

"I wasn't a part of it, but it was meant to show the anger of the masses against the magisters. Our own show of force, you might say."

"How did the mob escape? The newspaper said they just vanished."

"It's only a mob when they're all together, causing trouble. No one takes much notice of individuals coming and going if they disperse before the authorities arrive."

I wasn't sure I believed that, especially since I detected a hint of amusement in his voice that implied there was more to the story that he couldn't—or wouldn't—tell me. "Did they spare my house on purpose, because of me?"

"That I can't tell you, but the leaders of the movement know about you. In fact, this ship is named for you." He braced me so I could lean farther over the rim of the basket to see the name painted on the side in red lettering: *Liberty.* "Well, Everett named his ship for the cause, but between you and me, it's all about you."

The basket itself was painted a mottled grayish-blue color, as was the lemon-shaped balloon above us. Against a partly cloudy night sky, it was practically invisible. "How does it run?" I asked. "You didn't steal a magical vessel, did you?"

"It's electric. We store the energy from the dynamo in a battery. This is a test run to see if it works on an airship."

"*If* it works?" I gasped, grabbing the side of the basket.

He grinned. "Don't worry, the ship's sound. Everett's had it for a while. It's the power supply we're testing. We'll stay in the air, no matter what. The question is whether we can go where we want. We should have just enough power to get around the island, but it's enough to give us a look at where they're placing the troops, and this is quicker than sending people all over the city." He leaned over to look at the ground below. "Looks like we're almost there."

I saw what he meant when I looked down. There was a clear division between the wealthy neighborhoods and the rest of the city. The wealthy areas were well lit with soft, steady magical lights. Less-wealthy areas had flickering, dim gaslights. The poorest areas had hardly any light at all in the streets, though sometimes the faint glow of candlelight showed through a window.

Alec took a pair of binoculars from around his neck and

studied the ground. Mick did the same on the other side of the ship. After a moment, Alec grunted in satisfaction and said, "Ah, there they are." He lowered his binoculars and took a notepad and a pencil out of his coat pocket and handed them to me. "Would you mind recording my findings?" he asked.

Pencil in hand, I listened as he reeled off locations and numbers. "Light barrier at Fifty-Seventh and Columbus, six men. Same on Amsterdam." He gestured to Everett, who pulled a lever. The ship angled to the east. Alec turned to me, his binoculars in his hand. "I owe you an apology."

"An apology?"

"For what I said the other day, when I was more worried about your loss as a spy than about the loss of your position if you were recognized. I—I suppose I get too caught up in the cause. Lizzie says I forget to be human, that I'll turn into one of my machines one of these days."

"I'd forgotten all about it," I lied. It had eaten at me, but now that he'd apologized, I hoped I could forget it.

He put his hand on my shoulder. "Of course, if you ever were to lose your position, you've got our help, even if you're no longer of use to us in that way. You're our friend."

In spite of the cold wind, I felt as warm as the inside of one of Alec's steam engines. I blinked back tears before they could smear the lenses of my goggles. "I appreciate that."

"Hey, you two, you aren't on a romantic moonlight stroll!" Mick called from across the ship. "Keep your eyes open."

Everett steered a zigzag pattern across the city, covering the entire island. Alec had a better grasp of the city's topography than I did, always knowing exactly where we were. I only got my bearings when I saw a major landmark, like the cathedral or the Croton water distributing reservoir. The wind whipped the loose tendrils of hair around my face, and my cheeks had gone numb from the cold, but my entire body tingled with exhilaration. I was flying!

The farther we went downtown, the more barriers and soldiers we saw. They were thickest in the area below Union Square and around the university. I barely had a chance to look down from frantically scribbling the locations and numbers Mick and Alec shouted to me. Everett cut the engines, and we hovered for a while, taking in the entire situation. After we'd noted it thoroughly, Alec handed me the binoculars and let me look. The streets were red with the coats of soldiers on patrol. Few other people were out at this time of night.

While I studied the ground, Alec went back to talk to Everett. "They're thick on the ground here, which makes me wonder how thin they are elsewhere."

"You want to go all the way down to the fort?" Everett asked.

"Think we can? They're more likely to have lookouts there."

I could hear the smile in Everett's voice as he said, "They won't be looking in the sky for us. They think that's their territory."

"We've got enough power?"

"We can get there and back, so long as you don't want too many sightseeing excursions."

Everett restarted the engine, and we drifted downtown. It was harder to make out landmarks below since these were poorer neighborhoods or commercial and industrial areas that weren't well lit. Alec tapped me on the shoulder and pointed out the graceful arches of the Brooklyn Bridge spanning the river.

"This really is a magic carpet," I said, tearing my gaze away from the view to smile at him.

"Only without the magic. This is powered by human ingenuity, which is far superior. You like it, though?"

"Very much."

"Bessie might get jealous if you like this better."

"It's impossible to compare the two."

"Very diplomatically spoken."

The southernmost tip of the city was mostly dark, with the exception of the lanterns illuminating the rigging of a clipper ship docked at a wharf-side warehouse. "What a beautiful ship," I said.

"It needs an engine."

"Not everything needs an engine."

"It does if it's to compete with the magisters' ships and airships. If you put a steam engine in a ship you don't have to worry about catching a good wind."

We'd gone out over the water to approach the West Battery fort from behind. The water was inky black, but the wave crests sometimes held an eerie glow for a split second. That gave the harbor a sparkling effect. I could have stared at it for hours, as it was utterly mesmerizing, but then something else caught my eye.

A small boat raced across the harbor, heading toward the Battery. It must have been magically powered, for I saw neither oars nor sails. I handed the binoculars to Alec and pointed out the boat. "It's military," he said after looking at it for a while. "They're wearing uniforms, and they've got something in the boat with them. Looks like a chest. I'll wager they're bringing the payroll over from Governor's Island."

"In the darkness? And by boat, when they have airships?"

"They'll be as stealthy as possible when hauling around large sums of money." Alec called to Everett, "Bring us over the fort. I want to see if there's any activity there."

He returned the binoculars to me while he went to direct Everett. We'd passed the small boat and were nearly back over land. Behind the fort lurked another boat, hidden where it wouldn't be visible either to the fort or to the approaching craft. It looked like a pleasure yacht, but it bore no lights. I was about to remark on it when I noticed movement on the ground by the fort.

At first, I thought it must be my imagination, or perhaps the shadows of trees stirred by the night breeze, because I soon lost sight of the figures I thought I'd seen. But then they crept forward as the payroll boat tied up behind the fort. That seemed odd. I would have thought anyone meeting that boat would come fully armed and show themselves.

I leaned as far forward as I dared and adjusted the binoculars, trying to bring more detail into view. The figures on the ground stepped out of hiding, and I cried out in dismay, for I recognized them—or, rather, I recognized their masks. The Masked Bandits were stealing the military payroll.

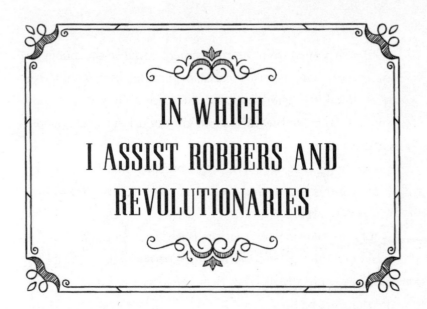

IN WHICH
I ASSIST ROBBERS AND
REVOLUTIONARIES

"It's the Bandits!" I cried out, then wished I'd kept silent when Alec rushed over and took the binoculars from me. While he scanned the ground below, I stared in frustration at the nearly featureless darkness that was all I could see without the binoculars.

"A robbery? Outta sight!" Mick enthused.

"Wait, are they using magic to freeze the couriers?" Alec muttered, frowning through the binoculars.

"Of course they are. They're magisters," I said, so distracted by worry that I spoke without thinking.

Alec pulled the binoculars away from his eyes to stare quizzically at me. "The Masked Bandits are magisters? How do you know?"

It was too late to take it back, so I explained, "They once robbed a train I was on, and they used magic then."

"But they steal from the government and give the money to commoners. The shop that makes my machine parts would have been closed if it hadn't been for their help. They've also contributed money to the cause. Sometimes they even help people pay their taxes."

"Really?" *That* explained why someone like Lord Henry would commit crime, and I felt giddy with relief to know that he wasn't wicked.

"Our movement would have collapsed without them. But why would magisters go against their own people?"

"They're not all evil. They're like anyone else. There are good and there are bad."

I waited to see how he'd respond, if he'd accept that truth—and possibly accept who I was—or argue against it, but he merely went back to watching the events below. I anxiously chewed my lower lip. *Oh, Henry*, I thought. No wonder he'd been so tense at dinner. But it was such an enormous risk, going right into the British military stronghold.

With a groan of frustration, I snatched Mick's binoculars away from him. He protested, but I ignored him. We were almost directly over the fort now, so I had to move around the ship to keep my eyes on events at the pier. The bandits had come out of their hiding places and were prying the chest from the hands of the entranced couriers.

I thought the lead bandit must be Henry. He was taller than the others and his bearing looked familiar, like the way he carried himself when he forgot to be clumsy. Two of the bandits carried the chest toward their boat. The couriers remained totally still as the remaining bandits—including the one I thought was Henry—slipped an identical-looking chest into their hands. Then they ran off toward the boat, leaving the couriers behind with the fake chest.

It looked like the bandits would get away with it and the couriers wouldn't realize anything had happened until the fake chest was opened, but before the bandits reached the boat, a soldier came out of the fort and spied the motionless couriers. A second later, he called out an alarm loud enough for us to hear in the airship. Before I could see what happened next, Mick snatched the binoculars away from me. "I want to see!" he said.

"Did no one teach you manners?" I huffed.

"Nope, not at all," he replied, without moving the binoculars from his eyes.

I turned to Alec, who was also watching intently. "We've got to help them!" I cried.

"What do you propose we do?" Alec asked me.

"We could create a diversion."

"And get ourselves caught?"

"Just enough to lead them in the wrong direction until the bandits can escape." I scrambled desperately for an idea, well aware that we were running out of time. Something from one of Rollo's discourses on airships struck me. "What kind of ballast do you carry?"

"Some sacks of sand and small rocks."

"We trickle a little behind us as we head into the city. The noise should distract the soldiers. It might sound like someone running away in that direction."

Alec glanced at Everett. "It's your ship," he said.

"We could stand to lose a little ballast," Everett said with a shrug and a grin.

"Mick!" Alec ordered.

"Aye, aye, sir!" the boy responded.

I grabbed the binoculars from him as he ran to get a sack. Soldiers rushed out of the fort, but they were still milling about in front while the couriers, who must have come out of their trance, gesticulated wildly. The couriers didn't seem to have seen which way the bandits went. Henry was almost to the boat, but if the soldiers moved even a little, they'd see him.

Everett steered us toward the city, and Mick dropped a small rock over the side of the basket, about fifty feet away from the gathered soldiers. They all reacted, glancing around in search of the source of the sound. Then Mick let a trickle of pebbles fall, dropping them in a rhythm like running footsteps and the soldiers ran in that direction. Our plan seemed to be working. No one had gone to the sea side of the fort, and now the boat was safely away.

Mick spilled a little more ballast, and I went to the other side of the airship to watch the boat. It rounded a bend, and then its lights came on, so it looked like just another magister's yacht on a nighttime pleasure cruise around the island. I suspected that if anyone boarded that boat, they'd find a group of wealthy young men much the worse for drink, possibly with a card game in progress. "They're away," I announced, letting out a long sigh of relief.

"And we should be away, too," Alec said, signaling for Mick to stop dropping ballast. "We don't want to give them a reason to look up." He peered down at the soldiers, who were fanning out to search the nearby streets. "I'm sure some of them are sleeping, but they seem to have almost everyone who isn't resting out on the streets. This is a small contingent." He lowered his binoculars and looked at me. "I don't suppose the governor mentioned which troops would be arriving, or when?"

"You got my message?"

"We did, and many thanks for that."

"He didn't give specifics. I got the impression he'd only just then received the news."

"Keep your ears open, and let us know right away if you hear anything."

"That's getting more difficult these days. Could you put a telegraph wire near my window and teach me to send messages? Then I could send you information without any of us having to move around the city."

He shook his head. "Too dangerous. Anyone who's tapped in can hear everything, and we don't want information that sensitive going out on the wires."

"It's safer to stick it in a hole in the wall?"

"Then it's not so obvious who's sending it." He smiled at me. "I trust in your ingenuity, Verity."

"The battery's running low, Alec," Everett called from the controls.

"Then we'd best get back to roost."

For the rest of the journey home, Alec stood with his arm around my shoulders and pointed out streets and landmarks. I almost forgot about revolutions and robberies as we soared through the night. I had the wind in my hair, air beneath my feet, and a good man at my side. I laughed out loud for the sheer joy of it.

The voyage came to an end all too soon as Everett guided the airship to the rear of the Lyndon mansion. Alec opened the gate on the side of the basket and lowered the tail of the ladder. I took off my goggles and handed them to him, then turned to wave farewell to Mick and Everett. "Thank you for bringing me along!" I said.

"This one's got the makings of an aviator," Everett said.

"I do enjoy flying."

Alec helped me over the side and knelt to hold me steady until my footing on the ladder was secure. "Hold on to the ladder," he cautioned.

"Thank you for a lovely evening," I said, smiling up at him. "It was the most amazing thing I've ever experienced—aside from the steam engine, obviously." Impulsively, I stretched upward and kissed his lips.

He returned my kiss, and when he pulled away, he said, "Just wait, there's more to show you." He started the mechanism that lowered the ladder and sent me away from him. The ladder stopped in front of my window, and he started to climb down to assist me, but I waved him back.

With one elbow crooked around the ladder, I reached for the window, caught the edge, and used that to pull myself closer to the building. I got one foot solidly on the windowsill, took a deep breath, and leaned forward into the room while I stepped off with the other foot and released the ladder, grabbing the other edge of the window for balance. When I was steady, I turned to wave at the airship's crew while they pulled the ladder up. I stood in the window, watching until the ship blended into the night sky and disappeared from view.

I stepped down onto my chair, then turned and shut the window. I felt horribly earthbound as I climbed down from the chair onto the floor. Once I was back in the ordinariness of my bedroom, I suddenly felt like I'd been up far too late. I removed and hung up my coat, took off my boots and stockings, and climbed into bed.

My last thought before I fell asleep was to wonder if Henry had made it home yet.

I woke the next morning with the sense that I'd dreamed the entire adventure. I'd certainly flown often enough in my dreams. The only tangible evidence that the night before had been at all unusual was a pair of stockings left lying beside my boots on the floor, which I knew hadn't been there when I went to bed the first time, and the chair that still sat under the window.

Lord Henry wasn't at breakfast when I went downstairs, and I couldn't help but worry. Had he been caught in spite of our efforts, or had he merely had a later night than I had? When he appeared in the breakfast room a few minutes later, I nearly forgot myself and ran to hug him. He looked much the worse for wear, with bleary, bloodshot eyes and a greenish tint to his skin, but there were no visible wounds. "Miss Newton," he greeted me tersely before asking for tea.

"Aren't you feeling well this morning?" I asked.

"Do I look that bad? No, don't answer. I know I do. That headache plagued me all night."

"I will try to keep Olive quiet this morning, then."

He gave me a rueful smile. "That's kind of you, but I have business out of town. I'm afraid I'll have to leave you alone tonight. If the children misbehave, think of whatever dire punishment you deem appropriate, tell them I said that's what I would do, and I'll carry it out upon my return."

"I'm sure they'll give me no trouble at all." I wanted to ask where he was going, but I doubted that would be a proper question for a governess to ask her employer, even one as friendly as mine. I suspected his business had something to do with the rather large sum of money he'd appropriated the night before.

I seldom saw him during the day since he usually stayed in his study when he was home, so I didn't miss his presence until dinnertime, when a referee for the usual arguments would have been nice. I let the children squabble while I daydreamed about flying, then I assigned reading to the elder two while I sent Olive to bed early.

Lord Henry hadn't returned by Thursday afternoon when Flora and I went to visit Lady Elinor. Daylight made a remarkable change to her room. It had seemed cavernous at night, but with the late-afternoon sunlight streaming through the windows the room was cheerful. Flora gave her aunt an obligatory greeting, but Elinor's focus was on me. "It is so good of you to come, Verity," she said. She bade us be seated, and servants brought an elaborate tea, with sandwiches, scones, and cakes. "I'm sure I'm ruining your dinner, but you dine so early. I refuse to adjust my schedule merely because Henry prefers to keep country hours. Verity, you may pour."

While I poured and passed around teacups, Elinor said, "I understand from my father that I knew your parents, Verity. I remember your mother. I was just a child then, and I'd lost my mother a few years earlier. I was quite the little duckling, following around anyone I thought might make a good replacement, and I attached myself to yours. I am truly sorry for your loss. You were very fortunate to have her."

"Yes, I was," I said.

"But enough of that! We have a book to discuss. Flora dearest, what did you think of it?"

"I thought it was preposterous," Flora said with a sniff. "No magister is going to marry the *governess*." She said the last word with a sneer and a pointed glance at me.

"But it was implied that Jane was from a magister family,"

Elinor said. "She'd merely been sent away to an ordinary school by her uncaring aunt."

"But if she had powers, why would she be working as a governess?" Flora asked.

Elinor smiled and said, "Not all magisters are as wealthy as we are, but perhaps I was letting my imagination run away with me. Being a governess must not be nearly as romantic as it is in novels, is it, Verity?"

Before I could respond, Flora rolled her eyes and said, "She works for Henry. Even if she were a magister, that wouldn't be at all romantic."

"Henry isn't that bad, though I will agree that he's not exactly a romantic hero," Elinor said with a laugh.

Without thinking, I leaped to his defense, blurting, "I could imagine him being quite dashing, under the right circumstances." They both stared at me, and I felt my face flaming. No matter what I said, my blush would make it sound like a weak denial of true feelings, and I didn't dare give the real reason I knew Henry wasn't as boring as they thought. Flora's glare chilled me, but Elinor gave me a little smile before putting the book aside and saying, "Enough about the book. We should discuss the truly important topics. There's to be a ball!"

"A ball?" Flora said, her eyes lighting up as she completely forgot about me.

"Yes! With all those soldiers coming in—they're bringing over the Third Division from England, which should arrive this weekend, and the Special Brigade from India, since they have experience with insurrections—Father feels he should host a ball to welcome the officers. It will be two weeks from yesterday. That's not much warning, but it's not meant to be a grand affair, merely an impromptu entertainment."

"Will I be invited?" Flora asked, wringing her hands anxiously.

"Of course, you goose. You're the governor's granddaughter. And with all those officers about, I'm certain you'll have to attend, as well, Verity. Magisters seldom enter the military, so I'm afraid few of the officers will be appropriate for you, Flora. They do make good dancing partners, though. But, Verity, you might find a husband. No one ranking below major, of course. You'll want some polish and seasoning."

"I'm not in the market for a husband," I said.

"Why ever not?" Elinor turned to Flora with a conspiratorial wink. "Do you suppose she already has a suitor?"

"She does seem to go out quite often," Flora said slyly. "Olive said she met a boy in the park once."

"Oh, really? Verity, do tell."

I would have preferred not to answer, but this seemed my best opportunity to recover from my earlier faux pas about Henry. "I do have a friend I see from time to time. He's a student at the university, and he's quite brilliant."

"Even if you do have a suitor, it will be good if he finds himself in competition with a dashing young officer. He'll have to work harder to win you." Elinor leaned back against her pillows and picked up a lace fan. "I don't know what having all those soldiers in the city will do to the civic order. Most of them are merely well-disciplined and well-dressed ruffians, if you ask me. There are far too many soldiers to fit in the barracks, even on Governor's Island. I hear they're commandeering the student housing around the university. That area seems to be where the troublemakers are, so I suppose that's a good enough plan. Though your friend might be inconvenienced, Verity."

Flora didn't give her a chance to say anything more about the military plans. She directed the conversation back to the ball itself. "It won't be a costume ball, will it? Those are so tiresome."

"Why would we have a costume ball when all the men will be wearing uniforms? Any man can be handsome in a uniform." Elinor smiled at me. "And now Verity is wondering how I know so much when I never leave my bed. I maintain a circle of friends. It's amazing how readily people share things with someone they don't think is in communication with anyone else in society."

"Their coats are red, so I should make sure my gown doesn't clash with red," Flora mused, off in her own world of modistes and fashion plates. "I would hate to form an unattractive picture while I'm dancing." Then she gasped. "Henry will allow me to go, won't he?"

"He'll have to come himself. This is one occasion when I doubt Father will allow him to plead illness—or any other excuse. You are, however, on your own when it comes to persuading him that you need a new ball gown. He'll insist that since the ball is to welcome newcomers, none of them will have seen any of your old gowns, and I'm afraid I can't disagree. Don't you have a lovely white gown? That would show well against the red uniforms. Since there's hardly any time, you certainly wouldn't be the only one without a new gown."

I didn't have any ball gowns at all. I wondered if I was expected, as a chaperone, to dress for the ball. I doubted I could count on Lord Henry's knowledge of society's rules for that. I thought I might be able to consult Lady Elinor on the subject, but I didn't want to sound like I was angling to get a new gown. I was sure Flora would interpret it that way, no matter what I said.

I could hardly believe it when Lady Elinor then said, "As it is, I hope there will be enough time for Verity to get a gown made. The invitations haven't gone out yet, so you'll have a head start with the modiste. I'll make an appointment for you with one I know. You may have to go to her studio as all these travel restrictions will make life difficult for her. She'll know what's appropriate for a chaperone these days. In my time, they were all bitter old hags, not lovely young ladies like you."

Elinor and Flora talked a while longer about the latest styles, until Elinor said, "Oh my, it's getting late. You should be getting home, but you must visit me again."

As soon as we were in the carriage, Flora said, "I don't know what Aunt Elinor was up to choosing that book, but don't get any ideas. It doesn't work that way in real life."

"Do you mean your uncle isn't keeping his mad wife in the attic?" I replied, perhaps more sharply than I should have.

"You know exactly what I mean," she snapped. "Henry may

be eccentric, but he wouldn't go that far in doing something that would disgrace his family."

"As you so kindly told your aunt, I have a suitor, so you have nothing to worry about on that account," I said, firmly enough to end the conversation. We traveled the rest of the way in silence as I stewed over what I should do with Lady Elinor's intelligence.

Lord Henry had returned while we were out. He, Olive, and Rollo were in the family parlor when we arrived home. Flora burst into the room with uncharacteristic enthusiasm. "Grandfather's going to give a ball! For all the officers! And I'm to be invited! Please, Henry, say I may go!"

Only after she'd blurted all this did she take in the situation. Henry and Rollo, both with large pink flowers in their lapels, sat on the sofa holding dainty teacups, while Olive wore a flower-bedecked hat and sat on a nearby chair. "We had our own tea party," Olive announced proudly. Rollo scowled, but Henry looked tired. Wherever he'd been, he hadn't been resting.

"I can hardly give you permission to attend when you haven't received an invitation," Henry said mildly.

Flora swept over to perch on the edge of the sofa next to her uncle. "Oh, but I must go!"

"I want to go to a ball," Olive said. "I could wear a pretty dress and dance all night." She sighed wistfully, then turned to her brother and said in a childish imitation of proper ladylike tones, "Would you care for more tea, Lord Roland?"

"No more tea; it's almost time for dinner," Lord Henry said.

He sent the children up to their rooms, and I moved to go to my own room, but he caught my eye, indicating he wished for me to stay. "How did Flora do?" he asked.

"Very well. Her aunt was pleased. I trust your journey was pleasant?"

"This one wasn't about pleasure, I'm afraid. But I may have to travel again soon."

I hoped he would stay home for a few days. When he was away, I had more responsibilities with the children, which complicated my efforts to communicate with the rebels, and I needed to pass on my new information as soon as possible.

IN WHICH
I DISCOVER A DREADFUL
DECEPTION

Much to my surprise, Flora provided the opportunity for me to meet the rebels. The next day at lunch she informed me that she'd heard from Lady Elinor, who had arranged an appointment for me with her modiste that afternoon. "There really is no time to lose," Flora insisted. "It's already too late to have a new gown of the finest quality, but in two weeks she can do something for a chaperone that won't embarrass me."

The modiste's studio was near Union Square, not too far from the Mechanics' headquarters, and that gave me the perfect opportunity to deliver my intelligence. My hopes sank, though, when Flora continued, "And if I must wear an old dress, I need some new ribbons for it. I should go with Miss Newton and purchase the ribbons. There's one shop in the city that has what I want, and it is near the modiste's."

This time, I owed my thanks to Lord Henry. "I won't have you going down there," he said. "Miss Newton can purchase the ribbons if you write a note for the shopkeeper. I will call for a cab and provide a pass for Miss Newton to reenter our neighborhood."

He came down the front steps with me when the cab arrived, and for a moment I feared he would insist on coming with me, but instead he glanced around as though making sure no one was listening, then said softly, "I hope I'm not imposing on you if I ask you to carry out an errand for me, as well."

"Of course not. I would be only too happy to help."

He handed me a small parcel. "Please deliver this to a bookshop near the university for me. The address is on the tag."

"This person is expecting it?"

"Yes." He shifted uncomfortably, then didn't quite look me in the eye as he added, "But he doesn't know who's sending it. The transaction is rather, um, under the table, so to speak. Not illegal, though. The discretion is more due to, uh, class divides." He leaned closer to me. "I appreciate your assistance, but I also trust your good sense. Don't take any unnecessary chances. If it seems dangerous there, don't worry about either my errand or Flora's ribbons." He handed me up into the cab, negotiated a fare with the driver and paid it in advance, then gave me money for the return fare.

The modiste called herself Madame Flambeau, but she only smiled nervously when I greeted her in French, so I switched to English without comment. Her speech was accented heavily with Irish, with the occasional French word thrown in, not always used in a way that made sense, and her hair matched her name. Even if she wasn't truly French, she did seem to know her craft. "A chaperone's gown should be simple, not showy, no?" she said. "No lace for you." She lowered her voice like she was sharing a secret. "There's too much lace being used in this city, if you ask me, but that's what they want, and they're the ones paying the bills, so lace I give them. You are not a lady for lace, I think. Far too practical."

Although I didn't much like lace, I couldn't help but bristle at her assessment of me as too practical. I imagined her putting me in a slightly fancier version of the kinds of day dresses I usually wore, but she returned from her back room with a bolt of cloth the color of new leaves in springtime and draped it around my shoulders. The silk fell in supple folds, and I sighed with pleasure. "Yes, that is the color for you," she said with a nod. "It brings out your eyes." Then she showed me a fashion plate of perhaps the most beautiful gown I'd ever seen. It was simple, but so very elegant with a sweetheart neckline, snug-fitting bodice, a slight bustle, and a swirl of skirts. "Do you like?" she asked.

"Oh, yes!" I said, thinking it was a pity Alec wouldn't see me in this gown. Madame Flambeau took measurements and sent me on my way, telling me to come back in a week for a fitting, assuming the rebels hadn't burned down the city by then.

The shop selling Flora's ribbons lay beyond the barriers. British soldiers were checking credentials of people heading uptown, but they waved me into the downtown zone with a firm "Be careful, miss. There are ruffians about."

This part of town looked very different from the way I'd last seen it. Rebel Mechanics banners now hung from windows and fire escapes, along with the white banners smeared with red paint to symbolize blood. Almost every available wall surface was covered in posters and signs, pasted over each other in a mad collage. The posters urged citizens to resist British rule, reminded people that British troops had fired on colonial children, and promoted the benefits of machinery over magic.

The streets were oddly quiet, with none of the usual bustle, and most of the shop doors remained shut. I decided to carry out my errand for Lord Henry first, as I was nervous about having his parcel with me. The address on the parcel was a few blocks down Broadway. The bookshop didn't appear to be open. The front door was locked, and I saw no lights or signs of life through the small gaps between posters on the front windows.

I doubted Lord Henry would have sent me to the wrong address, so I pulled the bell and waited for a response. I jumped and barely swallowed a scream when an eye appeared in a narrow triangle between two Rebel Mechanics posters on the front window. I took the parcel from my bag and held it up. The door suddenly flew open and a hand reached out to grab me and pull me inside. Before I knew it, the door had closed behind me.

The shop was dim, lit only by the light coming through the transom. It took a few seconds for my eyes to adjust to the meager light so I could make out the tall, lanky man with sparse yellowish hair facing me. "I was wondering if we'd get that," he said, grabbing my parcel. "Were there difficulties?"

"I have no idea what you mean," I replied. "I'm merely a courier. Now I must be on my way. Have a good day, sir." He stepped out of the way and opened the door. It closed so quickly behind me after my exit that it nearly caught the tail of my skirt.

The ribbon shop was several blocks farther downtown. The front door was locked there, as well, and after I tapped on the glass, the curtains were pulled aside ever so slightly so that the proprietor could peer out at me. Then the door opened a crack. "What do you want?" a voice quavering with age asked.

"I'm on an errand for Lady Flora Lyndon. She needs some ribbon for a ball gown."

The door opened wider, and the voice said, "Please come in." A tiny white-haired man in a green apron then stood before me. "My apologies. One can't be too careful these days. I'm not sure which is worse, the British or the rebels."

I couldn't imagine why either group would have any interest in ribbons, but I gave him a sympathetic smile as I handed him Flora's note. "Here is Lady Flora's order."

"Right away, miss."

The shop was small and old, with a narrow wooden counter, behind which were towering shelves full of ribbons of all colors, fabrics, and sizes. The shopkeeper climbed a library ladder and reached for a spool of pale blue ribbon, which he brought down, measured against a yardstick nailed to the counter, and cut. He rolled the cut ribbon into a loop, wrapped it in white paper, tied that off with string, then wrapped that parcel in brown paper and tied it off with twine, leaving a loop like a carrying handle. All of this took only seconds. "Will there be anything else, miss?"

"Not if that is all Lady Flora requested."

"Very good, then." He handed me the parcel. "Thank Lady Flora for her custom," he said, darting around me and opening the door just enough for me to slip through. I'd barely made it to the sidewalk before the door slammed shut and I heard the click of a lock. If the shopkeepers were this nervous, I wondered how safe I was walking these streets. Conditions didn't seem all that bad. There were neither roving bands of rebels nor military patrols. But the streets being so empty made me feel exposed and vulnerable.

I checked my watch. I'd made quick work of my errands, so I thought I might add one more without being suspiciously late to return home. I hurried toward the Mechanics' headquarters and knocked on the door.

I had my insignia ready to show, but when the door opened, Nat greeted me. "Verity!"

"Hello, Nat," I said. "I've been wondering about you, since I haven't seen you selling newspapers this week. I suppose this has been a difficult time for newspaper sales."

"Are you kidding? It's been the best ever. I can't go up into magpie land, but I sell out first thing in the morning. If this keeps up, I'll be rich soon."

"That's good to hear. I was worried."

"You really are a nice girl, Verity. What brings you down here?"

"I've got some important information I need to pass on, if Alec, Colin, or Lizzie is around."

"I don't know about Lizzie, but Colin and Alec are in there." He stepped back from the door. "Go on through, you'll find them up in the balcony."

I found the stairs at the rear of the auditorium and made my way up. A large table at the end of the balcony held piles of documents, including maps of the city and diagrams of machines. Alec and Colin stood at the table, bent over a city map. Mick stood at Alec's elbow, leaning over the map like he was part of the planning.

"Alec!" I called out, my pulse quickening at the sight of him. He wore no coat and his shirtsleeves were rolled up to his elbows, which made him look like a man of action.

He straightened, turned, and moved toward me, saying, "Verity? What are you doing here?" Before I could answer, he'd caught me in an embrace and kissed me as though he'd been wanting to do so for days.

I was equally pleased to see him, so much so that I almost forgot my errand. My senses finally returned, and I pulled away enough to say, "I have information I thought was worthy of bringing in person."

He slid his hands from my back down to my waist and held me in the circle of his arms. "How did you get all the way down here?"

"I'm on an errand." I held up my parcel. "I had to buy some ribbon and, apparently, the only suitable shop is near here."

Colin whistled in appreciation. "That's good thinking, Verity."

"I would love to take credit for being so clever, but it was pure happenstance. The eldest girl was in desperate need of ribbon, and Lord Henry wouldn't let her come to this part of town."

"But he allowed you?" Alec's color rose, as though he was offended on my behalf.

I couldn't help but laugh. "Yes, and it's a good thing, too, so calm down."

"You said you had news?"

"Yes. They're bringing over the Third Division from England, and they'll be here this weekend. And then there's a special brigade from India that specializes in putting down insurrections. They're going to billet them in the student housing at the university!" My voice rose in pitch and volume as I reached the end of my message.

Alec and Colin exchanged glances, then Alec turned to Mick and said, "Mick, go get Verity some water." Once the boy was gone, he said to me, "How do you know this?"

"I heard it at the governor's house."

"How?" Alec asked.

"It came up when we were talking about a ball the governor is planning for the officers when they arrive."

"There's not much action we could take, though it is good for us to know," Alec said.

"I thought you could get your people on the staff of those buildings, perhaps set up ways to listen to or observe the soldiers," I suggested.

Colin laughed. "I believe we've created a monster. Next thing you know, she'll be leading the revolution, standing on top of the barricade with a banner, shouting defiance at the British."

"No, that would draw too much attention," I said, shaking my head with a smile. "Remember, my expertise is espionage."

"When is this ball you mentioned?" Alec asked.

"The Wednesday after next. I don't know the exact time, as the official invitations haven't been issued. I also don't know who will be invited, if it will be only the highest-ranking officers or only the newly arrived officers."

Mick arrived with the water, then leaned against the table, looking like he was trying to make himself inconspicuous so Colin and Alec wouldn't notice he was there and send him away again. I took a grateful sip. I hadn't realized how parched I'd become while walking around. "What I was worried about," I continued, "was having that many troops billeted so close to your headquarters. They'll have you surrounded. They might decide to search the theater again, and you'd have less warning to hide the evidence."

Colin and Alec exchanged a meaningful look, and while they seemed to be weighing their response, Mick laughed. "You don't have to worry about that!" he said. "The magpies would never think to look here."

The glare Alec shot him should have killed him on the spot. A little doubt in the back of my mind grew, taking form as I realized what was wrong with what Mick had said. "But didn't they suspect your headquarters were here when the police searched the theater the night of the party?"

Alec turned a purplish shade that didn't look healthy. Even his scalp was red beneath his fair hair. Colin went so pale that his freckles stood out like copper coins on his face. Neither of them spoke. "There was no raid, was there?" I said, breaking Alec's hold on me and backing away. The realization made me ill. "The police weren't searching the neighborhood. All that gathering evidence and escaping was merely a bit of theater to make the new recruits—what did you call us, 'sparks'?—feel like we shared your danger, to convince us of how horribly persecuted your movement was so we'd sympathize and be useful to you."

Alec regained his composure enough to ask, "Do you disagree with the cause, Verity?"

"No, I don't, because it's a good and just one. There was no need to trick me." That fateful day in the park flashed before my mind's eye, and I saw the roadster rush past after Alec swept me off my feet. The driver's hat had been pulled low, but I remembered red hair. "That was you that day in the park, wasn't it?" I asked Colin. "That reckless 'magister' who nearly ran me down so that you"—I whirled on Alec, my finger pointed in accusation—"could rush to my rescue. What did you do, steal the roadster from some unsuspecting magpie?"

"Borrowed," Colin insisted. "He was having lunch and never knew it was gone." He went a little misty-eyed. "Drove like a dream, too."

"You were a potentially valuable resource. We had to secure you," Alec said stiffly, ignoring Colin. "We weren't likely to find another person placed that high in the magpie world who might sympathize with us. After Nat told us where you were employed, we had to get you on our side, right away."

"So all of it was a lie?" My eyes stung, but I refused to cry.

"Not *all*. It may have started that way, but it came to be true." Alec looked genuinely distressed as he reached out to me. I wasn't ready to forgive him. He'd kissed me. I'd kissed him. I'd thought it meant something, but I'd been such a fool. "What part was true, and what wasn't?"

Alec opened and closed his mouth, but no words came out. "We liked you from the start," Colin said. "What I said on the bus that day was true, that you're the kind of person we're doing all this for. Even if you hadn't wanted to get involved with us, Lizzie would have been your friend. She thinks you've got a good heart."

That was nice to hear, but it wasn't what I'd asked. I repeated to Alec, "What part was true? How many girls have you wooed into your cause?"

"You're the only one," he said, so softly I could barely hear him.

"Normally, that's my job, but you seemed more like Alec's type," Colin put in. "You'd like someone studious and clever."

"I think I still might have been interested in you," Alec said, not quite looking at me. "But I might not have been so forward about it."

Colin laughed. "Which means he might have worked up the nerve to talk to you by Christmas." The glare Alec gave him said he didn't think that was funny.

I wasn't laughing either. "You didn't have to pretend. You

didn't have to lie to me. You all lie so easily, how am I to know what's true? It's fitting that your headquarters are in a theater because you do seem to enjoy your performances. What is the cause, really?"

"Liberty," Alec said softly, but his tone grew more intense as he continued. "We want our freedom. We don't want to depend on magpies for everything. We don't want to have to beg for whatever crumbs they allow to trickle down to us."

"But how can your cause be just if you have to lie about it to recruit people or to make your points? How do I know I can believe what you're telling me now?"

"You'll have to take our word for it, Verity," Alec said with a shrug. "I won't lie to you anymore, I promise you."

"How can I believe that?" I firmly set my water glass on the table and stalked away.

I heard footsteps rushing up behind me, and soon Alec stood in front of me. "You're just going to walk out of here? You said you believed in the cause, but now you're giving it up because you got your feelings hurt? I thought you were better than that."

"No, you didn't, or you wouldn't have felt you needed to lie to me and trick me to get me on your side." I'd said it in anger, but the truth of my own words stung me as I stepped around him and headed down the stairs without a backward glance.

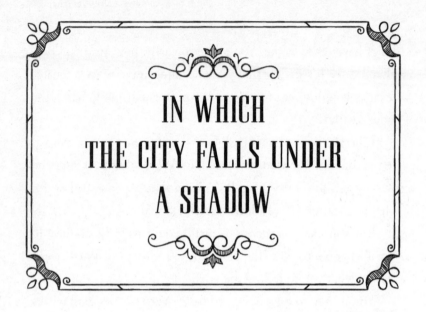

IN WHICH THE CITY FALLS UNDER A SHADOW

As I walked away from the theater, part of me wanted to turn back, even if just to prove to Alec that I was better than he thought, that I was fully committed to the cause. But I couldn't, not now. I knew I'd act more like a girl who'd had her heart broken than like a revolutionary, and I refused to let him see me cry.

Besides, there were other ways to further the cause. In fact, I'd just run an errand for Henry that I was sure was related to the rebellion, and I could continue to share intelligence without being friends with the Mechanics.

I must have been glaring so furiously as I approached the barricade that the British soldiers were intimidated, for they took a wary step back and allowed me to head uptown without asking for my credentials. I hailed the first magical cab I found, gave the driver the Lyndons' address, and settled back in the seat.

Alone at last, I could no longer hold back my tears. I let them fall with the hope that I would be through crying by the time I got home. Although I was angry at my false friends, I was most angry at myself for being naïve enough to fall into their trap. They had made me feel special and important, so I hadn't allowed myself to doubt them. I had always thought of myself as the clever girl who knew all the answers because I'd read so many books, and yet I'd been a simple fool.

But the worst blow was learning that Alec didn't care for me the way I'd cared for him. He might have liked me once he got to know me, but I'd always been first and foremost a tool. If I hadn't been useful to him, he'd never have given me a second thought. I should have known better than to think a mousy, unworldly governess would attract a brilliant rebel. He probably laughed about me with his short-skirted rebel friends.

When the cab passed the lower boundary of the park, I began scrubbing at my face with my handkerchief, and I took several deep breaths to get myself under control before I reached the Lyndon home. I might even have managed to hide my distress if Henry hadn't met me in the foyer. "Did you—" he started to say, but then he took a look at me and asked gently, "Ver—Miss Newton, is something the matter?"

"No, nothing," I said, tears threatening to form anew at his concern. "I'm merely somewhat fatigued. I never knew having a gown made would be so exhausting."

He stepped closer and lowered his voice. "You were able to carry out the errand? And you weren't in danger while doing so?"

"That went perfectly well."

"I thank you again for your assistance. You didn't have any trouble getting past the barricade?"

"It was hardly a barricade. They were only checking people heading uptown. The streets were strangely quiet, though, like everyone was expecting trouble."

"That's probably wise of them."

"Do you think it will be bad?"

"I don't know, but something's bound to happen." In an instant, he changed back into the vague, absentminded young nobleman he usually played, and I noticed Mrs. Talbot approaching. "Flora's about to burst from curiosity about your gown," he said, "but I've told her she must wait until dinner. You need time to rest."

"Thank you, sir," I said.

He drifted off in the direction of his study, and Mrs. Talbot said, "If you've got Flora's ribbon, I'll take it." As I handed over the package, she frowned at me. "You do look fatigued, my dear. I'll have some tea sent to your room."

I waited until the tea had arrived and the housemaid had left before I allowed myself to lower my guard and cry again. These tears, though, were more from anger than from heartache. I yanked open the nightstand drawer, grabbed Alec's handkerchief, and wished I had a fire I could hurl it into. The magically powered central heating offered few opportunities for destruction.

Then I took Lizzie's notebook and the Mechanics' insignia

from their hiding place. I wished I could destroy those, too, but I had to admit that the Mechanics had opened my eyes. I'd seen the injustices of British rule and the inequities among colonial citizens. I was a better person for having seen all that, and I did still want to fight for freedom. I would merely have to find another way.

On Saturday morning, I took Rollo and Olive for a walk in the park since I had nothing better to do on my free day and didn't want to be alone. Flora declined, waving Elinor's latest book as though she planned to spend the day reading it, but she didn't fool anyone. "Why didn't Uncle Henry come walking with us?" Olive asked as we entered the park.

"He went out," Rollo answered. "He said something about finding some beetle before it was gone for the winter. He and his scientist friends went to the country to look for it."

"Why couldn't we go to the country?" Olive asked. "We never get to go to the country with Uncle Henry."

I knew that was because "finding some beetle" probably really meant "committing banditry," and that was hardly an activity Henry could share with the children.

We reached the area where Alec had whisked me away from danger. It had become a habit for me to notice the spot whenever I was in the park, but now instead of the warm glow the memory once elicited, I felt a lump in my throat and a knot in my stomach from the knowledge that it hadn't been real.

I felt a pressure on my fingers and looked down to find Olive holding my hand. "You look sad, Miss Newton," she said.

"I'm sorry, Olive, I was merely thinking about something."

"Something sad?"

"Only a little."

Rollo, who'd wandered ahead, came running back to us. "Look! Look what's coming!"

"What is it, Rollo?" I asked.

"Come see!"

When we rounded the bend in the path and faced directly toward downtown, a vast object became visible in the sky. It was as though the moon had come down to hover just above the earth—that is, if the moon were shaped like a cigar. The largest airship I'd ever seen was flying over the city. It was several times as large as the ships that had brought the soldiers from Governor's Island, and the Mechanics' electric airship would have been a mere speck against it.

"I bet that's the *Hercules*, over from England," Rollo said, bouncing on his toes with excitement. "It's the biggest military airship ever made. Can we go see it up close, Miss Newton? Please? I'm sure Uncle Henry wouldn't mind. It's not a school day, and he encourages my mechanical interests."

"I don't think we'll have to go anywhere to see it," I said, craning my neck. "It appears to be heading straight for us." The sight of the giant airship blocking out the sky was awe-inspiring. The Mechanics had nothing that could match that.

We were now in the shadow cast by the giant ship. Unlike

the rebels' *Liberty* with its open basket, this ship had a closed gondola flush against the bottom of the balloon. It was flying so low that I could see windows in the cabin and people at those windows. Rollo jumped up and down and waved, and someone in the ship waved back.

Rollo grabbed my hand and tugged. "Can we go up to Belvedere Castle to look at it? Please? They've got a telescope in the tower, and we could see it so much better from there."

"It would be long gone by the time we got there," I said. The ship moved very quickly for something that massive.

"Then let's go home. I've got binoculars. I could watch it out the window."

"I don't want to go home," Olive said. "I want to walk in the park, not look at some ugly airship."

"Olive, you can walk in the park at any time," Rollo coaxed. "If we go home, then maybe we could come back out with a picnic for tea after the ship is gone."

Olive turned to me. "May we have a tea picnic? Please?"

"I will see what the cook can put together for us."

Rollo raced ahead, and I was just as eager to get home, but for a different reason. That ship made me nervous. It was an ominous cloud over our heads, forcibly reminding us of British domination, and it had brought with it soldiers to subdue the rebelling colonials. Its arrival was not a happy occasion.

The ship was so large that Rollo had plenty of time to observe it with binoculars from the schoolroom window. I half listened to him rattling off statistics about the ship while

I supervised Olive's piano practice. His mechanical interests reminded me of Alec, and I couldn't think of Alec without a pang. I wondered what he was doing—and whether he was wondering about me. Probably not, I decided.

When the ship was gone at last, I collected our picnic basket from the kitchen and we headed out to the park again. I stopped by the family parlor to invite Flora to join us but, as I expected, she declined the invitation. "Eating out of doors doesn't sound very sanitary," she said with a haughty sniff.

"What's sanitary?" Olive asked.

"It means clean—the kind of clean that keeps you from getting sick," I explained as we went down the stairs.

"Will eating outside make us sick?"

"Only if you drop your cakes in the dirt and eat them anyway," Rollo said.

"I won't drop my cakes. You'll drop yours."

"Then I'll eat yours."

"Miss Newton won't let you."

I was so busy trying to stop the argument that I didn't notice Lord Henry entering the house until he was upon us. He wore sporting attire and his face was pink, either from the sun or the wind, or possibly from exertion, as he appeared quite out of breath. One of his sleeves had a small rip in it, just above the elbow, and the cuff of one of his trouser legs was dirty and damp.

"Uncle!" Olive called out, forgetting her spat with her brother. "We're going on a picnic in the park! You can come with us!"

"I believe I would like that very much, if you don't mind my company." He addressed that last part to me, and I thought I detected a note of desperation in his tone.

"There's plenty of tea and cakes for all," I said.

"That's if Olive doesn't drop hers in the dirt," Rollo said with a laugh.

"I won't!"

"Children!" Henry warned. He turned to me and held out his hand. "If you will allow me, Miss Newton." I handed him the picnic basket, and then he held his other arm out to me. I hesitated before taking it. He should have escorted Olive, as she was the ranking lady present and I was merely an employee, but Olive seemed perfectly content hanging on to my other hand.

Henry selected a picnic site near one of the main paths, where we were quite visible, and though I'd never seen him socialize much, he made a point of waving and speaking to almost everyone who passed. I suspected he was establishing an alibi—making enough show of his presence that anyone who was asked would remember him having been in the park that afternoon. I bit my tongue to keep from smiling at the thought.

While I poured tea from a flask and passed out cakes, Rollo told his uncle in exhaustive detail about the airship. Henry looked as alarmed by the news as I felt. "Where do you think it will dock?" Rollo asked.

"I doubt it will stay. It will unload the troops and return to England, perhaps making a stop in the south for cotton."

"Do you think Grandfather could get me a tour of it while it's here?"

I nearly choked on the sip of tea I'd just taken. If I could get on that ship, it would be the perfect opportunity to gain useful intelligence, and I knew if I was with Rollo, I'd get all the technical specifications. "I'm sure it would be very educational," I said mildly. "And it's not an opportunity that comes along often."

Henry nodded to Rollo. "I'll send a message to your grandfather and see if he can arrange anything. It will depend on how long the ship stays."

Rollo put his binoculars to his eyes and scanned the sky, then said, "It's coming back!"

"It may have left some troops north of the city to guard the major roads and railroads," Henry said, taking his handkerchief out of his pocket, lifting his hat, and wiping his forehead. He looked ill, with beads of sweat forming on his upper lip and his skin a pale, grayish color. He went even paler when a pair of policemen on patrol appeared, and his sigh of relief when they passed was audible.

While Rollo watched the approaching airship, Henry rose to take a turn around that area of the park, stopping to talk to several people he knew. I couldn't help but muse upon what he was so anxious about. When he returned to us, I asked, "Did you find your beetle?"

"My beetle?"

"The one in the country that's about to go away for the winter."

"Oh, that beetle. Yes, we found a rather extensive colony of them, but I'm afraid that will be the last we'll see of them for a while."

"Winter must not be a good season for entomology," I said sympathetically.

"Oh, there's always work to be done," he said. "Cataloging, sketching, that sort of thing." He looked up, and when I heard the catch in his breath, I turned to see what had alarmed him. A group of uniformed British soldiers was approaching. Henry abruptly leaned over to study the ground beside our picnic blanket. "Will you look at that? What an interesting specimen." He took a pad and pencil from his coat pocket and began sketching. He didn't look up from the notebook until the soldiers had passed.

I wished I dared tell him I knew his secret. I thought it must be exhausting maintaining his façade, and I hoped for his sake that he really did have some interest in insects, or surely he must go mad having to learn enough to convincingly feign an obsession. He took off his hat with a trembling hand and set it aside as he leaned over his sketchbook, his unruly hair falling across his forehead.

"Uncle! Draw me!" Olive cried out.

Henry gave her a shaky smile. "It's been a long time since I've drawn something that only had two legs, but I'll try. Don't be alarmed if I give you wings, though."

She giggled and leaned against me. Rollo barely noticed the rest of us as he watched the airship come closer on its way downtown. A shadow fell on us as it passed overhead, and I shivered.

When I glanced down from the sky, I found myself looking directly into Henry's eyes. He looked as pained as I felt, but then he forced a smile and turned his notebook around to show us what he'd done.

"Does this meet with your approval, my lady?" he asked Olive. He'd drawn not only Olive, but also Rollo and me, and although it was a quick pencil sketch, it seemed very lifelike, capturing Olive's wide-eyed innocence and Rollo's fascination with something that lay beyond the edge of the page. I looked prettier than I was accustomed to seeing myself in the mirror. The loose wisps of hair around my face looked like winsome tendrils instead of untidiness, and he'd drawn me with a mysterious smile that made me wonder what I'd been thinking.

"Oh! Can I have it?" Olive asked.

"May you have it," I automatically corrected even as I stared at the sketch and wondered if that was how he saw me.

"Yes, you may, but wait until we get home before I take it out of the book, so it won't get crumpled," Henry said. He glanced at me. "Did it meet with your approval, Miss Newton?"

I couldn't look him in the eye because I knew I'd blush furiously. "You're wasting your talent drawing bugs. That's quite good."

"A proper young nobleman can't do something so common as take commissions or have a gallery show."

"But I'm sure the young ladies in your circle would love to have their portraits drawn. It would give you an excuse to spend time with them."

"Why do you think I started drawing bugs?" he asked dryly. "I'm much better at those than people. See?" He flipped a page in his notebook to show me a series of studies of dragonflies. These were more precise than his hasty sketch of us. As he flipped to another page, I glimpsed a drawing of a girl with her hair hanging loose around her shoulders, but he quickly moved past that to show me some finely detailed drawings of ants. Who could the girl be, I wondered, and then I despised myself for the surge of jealousy I felt. I had no claim to him, no hope with him. I hadn't even realized I felt that strongly for him, but the fact that I wanted to rip that portrait out of his sketchbook and rend it to pieces told me I must. Suddenly, our easy camaraderie seemed strained, at least on my part, and I couldn't think of anything to say to him that didn't sound foolish. Oh, but this was most inconvenient.

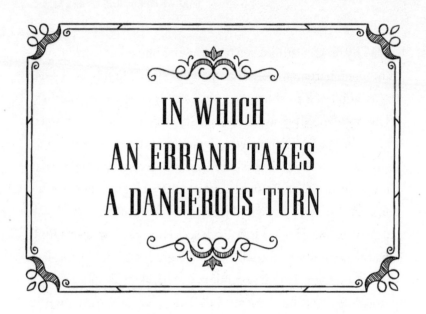

IN WHICH
AN ERRAND TAKES
A DANGEROUS TURN

The next afternoon was too rainy for walking in the park. Henry, Rollo, Olive, and I were playing a game and Flora was practicing the piano when Mr. Chastain came to the door of the family parlor. "Lord Henry, there is a gentleman here to see you. He says it's urgent."

Henry blanched. "Did he say what it was regarding?"

"No, sir, just that it was essential, and he needed to speak to you privately."

"I'll be down in a moment." Henry's hands shook as he straightened his tie and shoved his glasses back up on his nose before standing.

He'd only been gone for a few minutes before Mr. Chastain returned. "Miss Newton, you're needed as well."

I stood and smoothed my skirts, feeling I must have gone as

pale as Lord Henry had. Had they discovered the source of the rebels' intelligence or the identity of Liberty Jones? Lord Henry and another man both rose as I entered the formal parlor downstairs. "Miss Newton, this is Detective Vincent of the city police department," Henry said. "Detective Vincent, Miss Newton, my governess."

"Good day, miss," the detective grunted, then he gestured for me to sit next to Henry on the sofa. "I have a few questions for you. These are just a formality, but I have to follow all the angles, you know."

"Yes, of course," I said, trying to keep my voice from shaking. I clutched my skirt so I wouldn't give in to the impulse to reach for Henry's hand.

"Now, I understand Lord Henry was with you yesterday afternoon?"

This visit wasn't about me after all, I realized, going weak with relief. I tensed again with the thought that the detective was likely investigating the bandits. I'd worried what I should do with my knowledge about Henry, but now that a police officer was interviewing me, I had no doubt. "Yes, sir, he was. We took the children for a picnic in the park," I said, trying to sound as though the matter was inconsequential to me.

"Do you know what time it was?"

I gave a little laugh that I hoped sounded casual. "Oh my, I'm really not sure. I have to pay such close attention to time on school days that I completely forget about it on weekends. I do recall that the large airship—the *Hercules*, I believe it's called—

was traveling past, because Rollo—Lord Roland—was fascinated with it. He would talk of nothing else."

"I see." The detective made a note in his notebook. He didn't ask which direction the airship was going when we were on our picnic, and I decided not to clarify that for him. I hoped my instincts about Henry were correct and that I wasn't abetting some horrible crime. The detective snapped his notebook shut and stood. "That should take care of matters for now, my lord," he said. "You will notify us if you think of anything else?"

"Yes, of course I will." Lord Henry rose to walk him to the door, where he handed him over to Mr. Chastain to see him out.

When the detective was gone and the door firmly shut behind him, Henry sagged against the wall. "That was unnerving," he said.

"What was that about?" I asked, fearing the answer but not expecting the truth.

"One of my friends was arrested after a robbery yesterday. There were others with him who got away, and the police are talking to all of his known associates."

"How awful!" I said. "Had you any idea he was involved in criminal activities?"

His lips twitched. "I had a few suspicions."

"Well, it's most fortunate that you were with us yesterday. And if my word wasn't good enough for the detective, there are dozens of other people who saw you in the park."

I wished I could see his eyes behind his glasses, but he stood at just the wrong angle, with the light from the chandelier creating a glare on the lenses. "Yes, that is very fortunate," he agreed.

"Imagine if I'd come home and gone straight to my study while you were out, and you weren't able to vouch for my whereabouts. I might not have been able to persuade him of my innocence."

For a moment, I considered telling him I knew about him so he wouldn't have to lie to me anymore. I allowed myself to imagine what might happen between us if we shared that enormous a secret, and then I remembered that it couldn't really change anything. Falling for my employer was even more foolish than believing a rebel's lies. I was through behaving like the heroine of a novel.

The *Hercules* may have left, but the airships from Governor's Island maintained a steady patrol over the city during the following week. That meant getting Rollo's attention was a challenge. I handed him directly over to the headmaster each morning to ensure that he went into the school instead of sneaking away to watch the ships. He probably spent the school day staring out the window, but that wasn't my problem.

Henry was unusually social during that time. He hardly ever locked himself away in his study, and he dropped by the schoolroom several times a day. He never left the house without taking one of the children with him, and he still flinched and went pale whenever the front bell rang. Even Olive seemed to notice his tension, though that didn't stop her from demanding he play with her or read stories to her. I occasionally heard piano music coming from the schoolroom or the family parlor that was louder and more robust than Flora's delicate touch, and I recalled what Henry had said about playing when he needed to think. I wondered what he was thinking about.

Flora, though, seemed entirely oblivious to either the military activity or her uncle's strange behavior. The official invitation to the ball arrived Monday, and Henry had immediately written to accept. Flora and her lady's maid spent hours each day adding ribbon trim to the hem and flounces of her ball gown.

My initial hurt and anger about Alec's lies had eased, and now I felt his loss keenly. I hadn't realized how much I'd enjoyed having friends. I took my usual walks in the park, but I saw no one I knew. That convinced me that they'd lied about having come to care about me. As soon as I was no longer an asset, they'd dropped me entirely and were making no effort to mend fences.

My ball gown was ready for a fitting on Thursday. I saw to it that the girls were occupied with their music and drawing lessons before collecting my hat, coat, and gloves. When I stepped out of my room, I nearly ran into Lord Henry, who was lurking outside my door.

"I must ask another favor of you," he said, his voice fraught with tension. "I wouldn't impose upon you again if this weren't so very important and if I could think of any other way."

"Do you wish me to deliver another parcel?" I asked, nodding toward the one he held.

"If you would be so kind. It goes to the same place, with the same stipulations."

"It's no bother at all," I said, taking the parcel from him.

He then handed me a banknote. "Buy something for yourself while you're there."

I tried to give it back to him. "That's not necessary. I am only too happy to do a favor. You've been so kind to me."

"This isn't payment for the service. It's a reason for you to be there. If anyone asks why you were in that shop, you'll need something to show for it. You can look like you were selling and buying books."

Even though I was fairly certain of the truth—and that his answer would be a falsehood—I asked him, "Are you in trouble?"

"These are dangerous times and it is better to take precautions," he said evasively. Coming so close to being caught seemed to have frightened him into being more careful.

I nodded as I took the money from him and deposited it in my purse. He went with me down to the street, where a cab waited. As I rode downtown, I wished I knew a magic spell for looking inside a parcel. Seeing his fear and knowing that one of his associates had been arrested worried me. What would become of me if I were caught with this parcel?

As the cab neared Union Square, I noticed something in the sky. At first, I thought it was one of the airships that had been patrolling the city, but when I reached my destination and alighted, I got a better look and realized this must be the ship bringing the soldiers from India who had experience with insurrections.

This was a smaller ship, but it looked crueler. The *Hercules* was meant for carrying passengers and cargo, but this was a fighting vessel. I doubted it would be leaving, and I doubted that even his grandfather's influence would get Rollo a tour of this ship. The front, rear, and underside of its gondola bristled with weapons, and the balloon itself had great jagged scimitars protruding from it.

The ship was moored to the tallest building on the university campus. Soldiers swarmed down rope ladders onto the building's roof. It was difficult to see how many there were from nearly ten blocks away, but I didn't have time to go closer. With a sigh of regret, I entered the modiste's shop.

The ball gown was nearly complete, wanting only the finishing touches. Once I had removed my dress, Madame Flambeau tightened my corset before putting the gown on me. "For a ball, you want the tiny waist, no?" she said, and I was so lost in thought about the warship moored only blocks away that I didn't even argue with her about the corset lacing, as uncomfortable as it was.

When she threw the dress over my head, I momentarily forgot about the airship and impending revolution. "Oh, I've never worn anything so beautiful," I said. The image in the looking glass was that of a stranger. I wished I could turn and admire the way the dress moved, but Madame Flambeau was busy making little tucks and sticking pins in the dress.

"You've got a lovely figure, and in my gown you'll catch an officer's eye, that's for sure," she said. "You won't be a governess for long."

"I will be at the ball as a chaperone," I reminded her. "I won't be trying to catch an officer's eye."

"Aye, but you'll be one of the few ladies present they'll be allowed to touch. With all those magister girls around, there won't be many ladies who aren't forbidden."

"And that is why I imagine I will be very busy with my chaperoning duties at the ball."

She laughed. "Not if I know Lady Flora. She won't notice those who aren't magisters. Chaperoning her is the easiest job in the city."

I wished she would hurry and finish the fitting because I needed to carry out Lord Henry's errand as soon as possible. With all those soldiers in the area, getting to the bookstore unnoticed might be more difficult. I was in such a rush to get out that I forgot to loosen my corset again before dressing, so hurrying down the sidewalk left me short of breath. I leaned against the wall to recover, then moved more sedately toward the barricades.

The British barrier was still in place, but there was more activity in the streets in the rebel area than there had been during my last visit. Mechanics ran past in small groups, pausing at each corner to look around before running ahead. A shrill whistle made me jump, and I turned to see the smaller steam engine that had pulled the hayride at the picnic coming down the street, pulling a cart filled with men rather than hay.

The rebels were all heading toward Greenwich Square, where the airship was still unloading soldiers. I doubted they were going to give the new arrivals a friendly welcome. Fighting could start at any moment. I knew Lord Henry would understand if I couldn't carry out his errand. He had even instructed me not to put myself in danger, but it shouldn't take too long and I was several blocks from where the fighting would be. I didn't want him to think me a coward, and I wanted to prove to myself that I was still committed to the cause. Clutching the parcel tighter, I hurried on to the bookshop.

The windows of the bookshop were even more papered over than before. In addition to all the political posters, there were several advertising a theatrical extravaganza the night of the ball at an address I recognized as the Mechanics' theater. I suspected it was a diversion to occupy the soldiers. If the officers were at the ball and many of the soldiers were at the theater, it would be the ideal time for the rebels to raid British facilities.

The door of the bookshop opened before I had a chance to ring the bell. The same man was there, as were several others. I recognized one of them from among the Mechanics who'd been at Battery Park. He wore their strange garb mixing work clothes and formal wear—a brocade waistcoat over a red flannel union suit and striped trousers tucked into tall boots. He had a pair of goggles pushed up onto his forehead and a squashed top hat with a giant gem in the middle of the hatband resting on the back of his head.

As soon as I was inside, the yellow-haired man snatched the parcel away from me. "We were wondering if we'd ever see this," he muttered. "It's been days. Were there difficulties?"

"I told you before, I'm just a courier," I said stiffly. "And now, if you don't mind, I would like to purchase some books."

"Purchase some books?" he asked, raising an eyebrow.

"This is a bookshop, is it not?"

"She needs to buy something to have an excuse for having been here," the Mechanic said wearily, like he was accustomed to the yellow-haired man being obtuse.

"What sort of book?" the proprietor asked.

"I don't suppose you have any new paperback novels? I prefer adventure or detective stories. A romance will do in a pinch."

He went to a shelf and brought out a stack of books. "You can look through these and choose which ones you want."

"That won't be necessary. I'll take them all. Please wrap them up for me." I handed him the banknote Henry had given me. While he counted my change, there was a loud crash outside the store. The Mechanic rushed to the window to peer out through a slit between posters.

"What's happening?" I asked.

"The fighting may have started. I'd better check before you go out there, miss." He pulled the goggles over his eyes, straightened his hat, then opened the door ever so slightly and slid out sideways.

The bookseller took his time wrapping the books in brown paper, whistling tunelessly between his teeth while he wound the package with twine and tied it off neatly. There was more noise outside, with some bursts of gunfire and at least one explosion.

"It's about time," the bookseller muttered as he handed over my books. "Will there be anything else today, miss?"

"This should cover my reading needs for some time, though that might not be a problem if I'm trapped here." I attempted a smile. "I suppose if you have to be trapped someplace when a revolution breaks out, a bookstore isn't a bad place to be." He didn't return my smile.

The Mechanic returned a moment later, shutting and locking the door behind him. "There's fighting over by the square," he reported.

"Then I should go before the fighting spreads," I said, unsure if my racing heart was due to panic or excitement.

He shook his head. "No, miss, I won't have you going out into that."

I put my hand on my hip. "Then what do you propose I do? I can't stay here forever."

He grinned at me. "Don't you worry about that, miss. There's a good reason they call us the Rebel Mechanics. We've got far more than steam engines up our sleeves."

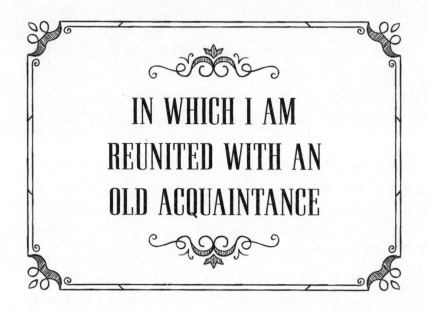

IN WHICH I AM
REUNITED WITH AN
OLD ACQUAINTANCE

The bookseller glared at the Mechanic. "You can't show her that! It's our biggest secret!"

"Well, unless you plan to adopt her, she has to get out of here somehow, and she can't go by the streets."

"You'll take precautions?" the bookseller asked.

"Do I look like an idiot? Besides, she's one of us. I've seen her before."

With a deep, groaning sigh, the bookseller took a key out of the cash register drawer. He gestured for us to follow as he led us to the back of the shop. There, he unlocked a door and held it open for us. It led to a steep staircase going down into a basement. The staircase was unlit, so whatever lay at its foot remained a mystery. "Down you go," the bookseller said.

"After you, miss," the Mechanic said to me. He took my

parcel so I could hold up my skirts with one hand and keep the other hand on the rail. The closer I got to the bottom, the darker it was. The Mechanic came behind me.

When he reached the bottom, he handed my parcel back to me, then he untied the kerchief from his neck and said, "Apologies, miss, but we do have to be careful." He wrapped the kerchief over my eyes and tied it at the back of my head. "This isn't too tight, is it?" he asked, his voice gentle.

"No. It's merely disconcerting."

"Don't worry, I'll have it off you in a minute."

Even with the blindfold, I could tell when he lit a lantern. I wasn't sure how he carried it because he took my parcel from me and tucked my hand into his elbow so he could guide me. He was a considerate guide, warning me when there was a step up or down and steering me around obstacles.

I tried to track each turn and how far we walked between turns, but I was soon hopelessly confused. I had a sneaking suspicion that he led me in circles a time or two to throw me off. Wherever he was taking me, it must have been a great secret.

At last, we entered what I presumed from the sound of our footsteps to be a large chamber. My guide removed my blindfold, and I saw that what I'd taken for an ornament in his top hat was the lens of a lantern. I thought that was remarkable, but then I noticed my surroundings.

I was in a first-class railway station waiting room—or, rather, what one might look like deep underground. There were rows of high-backed benches made of ornately carved dark wood up-holstered with red velvet. Brass chandeliers dangled from a rough stone ceiling, and travertine tiles lay underfoot. The walls were paneled in dark wood to just above head height, with rough stone above that.

Beside the waiting area stood an odd vessel that looked something like a boat, with a pointed wooden prow and a curved glass window at the front. A steering wheel stood between the prow and the window, and there was a long red-velvet-cushioned bench behind the window, with a single back down the middle, so the passengers would sit back-to-back.

A tunnel stretched ahead of the vessel, narrowing as it left the waiting area, with a set of railroad tracks leading down it. Behind the vessel at the far end of the cavern was something that looked like the steam-powered dynamo in the theater's basement. A group of men fed coal into it. About a dozen Mechanics sat in the waiting room.

"Can you take a couple more?" my guide called to the men working on the dynamo.

"Can you drive for us? Our scheduled driver hasn't shown."

"He may not make it—there's fighting. And you know I'm always up for a drive."

"Then we can take your passenger. We've room on this run. We'll be leaving as soon as we get her charged up."

"If you've got a line open, we'll need a cab at the other end." My guide came back to me. "We'll have you home in no time."

"What is this?" I asked.

"Our biggest secret—and it is a secret, mind you. Don't go telling anyone."

"My lips are sealed," I promised.

He gestured me to a seat in the waiting area and sat beside me. "About a dozen years ago, when they lived around here, the magpies thought an underground magical railroad would be a good way to get around town, out of the elements. But no sooner did they dig the tunnel and lay the track than they started moving uptown. And apparently there's no point in being a magpie without your own carriage, so the project fell by the wayside due to lack of interest. We found the tunnels and the rails, and we've built our own machines. We can't use steam engines in the tunnels, so we use dynamos to power the system in places where we can put chimneys without anyone noticing. They use electricity from the dynamos and magnetism to make the cars go, but you'd have to ask someone more clever than me to know how it all works. I just know how to drive it."

"This is amazing!" I said. "To think all this is going on beneath the surface, and nobody knows." I thought I now had a very good idea of how the rioters had come and gone so mysteriously.

"We're ready to go, so all aboard!" one of the men on the engine called out, and the passengers boarded the vessel. The padded bench was far more comfortable than any bus I'd ridden, but I felt exposed, as the vessel had neither roof nor sides. My guide pulled his goggles over his eyes and lit the lantern in his hat. My fellow passengers braced themselves, and I followed their lead.

The vessel shot forward on the rails, zooming into darkness lit only by the pilot's hat. I couldn't tell how close the tunnel's walls were or how fast we were going. We slowed as we entered another waiting area as elegant as the first, but we didn't stop. Suddenly, we were slung forward again. The next time we slowed, the cavern was unfinished, with only a dynamo and a few wooden benches. We shot forward, and this time when we slowed, we came to a stop.

This waiting area was barely carved out of the rock, with few furnishings. Electric globes hung from the ceiling. The tunnel extended a little farther beyond the station in a bulb-like shape that I realized was a roundhouse for turning around the cars. A few other cars like ours and some large flatbed cars without seats sat nearby on sidings.

"End of the line, all off," my guide called out. I waited until the other passengers had disembarked before I stepped off, and my guide joined me. "What did you think about that, miss?" he asked me.

"It was incredible! If it didn't have to be a secret, if you could use that for transit, it would greatly diminish the traffic and noise on the streets, wouldn't it?"

"We think so. But we're not supposed to be using it, as the tunnels don't actually belong to us, and they certainly don't want us moving about the city freely." He glanced down at his feet somewhat bashfully, then said, "Um, miss."

"Yes, I know, put the blindfold on me."

"I appreciate your being so understanding about this, miss. It's not that we don't trust you."

"I know. You can't be too careful these days."

After blindfolding me, he led me down passageways, taking a few twists and turns, until finally we came up a flight of stairs into what felt like a somewhat enclosed outdoor space, like an alley. We stepped briefly into the noise of the street, and then he removed my blindfold and handed me into a cab. I opened the grate between the passenger compartment and the driver's seat and gave the Lyndons' address.

While we traveled, I used the small mirror in my bag to straighten my hair after the blindfold and the wild underground ride. I was still smiling from the adventure, which had reminded me why I'd been drawn to the Mechanics in the first place. I might disagree with some of their methods, but their accomplishments impressed me.

Within minutes the cab stopped, and the driver helped me down. Mr. Chastain came out and paid the driver, and an anxious Lord Henry came rushing down the stairs as I entered the foyer.

"Everything went well?" he asked breathlessly.

"Perfectly."

"I heard the *Ares* arrived."

"That's the warship? Yes, it was there, with a great many soldiers."

"But you made it home safely?"

I gave him a patient smile. "Obviously."

He noticed my parcel, and his eyes went wide. "Were you able to . . . " His voice trailed off in worry as Mrs. Talbot approached. "These are some books I purchased," I said, loudly enough for Mrs. Talbot to hear. "I found a bookshop with all the latest paperback novels. They're my weakness, I must confess. They're probably not appropriate reading material for a governess, but I believe that if I can read the classics in their original languages, then I should be allowed the occasional adventure story in my spare time."

"I quite agree. If you don't mind, I may want to borrow one. I could use some light reading." He turned to the housekeeper. "Yes, Mrs. Talbot? Is there something you need?"

"I have just received word that our dinner menu may have to be altered tonight, as there was a problem getting supplies from the greenmarket. There seems to be some unrest downtown today."

"We'll manage," Lord Henry said. "It's sure to blow over soon enough."

I was surprised that he turned out to be right. The authorized newspaper reported that a minor skirmish near the university had been quickly put down. I couldn't imagine that the rebels would give up that easily. I might have accused the Mechanics of playacting, but they were serious about their cause, so I suspected any apparent surrender was part of a greater plot. Unfortunately, the new restrictions still made it impossible for Nat to sell papers in my part of the city, so I didn't know what the rebels were saying. After being so active, it felt odd to have nothing to do as the rebellion actually started, but I heard no useful information to pass on to them. I hoped perhaps I'd learn something at the ball, where I'd be surrounded by soldiers.

That is, if there was a ball. Would they really send the officers to a ball when a rebellion was brewing and there had been fighting in the streets? Or was that why the rebels had fought and then backed down, to make the British overconfident? If that was the plan, it had worked, because there was no talk of cancellation when the day of the ball arrived.

Flora had her maid, Miss Jenkins, help me dress. She arranged my hair in a style that was less severe than my usual tight knot. Curling tendrils framed my face, and others were pinned into a complicated style at the back of my head. I had a feeling I'd be finding hairpins for days after the ball.

Flora came to my room to check on me before we went downstairs. "You'll do," she said curtly, and then she tilted her head and frowned at me, making me wonder if there was something wrong with my appearance.

In spite of her frown, I felt like a princess as I swept down the stairs, my skirts rustling around me. Henry waited for us in the foyer, looking rather handsome in a white tie and a tailcoat. He'd attempted to tame his hair, but a few cowlicks had already rebelled. He was adjusting his cuff links, and when he glanced up to see us, his jaw dropped. Flora noticed his expression, turned to study me, then frowned. "Miss Newton, you have no jewelry," she said.

"Miss Newton doesn't need jewelry." Lord Henry's voice was strangely hoarse as he said it, and his eyes never left me, even when he spoke to Flora. I wondered if I'd done something wrong or chosen the wrong style of gown, but he didn't seem displeased, merely disconcerted.

Mr. Chastain opened the front door, and Henry offered his arm to Flora to escort her to the carriage. I followed, conscious of my true position in the household for perhaps the first time since I'd been employed. The driver helped Flora up into the carriage. She situated herself in the forward-facing seat. Henry took my hand to help me up, and I took the rear-facing seat. When Henry boarded, he turned to sit beside Flora, but she raised a hand to stop him. "No, you'll squash my skirts. Sit with Miss Newton."

He raised an eyebrow and smirked. "As you wish, my lady." I moved aside and gathered my skirts to give him room. None of us tried to converse during the drive. I grew increasingly nervous about what I would face that night since I had no real idea of what a chaperone should do at a ball. The tight lacing of my corset didn't help when my breath was already short.

There was a long line of carriages at the governor's manor, and we spent as much time waiting to reach the doorway and disembark as it had taken us to make the drive up to the tip of the island. I passed the time by looking out the window. From here, I had a commanding view of the city. It was almost like seeing it from the airship. Everything looked calm from this vantage point, but I had a feeling *something* would happen that night, given what I was sure was a diversionary show at the Mechanics' theater and the officers being at the ball.

At last, it was our turn to stop under the porte cochere and leave the carriage. Here, as at the Lyndon house, Henry escorted Flora, with me following. A footman announced the arrival of Lord Henry Lyndon and Lady Flora Lyndon as we entered the ballroom down a short flight of stairs.

I'd read plenty of books in which the characters attended grand balls, but the words on the pages hadn't prepared me for the splendor of the ballroom. Elinor had referred to it as an impromptu gathering, but if this was something just thrown together, I couldn't imagine what a true grand ball would be like. Even if the room had been bare, the profusion of elaborate gowns in bright colors, along with the brilliant red of the military uniforms and the gleaming brass of buttons and medals, would have been overwhelming.

But the room wasn't bare. Its walls were mirrored, the mirrors reflecting light from half a dozen magical chandeliers dripping with crystals. The effect was like sunlight striking water on a windy day. Nearly every surface in the room held densely packed arrangements of roses. The air was heady with the scent.

An orchestra played music that made me want to dance, but nobody was dancing yet. Lord Henry led us to a grouping of chairs where we could see the floor but were out of the way of most of the people milling about the room. Once seated, Flora snapped open her fan and used it to shield her face while she studied the attendees.

"The officers aren't very handsome," she commented.

"Don't be rude, Flora," Henry said absently, as though it was an automatic response that came up even when his mind was elsewhere.

"They can't hear me, it's so noisy in here. And I don't care if they know what I think of them."

"That's still no call to be rude."

"What do you think, Miss Newton?" she asked, turning to me. "Do you see any who are particularly handsome?"

I had to agree with Flora. There was a hardness about these men that made them unappealing, even if their faces and forms were pleasant. The ones who weren't hard seemed far too soft to be military men. I guessed that these were noblemen who got their rank through their positions. I pitied Flora if those were the only magisters in the group. "These men aren't to my taste," I said. But that didn't mean I would have minded dancing with some of them. It would be a valuable intelligence-gathering opportunity. Not to mention, it would be a pity not to dance at my first ball.

The orchestra played a fanfare, and the guests applauded as a small group of people went to the center of the floor. I recognized the governor and General Montgomery among a few other men in uniform with their ladies. "It's the quadrille," Flora explained. "The host and the top guests do this to start the dancing."

When the quadrille was over, the orchestra struck up a waltz, and the mass of red uniforms fanned out around the room in search of partners. Flora was easily one of the prettiest girls in attendance, so she was much in demand, and in spite of her earlier dismissal of the men, she accepted them all politely. None of them acknowledged my presence. Henry didn't go in search of a partner, instead staying near me with his eyes on the dance floor. I wished I'd had a better look at the sketch I'd seen in his book so I could recognize whichever lady had caught his eye.

When Flora took a break from dancing and returned to us, the governor came over to greet his granddaughter and Henry. "You are enjoying yourself, my dear?" he asked Flora.

"The officers are good dancers," she said, fanning herself, "but I don't much care for their company."

The governor roared with laughter at that. "You have your mother's sense," he said. "Good girl, you stay just like that, and you'll keep out of trouble." He wished us a curt good evening, then turned and moved away. He was only a few feet from us when a footman approached him with a note on a silver tray. The governor read it and reacted with shock, then signaled across the room to General Montgomery. They met to the side and spoke for a moment, their heads close together, then the general signaled to a couple of the other officers, and all of them left the room.

"I wonder what that's about," Henry said under his breath. He moved away into the crowd, disappeared for a moment, and then returned to us. A few minutes later, he barely suppressed a smile as another footman approached us with a message for Henry. He merely glanced at it before saying, "Matthews is here, says he has an urgent message to deliver. I'll be back in a moment, ladies."

Soon after Henry left, the governor, the general, and the

officers returned. The officers worked their way around the room, stopping other officers and speaking briefly. The officers then began departing. "All the dancing partners are leaving," Flora grumbled. Dancing wasn't my concern. If they had withdrawn the officers, it had to mean something was happening elsewhere.

Elinor's maid came up to me with a curtsy. "Miss Newton, Lady Elinor has asked to see you."

"I'm afraid I can't," I said. "Lord Henry has stepped out, and I must chaperone Lady Flora."

"Oh, go on, Miss Newton," Flora said with a flick of her fan. "There's no one left to dance with, and I'm in my grandfather's house. I'm the safest girl here. I promise to stay right where I am."

Although I'd been there before, the maid gave me a brief tour of the house on our way to Lady Elinor's room. She pointed out the library, the parlor where we'd gone the first time I was there, and the closed door to the governor's study. The latter caught my eye as we passed it. Whatever information had been brought to the governor might be in there.

Lady Elinor was sitting up in bed when I reached her room. "I hope you don't mind me pulling you away from the ball, but I had to see your gown," she said. She gestured for me to turn around so she could see it from all angles. "I approve. You look lovely. Are you having a good time?"

"It's a very nice ball," I replied.

She laughed. "You haven't danced a bit, have you?"

"I'm afraid not, and most of the officers have already left."

"So soon? But this is early! I wonder what happened. I shall have to ask Father later. Now, run along back to the ball. I don't want to keep you. Promise me that you'll dance at least once. Make Henry waltz with you. You wouldn't think it from the way he bumps into walls, but he's rather good if he keeps his mind on it."

"I will try," I said, not meaning it. My awareness of Henry was unsettling enough without knowing the feeling of dancing with him.

"Do you think you can find your own way back, or should I ring for my maid?"

"I'm sure I can find my own way."

When I passed the governor's study, I paused. There was no one in the hallway to see me, and I thought I had a few minutes before my absence would be noticed in the ballroom. I sidled closer to the door and pressed my ear against it. There was no sound from inside. If someone was in the study, he was being very quiet.

I put a cautious hand on the doorknob and found that the door was locked. I could probably have unlocked it magically, but with so many magisters about, I was afraid to risk them noticing the magic. With another glance up and down the hallway, I pulled a pin from my hair and inserted it in the lock. I'd become an expert on unlocking doors that way when I had a young pupil who had a habit of locking himself in his room to avoid lessons. With a satisfying click, the door opened for me, and I returned the pin to my hair, hoping I hadn't ruined the elaborate arrangement of curls.

The room was dark, but moonlight and lanterns in the garden shone through the window, casting a silvery glow that enabled me to find my way. This study was far neater than Henry's. The giant mahogany desk was clear, except for a large blotter pad. A single sheet of paper, creased as though it had been folded, lay on top of the blotter. I moved over to the desk and bent to read the message on the page, but then a noise from behind startled me. I whirled to see a masked man climbing through the window—the masked bandit I'd encountered on the train.

He froze when he saw me and blurted, "Verity? What on earth are you doing in here?"

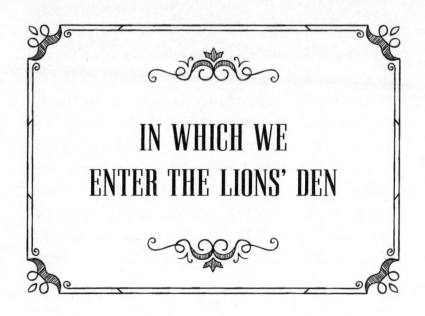

IN WHICH WE ENTER THE LIONS' DEN

It was Henry's voice, but that only confirmed what I'd suspected from the start and had known for a while. "I'm doing the same thing you are, helping the rebels," I snapped. "Now, Henry, get in here before someone sees you."

He climbed the rest of the way through the window and pulled the mask off, revealing a sheepish expression. "You knew?"

"I figured it out long ago. But this isn't the time to discuss it. I think the message the governor received is there on his desk."

Henry conjured a small light in his hand and moved to the desk. Even as close as I was, I could barely sense his magic, and I admired his control. We bent over the piece of paper together and saw that the message was from a downtown garrison. The rebels had struck that night while the officers were at the ball and many of the soldiers were attending the theater, and the situation had become desperate.

"That would explain the rapidly disappearing officers," Henry whispered.

I ran my fingers lightly over the blotter, feeling the indentations from a pen. "It looks like he's written something here recently—his orders in response?"

"Let's find out." He waved his hand over the blotter, and letters became visible, glowing against the paper. "Forget about fighting the people," the words said. "Seize the machines. I don't care if they're technically legal. Tear up every building in that area to find them. It's the only way to end the rebellion."

Henry and I looked up from the page to each other. "Oh, no," I breathed. "He's right, though. The machines are what give us a chance against magic. If they take the machines, it's over. We have to warn them."

"I'm assuming you know how to get to them, and that they'd trust you?"

"Yes, I know them, and I think they trust me. We just have to get to them in time."

"And then find a way to hide the machines or get them away. How many do they have?"

"I don't think I've seen them all, and I don't know where they all are. But there are a number, and they're not the sort of thing one could slip under one's coat and walk off with. They're large and noisy."

"We'll get away from this ball as soon as possible, and then we'll go warn the rebels." He pulled out a pocketknife and carefully slit the top page off the blotter, folding it and tucking it away in his pocket before returning the message to its original position.

He tied his mask back on, speaking as he did so. "Get back to the ballroom. I'll join you soon, and when we can leave without looking suspicious, we will." With a wry smile, he added, "When all this is over, you and I have much to discuss."

He headed for the window, and I followed him. "Are you going to dismiss me for being a rebel spy?" I asked.

He paused with one leg over the sill. "Heavens, no. I think it's excellent." Then he disappeared over the side.

I listened at the door, determined that it was safe to leave, relocked the door with my hairpin, and hurried back to the ballroom, hoping I didn't look as flushed and anxious as I felt. Flora was where I left her, looking more bored than she did when reading a book. "Did Aunt Elinor approve of your gown?" she asked.

So much had happened since I saw Elinor that it took me a moment to remember why I'd left the ballroom. "She did. And she took me to task for not dancing."

"Chaperones seldom dance. Only at very small balls where there are few ladies." She frowned at the dance floor, then added, "Though this was one of them. I'm surprised none of the officers asked you to dance. Henry probably scared them all away."

"Where *is* your uncle?" I asked, trying to sound only mildly curious, even as my heart pounded madly against my stays. "Hasn't he returned yet?"

"No, he hasn't. If I know Henry, after he talked to Matthews he wandered into the library and forgot he was attending a ball. We'll have to send servants to find him so we can go home."

Henry entered the room then, looking mostly the way he had when he left, though his hair was more rumpled. He stopped and spoke briefly with a few young men as he made his way to us. "My apologies for leaving you ladies alone," he said when he reached us.

"I hope there's nothing the matter," I said. I couldn't bring myself to meet his eyes because I knew I wouldn't be able to keep a straight face if I did.

"Only a minor situation that required my immediate attention."

"And you were eternally grateful to have an excuse to leave," Flora teased. "I know what you think about balls."

"I'm surprised to see you sitting," he replied.

"I've decided soldiers are even worse than scientists when it comes to conversation."

"I suppose soldiers aren't very good at talking about gowns."

I wished I had Flora's fan as I tried to hold back a smile. They sounded just like Rollo and Olive.

After bickering a little more with Flora, Henry turned to me. "Miss Newton, have you danced at all this evening?"

"I am here as a chaperone," I demurred, but he stood in front of me and held out his hand.

"Please do me the honor, Miss Newton."

"Oh, I couldn't."

"I insist."

Flora glared daggers at me, and I knew it would be wisest to refuse, but I did want to dance. It was, after all, my first ball. I tried to tell myself it had nothing to do with Henry, but I didn't believe it.

The orchestra finished a song, and there was polite applause from the guests. "Come now, they're about to start another song," Henry said, taking my hand, so I felt I had no choice. He led me to the dance floor, then bowed to me before taking my right hand in his left and resting his right hand against my back. I placed my hand on his shoulder as the music began.

Elinor was right, he was a good dancer. We made one circuit of the floor before he spoke. "I know how we could move the machines," he murmured into my ear, nearly throwing me off rhythm.

"How?" I whispered.

"Magic. But I can't do it alone. I'll need help. I've begun notifying my gang." His breath was warm on my cheek, and I was glad we both wore gloves because my palms felt clammy.

"I'll have a difficult enough time getting them to accept *you*. They *really* don't like magisters."

"I'll go alone with you at first, and then once we've persuaded them, I'll bring in the others."

"You're very optimistic."

"It's only logical. They can either accept my help or lose their machines and lose the revolution before it can go anywhere." He grinned at me, his eyes twinkling behind his spectacles.

"Besides, I have every faith in your persuasive abilities. If they won't listen to reason, you can hit them in the head with your bag."

I feared that people would get entirely the wrong impression from us murmuring to each other. He was so much taller than I that it was obvious he was bending to whisper in my ear. "People are giving us odd looks," I said. "Is it proper for you to dance with your governess?"

"They're probably wondering who this mysterious beauty is. They may not realize you're the governess."

"I wasn't announced when we entered."

"No one pays attention to that. We all know each other already." The song ended, and we applauded the orchestra. Then he took my hand and bowed over it. "Thank you for the dance, Miss Newton." Still holding my hand, he led me back to Flora.

"Now that you and Miss Newton have had your dance, do you think Grandfather would mind terribly if we left, even if it is barely midnight?" she asked.

"I think he'll understand." He released my hand and extended his hand to help Flora rise. The three of us made our way around the room toward the governor, where Henry and Flora thanked him for the evening and I, not sure what I was supposed to do, gave him a slight curtsy.

When we stepped outside, the view of the city wasn't nearly as serene as it had been when we arrived. There was a glowing red spot in the distance that had to have been made by either dozens of fires or one huge inferno. Henry glanced over his shoulder at me, a look of dismay on his face. The ride home was as quiet as the ride to the ball had been, but I felt like the quiet had an underlying tension to it.

As we entered the house, Flora said, "I'll send Jenkins to you in a moment to help you undress, Miss Newton."

As she swept up the stairs, Henry leaned over and whispered in my ear, "My study, as soon as the maid is gone. Dress for action." I nodded before following Flora up the stairs.

Although I would have preferred to undress myself, I did need assistance with the many tiny buttons and layers of garments. Miss Jenkins started to undo my hair, but I stopped her. I'd be there all night if she had to find and remove all those pins. "It's so beautiful, I'd like to keep it this way a little longer," I said.

"I'll help you into your nightgown."

"I'm perfectly capable of dressing myself for bed. I do it every night. You should get to bed. It's very late."

"Thank you, miss," she said. When she was gone, I put on a simple day dress, stuck a hat on my head as well as I could over the elaborate arrangement of curls, and tiptoed to Henry's study in my stocking feet with my coat over my arm and my boots in my hand.

He must have been listening for me, for he opened the door before I could knock and hustled me inside. He was dressed in sporting clothes, like he wore when he went out in search of bugs. "We should wait until we're certain the house has settled down for the night," he whispered.

"We don't have much time."

"It's just past one. I can get us downtown quickly, but we don't want to make Mrs. Talbot suspicious. I think she's a spy for the governor."

"Does he suspect you?"

"I'm not sure. I think—I hope—that he merely put her in place to report on how I'm doing as guardian. The housekeeper who'd worked for Robert suddenly got an excellent position elsewhere, and His Grace was so kind as to send someone who came highly recommended so I wouldn't have to bother hiring anyone when I had so many other responsibilities." His sarcastic tone told me how thrilled he'd been about that.

"And you would have looked more suspicious if you'd rejected her."

"Exactly. I felt that if I could fool her, that would only strengthen my cover. I don't know that she cares about politics or has the slightest inkling of my criminal behavior, but she would report it if she knew I was sneaking out of the house in the middle of the night with the governess."

He doused the single magical lamp in the room with a wave of his hand, and we waited in darkness and silence, straining our ears for any sign of life. "I think that's everyone in bed now," he breathed. I nodded, and then he helped me put on my coat, put on his own overcoat, picked up his shoes, and eased the door open. We tiptoed down the stairs, then he led me to the rear of the house, into the kitchen and out the back door.

We stopped to put on our shoes, then ran across the small back yard to the carriage house, where he opened a side door and gestured me inside. The family carriage was in there, along with a small, sporty roadster. "It's a relic of my bachelor days," Henry whispered.

"Aren't you still a bachelor?" I asked.

"Can one truly be a bachelor while bringing up three children? I know I certainly can't live like one." He gave a wistful sigh. "Alas, my wild bachelor days ended when I was barely twenty-one."

"You're a bandit," I reminded him. "I think you manage your share of wildness."

He didn't comment on that, saying instead, "The trick will be to get it out of the carriage house without waking the driver, who lives above."

"That should be good practice for spiriting steam engines out of the city."

"Very good point, Verity." He studied the carriage house door, rubbing his hands together thoughtfully. "First, I think a noise-dampening spell on the door." He placed his hands on the door, and it slid silently aside. He returned to the roadster, helped me into the passenger seat, then ran his hands along the vehicle, from front to back. Taking his seat behind the steering wheel, he brought the engine to life, and the roadster crept forward, the only sound the slight crunch of gravel. Once we were outside, he stopped to close the carriage house door, and then we were off into the alley and onto the side street.

Instead of heading to Fifth Avenue, he went a few blocks east, to an area that was less restricted. Traffic was light at this time of night, but it wasn't gone entirely, even with a curfew and martial law. The city was too busy to ever stop completely.

Once we'd blended into the flow of traffic, Henry asked, his eyes still on the road, "If you've known who I was all along, why didn't you ever report me?"

"Positions aren't that easy to come by, and having my employer in prison would have hurt my prospects. I have nowhere to go if I fail here. And then I learned what you do with your loot." I couldn't quite bring myself to tell him that I liked him too much to turn him in. "But why do you take such risks, especially when you're responsible for children? Are you that committed to revolution?"

He turned onto another street, and I thought he would avoid the question until he finally said, "It started because I was bored. I know it sounds terribly gauche to complain about having too much privilege, but if you're clever and ambitious, being the younger son of a nobleman isn't fun. It would be unheard of to have a career or trade, and yet there's not even the work of maintaining the family estate because that's the eldest son's job."

"Train robbery was the only other option?"

"We don't just rob trains."

"Yes, sometimes there are boats."

He turned to look at me. "How could you know?"

"I'm a spy. I know a great many things."

Henry slowed the roadster as we approached a military checkpoint. "This should be interesting," he muttered.

"Could we go around it?"

"There's probably something blocking every street heading downtown."

"Your name should get you through it."

"Only if you want everyone thinking I've eloped with the nonmagister governess." He turned to me with a grin. "That would get both of us in trouble. I have an idea, though."

He stopped when the soldiers flagged him down, but before they could speak to him, I felt a wave of magic. The soldiers went still, like the couriers at the fort had, and Henry sent the roadster flying down the street. He took a few turns so that we were no longer visible from the checkpoint, and then he leaned back against the driver's seat, letting out a pent-up breath.

"There was a gang of us in school, all of us in similar positions," he then said, continuing his story as though there had been no interruption. "We'd heard of the rebel groups, and to us revolution sounded like a good idea, mostly because if the social order was upset enough, we might get the chance to do something with our lives. We came up with the idea of stealing from the government to finance the revolution, and when we finished school and came home, we decided to see if all our intricately laid plans would work. When they did, we kept doing it. We talked of revolution and made enough connections with the rebel movement to anonymously send money to them, but we mostly did it for fun."

"How long have you been doing this?"

"Several years."

"And no one ever suspected?"

"That was part of the fun, acting in such a way that we would be the last people anyone would suspect of being the Masked Bandits."

"You did that very well. You almost fooled me. But didn't your family notice that you'd changed? Surely you weren't always the absentminded entomologist."

"I went off to England for boarding school when I was eight and stayed for university. I only came home for holidays, so they barely saw me for nearly ten years. Lily was the one who would have noticed a difference, but she died while I was gone. After her death, I'm not sure Robert would have noticed if I'd returned acting like a circus clown. The children were too young to remember me from before."

"Why bugs?"

"I'd always been interested in them. I'm not saying that if I had my choice of careers, I would have studied bugs, but I like them well enough that it wasn't too painful to spend so much time talking about them. The charade was easier before Robert died. Then I only had to play the obsessed amateur scientist in public. When I moved in with the children, in a house full of staff, I had to begin living the lie."

He saw a police carriage ahead and turned the corner. "We're getting close now, aren't we?"

"You know the old theater on Eighth, just east of Broadway?"

"That's it? You're sure?"

"I've been there several times."

He gave me a sidelong glance, then said, "Your charity

project a couple of weeks ago—you were on the Battery when the troops fired on the children, weren't you? That was why you were so shaken when you got home." It was a statement of fact, not a question.

I nodded, even though he was focused on the road and wouldn't see. "Yes. We were acting on information I overheard when I was at the governor's house for that dinner party. The rebels decided to counteract the governor's show of force and prevent a confrontation by having children there. I don't think anyone counted on the soldiers being so spooked that they'd fire on the children."

"That was what made the difference," he said softly. "I'd been playing at revolution before, paying lip service to the cause. But that changed things. I don't want my brother's children growing up in a world where that could happen."

"You almost got caught last weekend, though."

"We got reckless, and one of my friends paid the price. We're having to rethink our strategy now that the authorities know magisters might be involved." With a shaky smile, he added, "And you withheld information from the authorities for me." He stopped the roadster on the side of a residential street. After a long, serious look at me, he said, "To be honest, I initially hired you because I thought it wise to keep you under my power. You'd be dependent on me for a job and think twice about turning me in if you did figure it out."

"You were right."

He smiled again. "But I also liked your spirit. You were the first person to fight back, in all the robberies we'd done. I had no idea how wise a decision hiring you would turn out to be."

He got out of the roadster and came around to my side to help me out. "I doubt we can get much farther on the road. The barricades will be much tighter. We'll have to figure out a way to get there on foot."

"Leave that to me," I said, taking his hand to lead him. We reached Fourteenth Street and crossed it, then I looked for a familiar door and hoped it would be unlocked. If it wasn't, I had plenty of hairpins. But it opened, and we made our way through the basement, which was even darker at night—that is, until Henry lit our way magically. He doused his light when we reached the yard. The next door wasn't locked, either, and soon we were within the rebels' zone.

There were sounds of fighting and the flicker of flames in the distance, closer to the university, but this area seemed to be relatively peaceful. Then we rounded a corner and saw a group of British soldiers approaching. Henry pulled me into a doorway, where we hid in the shadows as the soldiers banged on a door across the street and shouted. When there was no response, they kicked the door in and rushed inside. While they were in the building, we left our hiding place and ran. We saw several more groups of soldiers making a systematic search of the area. They were coming uncomfortably close to the theater.

When we reached the theater, I knew I'd never get Henry past the lookouts at the main entrance. Instead, I led him around the building, looking for the alley where Alec and I had escaped from the raid that never happened. I'd been blindfolded then, but now that I knew where the theater was, I was able to find it. Deep within the alley, I spotted the open basement window and peered through to ensure it was the room I remembered. "I'd better go in first," I said.

"That looks like a long drop. I should go first and assist you."

"They're less likely to shoot me on sight, if anyone's there."

"Then be very careful with that drop."

He knelt beside me and helped me get my skirts through the small window. My feet found the ladder that was still below the window, and I got my footing, then took stock of the room, making sure no one was there before signaling for Henry to come down.

When he stepped onto the floor, I tugged on his necktie to make him bend so I could speak directly into his ear—the only way to be heard over the sound of the dynamo without shouting. "Follow my lead, and let me do the talking." I paused. "Maybe I should go up alone first."

He shook his head, then said into my ear, "You're not going anywhere without me."

We went up the narrow stairs to the auditorium, which looked like any other theater after a performance. Some of the chairs had been knocked over or shoved aside, as though the audience had left in a hurry. The floor was littered with programs. There were no signs that the Rebel Mechanics had ever been there. A light came from the balcony, and I could see people up there. Gesturing for Henry to be as quiet as possible, I led him up the side aisle to the balcony stairs. As we climbed the curved staircase, I felt like I was leading a cat into a mouse hole. They would see this as a betrayal.

Then, I reflected, they would know how I felt about what they'd done to me, only I was doing this to help them, not to trick or use anyone. The closer I got to the top of the stairs, the more uneasy I became. This would be the first time I'd seen Alec since I'd learned the truth, and I wasn't sure if I wanted to hit him or kiss him. I'd imagined bringing him some important piece of information and him being appropriately penitent about how he'd treated me and awed about what a brilliant spy I was, but now that I was actually doing so, I felt certain he wouldn't react the way I wanted him to. I only hoped that I didn't reveal how hurt I was to Alec or show enough emotion that Henry would infer anything about our relationship.

At the top of the stairs, I nearly ran into Nat. "Verity!" he said. "What are you doing here so late? Don't you know there's a revolution on?"

"I have news. It's important—urgent."

Nat turned to shout, "Alec! Colin! Lizzie! It's Verity. She says it's important." Then he turned back and noticed Henry behind me. "And she's brought a magpie with her!"

He backed away to join the circle of Mechanics that came to loom at the top of the staircase. As I saw their decidedly unfriendly expressions, it occurred to me that this might be more like bringing a mouse into a group of cats.

IN WHICH
WE MUST LIGHTEN
THE LOAD

Alec stepped forward, gesturing for the others to stay back and, I hoped, not do anything rash. "What is this, Verity?" he demanded, his voice harsh. He seemed a very different person from the one I'd known. Henry wasn't the only one who maintained a mask.

It was easier to face this near-stranger than the boy I'd been falling in love with, but I still fought to keep my voice calm so it wouldn't betray my emotions. "The British are going to seize the machines. They're searching the whole area door-to-door, quite thoroughly, and they're closing in on you."

He glanced at Henry, who stood silently beside me. "It must be easy for them if you lead them straight to us," Alec said with a sneer. "Is this your revenge?"

"Don't be stupid," I snapped, forgetting my vow to keep my

emotions in check. "This is Lord Henry Lyndon, and he's here to help."

"Help how?"

"Do you really think you can get your machines out of the city under the noses of the British troops without magical assistance?" Henry asked evenly.

"Let's hear what he has to say," Colin said with a shrug. "We don't have to let him leave if we don't believe him."

Although he was in far more danger than I was, Henry stayed protectively next to me as the rebels escorted us to the table where they'd been gathered. Colin rushed forward to hide the papers that had been spread out on it. Alec gestured for Henry to sit at the head of the table, and then other rebels filled in next to him, with one standing behind him. I took an empty seat farther down.

If Henry was flustered by such hostile surroundings, he didn't show it. This was, after all, the man who hadn't reacted when the girl he'd encountered during a train robbery showed up to interview for a position in his home. He didn't play the fool this time, though. This Henry was the Masked Bandit, only without the mask, regarding the rebels as though he was the one who had them at a disadvantage. Even in the dim light, his eyes showed icy blue.

"Now, tell us why we should believe you," Alec said to him. "The soldiers were just here for the show. They'd think there's nothing here to seize."

"We were at the governor's ball when the governor received

a message and gathered a few officers for a conference in his study. I presume this was in response to whatever action you carried out tonight. I manufactured an excuse to slip away so I could see what was in the study, and Verity likewise went snooping—quite independently from my activities, I assure you. I had no idea of her efforts on behalf of the cause."

Alec leaned forward. "What did it matter to you?"

Henry paused, considering for a moment, then he grinned and said, "I'm as much a rebel as any of you. Have you heard of the Masked Bandits?"

There were gasps around the table, and Alec turned to me. "That's why you wanted to help them at the fort? You knew who he was? And you said nothing?"

"I'm very good at keeping secrets," I said.

"You were the ones who helped that night?" Henry asked, his composure slipping a little. "I knew someone must have created a diversion. Verity, that's how you knew about the boat? Were you there?"

I started to respond, but Alec held up a hand, signaling for silence. "So you're one of the Masked Bandits," he said to Henry, sounding skeptical.

"I *lead* the Masked Bandits." Henry gestured around the room at the various bits of machinery. "Who do you think's been funding your merry band of Mechanics all along? But this is hardly the time to argue about who's more revolutionary than whom. I've gone to quite a bit of risk to ensure that you people succeed, and I won't have you throw it away over petty prejudices. Verity and I saw the governor's order to search this entire area and take the machines." He pulled the blotter page from his pocket, unfolded it, waved his hand over it to make the letters glow, then threw it on the table. The Mechanics shied away from the magic, even as they tried to read the message.

"This time, the raid is real," I added, giving Alec a frosty glare.

"Now, do you want my help getting your machines out of the city or not?" Henry said. "I've got my entire gang ready to come at a moment's notice."

"They know where we are?" Colin asked, rising from his seat.

"The exact location would have to come when I tell them they're needed."

"How do you think you can get the machines out of here?"

"I can magically make them silent. I can use glamour to make people not see them. I can entrance soldiers so they'll do nothing as we go past."

"Wait a second!" Mick, who had remained quiet at Alec's side this whole time, jumped to his feet and pointed at Henry. "Why is he so fired up about getting the machines out of the city? It could be part of their plot to steal them!"

"That is a good question," Alec said.

"They'll tear the city apart to find those machines because without them, you have no revolution." Henry shrugged slightly. "Really, even *with* the machines you haven't much of one."

"Then what's that going on out there?" Colin asked, gesturing in the general direction of the fires.

"It's fighting. That's different from revolution. Do you have a plan to bring down the colonial government? If you do, do you have a plan for what will replace it? Do you have plans for extending the fight beyond this one small part of the city and into the rest of the colonies so that you stand a chance against the British Empire? Or do you expect the colonials to spontaneously rise up at your example and take matters into their own hands?"

"I suppose *you've* got all that worked out?" Alec asked, his voice sharp.

"Not yet, which is why I've been laying the groundwork instead of provoking fights with the British and showing off what I have in my arsenal. Tonight's little foray is driving you out of town and could have lost you your machines. Was it worth it?"

Alec smiled tightly. "You have no idea."

I stood and pounded on the table. "Boys!" I shouted in my sternest governess voice. They stopped arguing and turned to look at me. More conversationally, I continued, "We can debate the merits of our respective revolutionary plans later. But for now, the soldiers are closing in on us, and you're running out of time. We're offering assistance. Do you want it?"

Alec stood and gestured to his comrades. They went off into a corner, and muffled sounds of discussion came our way, but I couldn't make out any words. "So these are your friends?" Henry asked.

"I thought they were, at one time. But that's too long a story for tonight."

"If they don't let me help, this will become more difficult."

"How so?"

"Stealing their machines would be the biggest heist I've ever managed."

"You wouldn't!"

"I'd have to. We don't have the slightest chance of winning a revolution without those machines, even with some magisters on our side."

The Mechanics returned to us, and Alec stood facing Henry. "We will accept your help."

"Very sensible of you," Henry said, rising and reaching into his pocket. "Allow me to contact my colleagues." He went into the corner the rebels had just vacated and spoke briefly into something that looked like a small pocket mirror. He came back to us, putting the object in his pocket as he walked. "They should be here soon, but in the meantime, I can help you get started. The hard part will be getting everything out of this part of town."

Alec grinned. "Actually, that will be the easy part. Where we'll need your help is getting out of the city."

We trooped down to the basement and into a corridor I'd never seen. It smelled familiar, though, and I suspected I knew where Alec was leading us. We came out into the underground railway station. "This leads uptown, past where you live," Alec told Henry. "We use it to transport machines within the city."

Henry gazed wide-eyed around the chamber and at the machine powering the railway. "Remarkable!" he said with a huge grin. "So we'll merely need to load the machines onto your railway to get them out of the immediate reach of the soldiers."

"That won't be easy," Colin said. "The dynamo is heavy, and it isn't on wheels."

"That's where I come in," Henry said cheerfully.

His friends had arrived by the time we made it back to the theater's basement, where the machines had been hidden during the diversionary theatrical production. The dynamo had already been disconnected, and the group of magisters soon had it floating into the rail station, where it landed light as a feather on a flatbed car behind the pilot car. Once it was loaded, the car shot down the tunnel.

The Mechanics pushed the smaller steam engine into the cavern, with much effort, but the magisters stepped in and had it gliding along under its own power. After that demonstration, the Mechanics' resistance to magister help faded. Getting Bessie onto a flatbed car took a combined effort from magisters and Mechanics. While the magisters and Mechanics worked with the heavy machinery, Lizzie and I went around the theater, gathering all evidence of the Mechanics' presence there. It had mostly been cleared out for the performance, but in the balcony, basement, and dressing rooms we found some banners, maps, and machine diagrams that we added to the loads heading up the tunnel.

We worked in uncomfortable silence for a while before Lizzie finally said, "I know you're angry at us. Maybe we should have just honestly recruited you instead of staging all those little dramas for you, but you must admit that you were alarmed to learn we were Mechanics. Why should we have thought that you'd be open to joining us?"

"I didn't know anything about the Mechanics then, nothing more than was in the newspaper," I said, rolling up a map. "But you may have noticed that I didn't snub you when I saw you again, and I accepted your invitations. You could have told me the truth at any time."

She gathered several rolled charts into a bundle. "I suspect that what you're really angry about is Alec. That might have been going too far. That's my fault. I thought that would be the best way to reach you, and I pushed him into it."

"So he *wasn't* interested," I said with a grim nod.

"That's not what I meant. He didn't want to recruit you by seducing you."

"And yet he did." I had an armload of papers and maps, so I left the balcony.

She came behind me. "You're a good writer. That wasn't part of the recruitment plan—well, asking you to help was, but keeping you doing it wasn't. I hope you'll keep writing for the paper. I'll find you a new contact if you don't want to talk to me. But I hope you'll want to talk to me."

"Can we discuss it later?" I asked. "We have other priorities right now—such as the British troops who'll be here at any moment."

When we returned to the station, the others had sent several more loads and were working with the calliope, which required some tricky maneuvering. It wouldn't fit through the tunnel to the rail station, so it had to be partially dismantled. While the Mechanics were frantically separating the largest pipes from the machine, Nat ran into the tunnel, shouting, "The soldiers are coming! They're almost at the theater!"

"This will have to be the last load, then," Henry said.

"This is almost everything. Our other big machines are stored out of town," Alec said.

"We can buy some time," Henry said, gesturing to one of his friends. They ran to the door, and I wasn't sure what they did, but I felt the magic. The Mechanics doubled their efforts on the calliope, while Lizzie and I made one more pass around the theater to make sure we had removed every last trace of the Mechanics' presence.

The soldiers were pounding on the theater's front doors when the calliope at last made it through the tunnel into the station. "It will take them a while to get past those seals," Henry said when he rejoined us.

Alec and the Mechanics closed the door that led into the tunnels and bolted it from the inside. "With any luck, they won't find the passage," Alec said. "I'd hate to lose the railway."

With a grin, Henry placed his hand on the door, and I shivered as his spell took effect. "Unless they have a magister with them, they won't see it," he said.

I heard shouting in the theater as we ran down the tunnel into the rail station. It seemed like an eternity before the pilot car came back from its last trip uptown, and the entire time we waited, I cast frequent glances at the tunnel, fearing that the locks and Henry's spells wouldn't hold. I went weak with relief when at last the car arrived. The Mechanics got it turned around, then connected it to a flatbed car loaded with odds and ends and small machines. "Looks like we'll have to find a new headquarters," Alec said wistfully as he took a seat on the pilot car.

"I don't think I was cut out for a life in the theater," Colin quipped. Then he looked at his sister, who hadn't yet boarded the car. "Aren't you coming, Liz?"

She shook her head. "No, I've got work to do here, and I'm useless with machines. I'll get out through one of the other exits. Someone will have to report on how the mysterious disappearance of the Rebel Mechanics baffled the British."

Nat stood by her side. "And that's gonna sell a lot of papers for me."

"Verity, we'll talk," Lizzie said, her tone pleading. I gave her a curt nod before boarding the car with the others.

When the car shot down the tunnel, Henry threw back his head and laughed. "Amazing!" he shouted, grinning widely, and some of the Mechanics grinned back at him. Alec still gave him wary glances, but the others had warmed to him. I couldn't blame them. This Henry, a blend of the boyish enthusiasm of his cover persona and the daring intensity of his Bandit identity, was irresistible.

Some of the Mechanics and magisters had gone ahead with the other machines, and they were waiting at the end of the line. They'd hooked the flatbed cars carrying the machines that didn't move of their own accord to the engines. Now we had to get them out of the tunnels and into the city—and then out of the city.

Alec sent a scouting team that included the Mechanic who'd been my guide the week before and one of the magister bandits to reconnoiter. They returned with a report that the immediate area was clear. At that signal, the Mechanics opened a wide set of doors at the end of the tunnel.

The doors led to a ramp, and the magisters got all the machines moving up it. The ramp ended in a barnlike building. The magisters gathered around the machines and did the silencing spell Henry had performed on his roadster, and then at Henry's signal, the mechanics opened the doors, and we went out into the street.

Henry and I rode on Bessie with Alec at the head of the line. It had seemed as though we'd been underground for hours, but it was still pitch-dark, just past three in the morning. The city slept as the machines moved silently through the streets.

There weren't any barricades this far uptown because the police and soldiers assumed all the other barriers would have stopped any rebels, and they were focusing their efforts downtown in the rebel stronghold. It looked like we might be home free, until the scouts who'd traveled ahead returned, reporting that the bridge leading off the island to the north was guarded.

Alec turned to Henry. "Now what do we do?"

"Let me take a look," Henry said. He climbed down off the engine, and I went with him. I felt like he was my responsibility, and I wanted to make sure he neither came to harm nor did anything foolish. We went down the riverbank to where we could observe the bridge unseen. Henry took a pair of field glasses from his coat pocket and studied the bridge. "They're only guarding this end," he said. "Looks like half a dozen men." He put the glasses in his pocket and turned to head back to the machines.

"Do you have a plan?" I asked as I hurried to catch up with his rapid, long-legged stride.

"I think so." When we reached the machines, he gestured for everyone to gather around him. "It will take at least two of us to entrance that many guards long enough for us to get by. I think the rest can move the machines magically so they make no noise, but it will be a strain. We won't be of much help beyond the bridge."

"We'll be fine from that point," Alec said.

"Why don't we just shoot the soldiers? Or conk 'em on the head?" Mick asked.

"Because then they'd know someone had been past, and they'd know to look for us," I said. "This way, no one will know the machines left the city."

Henry gave me an appreciative look. "Yes, Verity's right," he said. "If they find dead or injured soldiers, you'll have a manhunt. They won't realize they've been entranced, so you'll disappear—as if by magic."

"I don't suppose you could just wave your hand and make us disappear," Colin said with a grin.

"I wish I could, but we're not that powerful," Henry said. "You're fortunate to find this many magisters who even know how to use their powers properly."

The magisters tasked with entrancing the soldiers went ahead. Once we'd moved out of the more settled parts of the city, the machines had run on their own steam power, but now the Mechanics cut the engines, and it was up to the magisters to power them. Even without the engines, the machines weren't entirely silent. The wheels crunched on the road surface, the moving parts clanked and squeaked, and the loose pieces of metal in the cargo rattled at every bump.

I held my breath as the engines approached the bridge. The soldiers stood there on either side, looking like they were on guard. I waited for them to raise their weapons and challenge us, but they didn't move at all under the spell.

The machines had to go over the bridge one at a time because they were so heavy. The smaller engine went first. The calliope was heavier, and while Bessie waited her turn to cross, Henry jumped off and joined the crew moving the calliope. The bridge groaned alarmingly as the calliope crossed, but it held. Henry and two other magisters ran back across the bridge to Bessie.

Henry swung himself up onto the engine to talk to Alec. "I don't think the bridge will take this engine and the dynamo."

"There's no other way off the island," Alec protested. "The railway bridge is too busy and the area around it too populated. I suppose we could find somewhere else to hide them. They won't look for them up here, but I'd rather have all the machines where we can use them instead of keeping them hidden."

"We could levitate them slightly, just enough to take some of the weight off the bridge," Henry suggested.

"You can do that?" Alec asked, his skepticism clear on his face.

"It will take a lot of power, but I believe we can."

"If you fail, we'll lose our most important engines. I'd rather keep them hidden," Alec said. "Now, are you absolutely certain you can make this work? Don't overstate your abilities, magister."

"We can do it," Henry insisted, his jaw set stubbornly. He waved to the rest of the magisters, and they gathered by the engine, discussing how to manage the spell. Then they took their places, some on the dynamo and a few on the ground to walk beside the engine and dynamo. Henry sent all the Mechanics other than Alec ahead over the bridge before climbing onto the engine with Alec and me.

"Verity, you should go on, too," Alec said.

"I told you, we can do this. She'll be safe," Henry said.

"I'd rather not take the chance with her life, and that will lighten the weight you have to lift."

"I need a lookout. You'll be steering and I'll be deep into the spell. She's hardly any extra weight. She stays." Henry's voice left no room for argument.

Alec glared at him, and I thought for a moment it might come to a fight. "I'm willing to stay as lookout," I said. "I'm not afraid."

"Then that settles it. We should get started," Henry said, rubbing his hands together, then placing them on the engine. I felt the surge of magic as the engine crept forward and onto the bridge.

I couldn't tell when they began lifting some of the engine's weight, but the bridge didn't make any frightening sounds, so

I assumed it was working. I shifted my attention back and forth between the group waiting at the other end and the group holding the guards in thrall. So far, everything was going according to plan.

Then when we were just past the middle of the bridge, I heard a distant drum cadence. "I think it's the shift change for the guards," I said, wondering if Henry could hear me, as deep as he was into the spell.

"We'll have to hurry, then," he said without opening his eyes. The engine moved faster, but the strain was showing on Henry's face, and the sound of groaning metal told me the bridge was taking more weight than it should.

IN WHICH
I MUST DECIDE
MY FUTURE

We weren't going to make it across the bridge.
More soldiers were coming, and the magisters didn't have enough power to move the engine faster while lifting its weight enough for the bridge to bear it. Either we'd be caught or the bridge would collapse and plunge us into the river below. I didn't know much about using magic, but I could channel power from the ether. Perhaps that would provide the needed boost. However, doing so would reveal my biggest secret. It was a revelation that could cost me my freedom.

The bridge groaned again, sounding like its metal trusses were crying out in pain. Alec kept the engine pointed straight down the bridge, but I could see the tension in his shoulders as he focused on the other end that seemed so far away. A look at Henry's sweat-beaded face convinced me I had no choice but to trust him. He knew a thing or two about secrets and breaking the law. If any magister could accept a half-breed in his household, it would be Henry Lyndon. I removed my glove and placed my hand on top of his, then lowered my magical shields and opened myself to the ether, pouring the power I channeled into him.

He gasped out loud in surprise as my power connected to his. A moment later, the bridge quit groaning and the engine gained speed. My instinct was to hold my breath until we were safe, but I forced myself to keep breathing to maintain the flow of the ether. All the while, the sound of approaching drumbeats grew louder.

At last, the engine moved off the bridge, so we no longer needed to levitate it. Henry signaled to the magisters enthralling the guards, and they ran across the bridge to join us. I felt as though I'd been drained completely by the time we were far enough away for Alec to fire up the engine. I sagged against Henry, and he turned his hand around to clasp mine. "Well done, Verity," he whispered in my ear. "You are full of surprises, aren't you?"

About half an hour later, the machines had all moved a safe distance from the city into the wilds beyond the Bronx. The engines stopped, and all of us—magisters and Mechanics—piled off to say our farewells before the Mechanics went on and the magisters returned to the city.

"Thank you for your help," Alec said, extending a hand to Henry. "It was a good plan." It looked as though the admission pained him, but he was being a good sport about it.

"You have good machines that helped it work," Henry said. "That underground railway of yours is amazing. What will you do now?"

"We'll go somewhere west—we have some allies among the native tribes, and they'll give us refuge in their land—and do what you said we should do. We'll make plans for a real revolution, build more machines, get ready to really turn things upside down throughout the colonies. You'll be doing the same?"

"I'll keep undermining the government, and we have other things in the works. I'm sure our respective groups will encounter each other again." He glanced around, then gave a sheepish smile. "There is one small flaw in my plan: how are we to get home?"

"Stewart's meeting us with his carriage," one of the magisters said.

"That's well enough for you. You're known for being out until the wee hours. But even if I left this moment, I'd be caught sneaking through the kitchen door after being out all night with my governess," Henry said. "The servants would be up by the time we drove home, and I'm sure my housekeeper is a spy for the governor."

"We can get you home faster without having to go through the kitchen door," Alec said. "As I told you, some of the machines were already out of town. Get back on board."

The carriage arrived and the rest of Henry's gang piled into it. We waved goodbye as the engines moved onward. A few minutes later, we stopped in front of an enormous barn, and the

Mechanics opened the doors to reveal the airship *Liberty*. Everett came out to meet us, and after Alec explained the situation to him, he said to Henry, "If you can get in through your bedroom windows, we can keep you out of sight of any nosy servants."

Alec turned to us and asked, "Will that do for you?"

"You have an airship? How is it powered?" Henry asked, looking and sounding very much like Rollo. "Wouldn't a steam engine be too heavy?"

"Everett can explain it to you," Alec said with the first real smile he'd given Henry. Henry's enthusiasm about the machine had apparently made a small dent in Alec's resentment of magisters. He paused, frowned, then seemed to come to a decision. "The fighting tonight wasn't really about revolution. It was a diversion to distract the soldiers who weren't at the ball or the theater so we could carry out our real mission." He reached into his breast pocket and pulled out a few sheets of paper. "We managed to get into their offices and copy their codebooks. I doubt they have any idea that we have these. They think we were just fighting a skirmish." He handed the papers to Henry. "You can probably make better use of these than we can."

Henry gave a soft whistle of surprise as he took the papers. "I owe you an apology, then," he said. "You were being more strategic than I gave you credit for. Thank you. I'll put these to good use. We've stolen a lot of dispatches we need to decode." He folded the papers and tucked them carefully into his breast pocket.

"And now, we'd best be on our way."

"Godspeed," Henry said with a jaunty salute.

Alec hesitated, then said, "Verity, may I have a word?" He pulled me aside and said, "I'm sorry for tricking you the way we did. I should have known what a piston you were. You really came through for us tonight in warning us, even if you did bring a magpie with you."

"You wouldn't have escaped without him."

With a deep sigh and a rueful smile, he said, "I know. I hate it, but you're right. Our machines couldn't have done it alone." He glanced at Henry, then back at me, paused, took a deep breath, and said, "You could come with us if you like."

"Wouldn't you be giving up a valuable spy who has access to the highest levels of magpie society?" I couldn't keep the bitterness out of my voice.

"I don't care about that." He took my hand and squeezed it fiercely. "I'd rather have you with me than have you being useful. I've missed you."

I weighed what he'd said, realizing what a sacrifice he was willing to make. I'd been so potentially valuable to them that they'd engineered an elaborate ruse to get me on their side, and now he was willing to give up the spy they'd worked so hard to create. But they'd done their job too well. I couldn't just leave now. I shook my head. "We've got a lot of work to do, and I think Liberty Jones has a lot more stories in her. Who knows what I might learn among the magisters?"

He looked disappointed for a moment, then he grinned. "That's my girl, Liberty. I'm sure I'll see you again."

As Alec boarded the engine, Henry came up behind me. "If

you want to go with them," he said softly, "I'd understand, even though hiring a new governess would be very inconvenient."

I turned to face him. "Do you want me to go, now that you know about me?"

"Only if going is what you want. Nothing has to change, as far as I'm concerned."

I glanced at Alec and the magnificent engine, then turned back to Henry. "No, I think I can do more in the city. Besides, there are the children, and there's my newspaper career."

"Newspaper career?"

"Just one of the many things we need to discuss later, but we're running out of time to get home safely."

Everett and his crew had wheeled the airship out of the barn, and he gave us goggles as we boarded. The ship was soon soaring upward. I could see the rebel engines below, snaking their way into the wilderness, and I waved, but I wasn't sure they could see me.

Henry was like an older version of Rollo as he moved around the ship, taking note of every detail of how it worked, and then looking over the side at the approaching city far below. "Rollo would be so jealous," he said with a grin. "I feel guilty for getting to do this without him."

"Maybe someday we can arrange it for him," I said.

"Perhaps. You're the one with the connections." He studied me for a while, then took my hand and said, "That, back there, is that why you had to come to the city, why you said you have nowhere else to go?"

I nodded. "I think my father always knew I wasn't his child, and when my mother died . . . " I gave a weak shrug, and he nodded. "He didn't even know about the magic, but that was how I knew."

"Do you know who your natural father was?"

"I have no idea. It wasn't the sort of thing anyone talked about. My parents pretended nothing was the matter, until my mother died and her husband didn't want anything to do with me anymore. I didn't know until I arrived in the city that what I am isn't accepted. I never found out what happens to half-breeds, but Mrs. Talbot hinted that it was dire."

"I think it involves isolation, to make sure the blood isn't further tainted. And they may be used to provide power for magical objects. Slave labor, essentially." I gulped in horror, and he gripped my hand tightly. "I hope you can trust that I'll keep your secret. You keep so many of mine."

"Isn't that the ideal relationship between a governess and her employer—each having enough knowledge to thoroughly destroy the other?"

"I think it's also the ideal foundation for a good friendship," he said with a laugh. "Think of it as us having a great deal of trust in each other."

"Oh, what about your roadster?" I asked, remembering one last loose end from the night's adventure.

"I'll send Matthews to retrieve it. He's in on all my secrets. If you ever need help and can't find me, you can always turn to him, and I'll let him know he can trust you as well. I suppose all of us have some planning to do—after we get some rest."

The sky was still dark, but lights were beginning to show here and there in windows as early risers woke, when the airship came in behind the Lyndon house. Since we had left through the kitchen door, the bedroom windows were closed, but Henry and I went down on the ladder together, and he magically opened my window for me and saw me safely inside before the ship moved farther down the building to his room.

The servants had assumed we'd be out late at the ball and let us sleep in, so I managed a short nap before I had to face the day. I was grateful that I'd accepted Mrs. Talbot's offer to walk Rollo to school in the morning because that allowed me to take my time getting up and dressing. It took me forever to pull all the pins out of my windblown and tangled hair, but eventually I looked like my usual governess self, and I felt safe going downstairs for breakfast.

Henry was already there, and after the way he'd been the night before, I was somewhat disappointed to see him in his familiar guise, with the spectacles on his nose and the vague, absent-minded air about him. I liked the real Henry so much better. "Good morning, Lord Henry," I said cheerfully. "Is there anything interesting in the papers?"

"Nothing much," he said. Then he lowered the newspaper and looked at me over the top of his spectacles. "But I understand there are some mad people about who plan to start a revolution."

I sat across from him at the table and poured a cup of tea. "Imagine that!" I said, unable to hold back a smile when I met his eyes.